HIGH FLYER

MICHELLE DIENER

ACKNOWLEDGMENTS

Thank you so much to Edie and Jo for your eagle eyes and great suggestions as always, as well as to my awesome reader team of J. Lee Conway, Diane, Christine, Lynn and Sandra! Thanks as always to EJR Digital Art for the truly beautiful cover!

THE VERDANT STRING SERIES

The eight planets of the Verdant String, the green, fecund sources of life spanning five solar systems, comprise the Verdant String Coalition.

This is the setting for a new science fiction romance series from award-winning science fiction romance novelist Michelle Diener.

While the people of the Verdant String know they have a common ancestor, a group of explorers who colonised the planets at the same time thousands of years ago, the mysteries of who they were, and where they came from, persist.

Each book in the series can be read as a standalone:

Interference & Insurgency Box Set

Breakaway

Breakeven

Trailblazer

High Flyer

CHAPTER 1

HANA HAD BEEN FLYING for Iver Sugotti for nearly six months, so she knew the drill.

As she approached the house, with the green hills and wooded valley blurring beneath her feet, Lancaster sent her a comm, telling her to come straight in.

She swooped the Sig in over the part of the roof Sugotti had modified to take a landing pad, and instead of landing as she'd been told, she executed the little dance she'd come up with, moving the Sig left, then right, then in an elegant pirouette before settling down on the tiny red square.

If anyone had been holding a gun to her head, or had already killed or removed her, and had taken the comm instead, they would have given themselves away. And knowing Lancaster, they would have been dead one second after landing.

As it was, Lancaster raised his hand in greeting as he stepped out from the atrium on the roof where he and Iver waited. Iver followed him out, and they exchanged a few words before Iver bent low to avoid the turbulence of the blades.

While he ran the few meters to her, she glanced up at Lancaster.

His eyes were on his boss, his face unguarded, and what she saw there made her blink.

Iver reached the door and pulled it open, hauling himself in next to her.

She waited for him to slam the door closed and then lifted off, banking right, and then punching it up so they shot over the gardens and were on their way before he'd even finished clipping his belt.

She said nothing until he looked settled. "Not working today?"

He'd sat up front with her a few times in the six months she'd been his pilot, she assumed to get to know her better at first, and once after that when his screen had gone on the blink.

She liked it better when he sat at the back, absorbed in his work, but she liked this job, so she was prepared to make small talk if he wanted her to.

"No. Don't feel like it."

She looked sidelong at him, and wondered if it was snowing somewhere on the plains of the Argin Desert. He hardly ever didn't feel like working.

"I thought Lancaster was coming with you on this trip to Touka."

"He was. Something came up I needed him to deal with."

She wondered what it was that had put such a look of fury on Lancaster's face as Iver had run toward her.

"Nothing serious?"

He shrugged. "No. Just needs doing."

She had no comeback for that, so she concentrated on the job, the challenge of flying on a planet that seemed to fight tech at every turn, tried to pull every ship out of the air. It was why the runners on Faldine had air blades. They had to go very old school here.

She banked again as they blasted out the valley, a sharp left, going low, just to keep things nice and unpredictable.

The military had drummed that into her, and Lancaster had asked her from the start of the job to keep flying as if she was still in combat. She was happy to oblige.

All the thrill, and so far, none of the danger.

In her last job, nearly a year with the mining giant HRP, she'd been under strict orders to always fly as level and smooth as possible. Some of the top HRP execs didn't fly so well.

Sugotti, on the other hand, perked up when she did the bob and weave. Sometimes, when she looked back to see how he was coping with her maneuvers, she could see him smile down at his screen when she did something particularly wild, even if he had to hang on and couldn't work as well while she did it.

Yeah, she could handle some chit-chat for those smiles.

"So, how are you doing, Hana? Got anything planned for the days you're waiting for me in Touka City?"

"A few things." She didn't remember chit-chat getting this personal. She wanted Iver at arm's length. Wanted him sitting behind her, working, and giving her a nod of thanks as he came and went, leaving the briefings, the comms, to Lancaster. She didn't want him right next to her, his shoulder rubbing hers as she took them up and over the range of low hills. "I was thinking of heading up the Spikes. One day up, one day down. I should be back, ready to take you where you need to go, before you need me next on your schedule."

She never knew where he was going until the day they left. Standard operating procedure. Another of Lancaster's precautions.

"The Spikes are good. I've been through them a few times since the war, looking for sky lane routes. Are you going with a group?" He stretched out his long legs, which wasn't as easy to do up front, and she hoped he'd get uncomfortable enough to move to the back.

"No. I don't know anyone in Touka. Not any more. Part of why I thought I'd hike it, actually."

That was a lie.

She was happy her friend Lucca had moved, because if he'd known about her trip up the Spikes, he'd have tried to come along.

She wanted no witnesses to what she planned to do in the mountains.

Iver angled himself toward her, and his leg pressed against hers. "I thought you had a friend there."

She nodded, shifting her leg away. "I did, but Lucca got a job in Permeo a couple of months ago. He's loving it there."

"Going up on your own isn't such a great idea."

She didn't know what to say to that. *That's none of your business* just didn't seem right. She shrugged. "If the weather looks dicey, I won't take chances, I'll come right down."

Another lie.

She would see her trip out, no matter what.

He didn't respond, and she concentrated on the job. They were over the hills and skimming the plains, something the autopilot would have taken care of on Themis, her home planet, or any of the planets of the Verdant String, for that matter. Here on Faldine, though, pilots were more than just window dressing in case things went wrong.

She hung onto the stick, leaning forward, her eyes on the horizon as the sun dipped lower in a blaze of oranges, purples and reds.

She caught a glint off to the right, the last flare of sunlight on something metallic on the ground below, and just because she wanted something to do, something to distract her from the subtle rub of Sugotti's shoulder against hers, the heat where they touched, she took the Sig straight up, all in the name of being unpredictable. Just following Lancaster's orders, if Sugotti should ask her what the hell she was doing.

The missile missed them by two meters.

She saw it literally fly beneath her feet through the clear bubble nose of the Sig as the collision detector squawked in her ear.

It would come back round, of course, so she followed it, banking sharp left and trailing in its wake, not giving it any room to maneuver.

Sugotti had gone still beside her, and when she glanced at him to gauge his reaction, she saw he had a dart gun in hand. Looked like a military standard SAL.

She had to twist and turn in the Sig to keep up with the missile, but it only had so much hard fuel and it would have to drop out the sky soon. She brought up the display, watching for a second Sweet-D, because if they were serious about taking out a Sig, they must know they'd need two.

She switched to voice command, and hunched her shoulders to get rid of the kinks. "Bring up guns."

"Bringing up guns." The smooth voice of Siggy, her onboard system comms, made the moment almost cool. She hadn't had cause to bring up the guns since the war ended, and never in a Sig.

But . . . no.

She'd rather skip the cool bit and not have a missile coming at her.

"Fire at target."

"Firing at target."

She caught the quick flash of laser fire as the two guns on either side of the front nose let loose, and then she lifted them almost vertical to avoid the shrapnel as missile number one blew into tiny little bits.

She heard Iver make an appreciative noise at the back of his throat, then go silent as the display in front of her began to beep.

Missile number two. Right on time.

"Well, damn."

Iver gave a snort, and put out a hand to brace himself as she spun them around and fired directly at the incoming.

It was a dicey move, but she didn't have much choice. No time, nowhere to go, and she felt the cold, queasy hand of dread grab her gut as an exploding piece of missile number two clipped one of the blades above the Sig's sleek body.

The Sig lurched hard left, and she was grateful she'd taken them so high to begin with.

It was a fight to the ground, but she had a few precious seconds to get them level, find somewhere flat to land.

And her little edge, her secret that she never talked about.

It had saved her more than once.

It looked like it was saving her again.

She watched the soft curve of a rise on the ground below disappear beneath them, and then dropped them down into the hollow beyond it. The plains didn't leave much place to hide, but this was better than nothing.

It wasn't flat, but it was relatively rock free, and they thumped down and tipped left, the nose digging into the soft, dry soil and flinging turf in all directions until they came to a halt.

The Sig groaned a little, as if in relief, in the absolute quiet that came after she disengaged. And then it was just the tick tick tick of the engine cooling down, and the quiet sound of water flowing in the stream she'd somehow noticed as she'd taken them down.

She leaned back in her seat, and turned her head to Sugotti.

His gaze was already on her, and for a moment, for the first time this trip, she looked straight into his eyes.

She turned away, frightened by what she saw there. What she'd suspected she'd see there from almost the beginning, which is why she'd never looked in the first place.

"Better get going," she said, lifting her helmet off. "They seem to be serious about killing you, so I'm betting they're on their way to finish the job."

CHAPTER 2

SOMEONE WAS, most definitely, serious about killing him.

Iver hauled himself out of the relatively unscathed Sig and gave it a grateful pat. The extra investment in the guns had really, really paid off. Lancaster had talked him into it, and for that alone, he should get a raise.

But the star of the show, the real reason he was standing on the sweet soil of Faldine, was clambering out the other side, unzipping herself from her fireproof jump suit. It was standard procedure to wear it, and he'd always wondered what she had on underneath.

Had spent rather too much time wondering, actually.

He watched her wriggle out of it, and found out it was a close-fitting white top with tiny flowers on it and a pair of shorts.

She reached into the Sig, behind her seat, and pulled out a backpack. The one she presumably had planned to take on her hike up the Spikes.

"You going to call Lancaster or shall I? The magfield is weak enough here, we should get a signal." She was already pulling out her comm unit.

He held up his own in answer and walked away from the Sig toward the outcrop of rocks nearby, giving the audio command.

Hana got into step with him, her head swiveling from side to side as she checked for any sign of pursuit.

Lancaster was on another call, and as Iver waited for him to switch across, he watched as Hana ran up a large rock almost as if gravity didn't apply to her and shielded her eyes as she swept the landscape from the top of it.

"Boss?" Lancaster's voice was as dry as ever.

"Someone took a shot at us. Two, actually. We're down."

There was silence, as if Lancaster was taking time to process the information.

"Two what?"

"What were they?" Iver called up to Hana.

"SD3s." She dropped lightly to the ground on the other side of the rock and he walked around it to join her.

They were now out of sight of the Sig.

Hana stopped walking and cocked her head, listening, and he stopped as well.

"You on the move?" Lancaster's voice was calm.

He didn't know why he took the extra precaution--Lancaster had made sure his comm unit was secure--but he always listened to his gut. "Not yet," he said. "We came down pretty hard."

Hana gave an approving nod at the lie, and he was ridiculously pleased by it.

He'd been trying to steer clear of his pilot since the first day he'd met her. She'd made it obvious she wasn't interested in anything personal with him, and he'd respected that, and respected Lancaster's hint that ex-military pilots of her caliber were almost impossible to find, but his restraint had burned away with that little look they'd exchanged when she'd brought them down.

At last he heard what she'd obviously already picked up on a few seconds ago, the roar of a runner's engine. He froze, and Hana grabbed his jacket and pulled him down, tight up against the base of the rock, as a whump shook the ground.

Another SD3.

And this time, it didn't miss the Sig.

They shared a look, and Hana opened her comm unit and pulled out the chip. She crouched down, moving smoothly and quickly, placed the chip on a flat rock, grabbed another rock and smashed it down hard. He handed his chip to her and she smashed that as well.

"At least we got that call in to Lancaster."

"It'll take him a few hours to get another Sig and get out here." She picked up the smashed chips and stuck them in her shorts pocket, then scuffed her boot over the rock she'd used to destroyed them, removing any sign of the carnage.

"You're handy to have around on the run." Iver started forward again, heading for the stream he'd seen moments before they'd hit the ground.

The runner that had taken out his Sig had landed behind them, just over the ridge, and someone would be coming to scout the area soon enough.

"Think they saw us?"

"They were coming from the opposite direction, and they hit the Sig before they landed, so chances are no." Hana fell into step with him again, and they took the sudden, steep descent to the stream, which was deep and fast, and cut into pure rock.

He waded in, wincing as the icy water climbed to his waist. Hana followed him without speaking, without so much as a squeak at the cold. She looked like calm competence personified, and as swift and brutal as the water battering at him, he felt something give way in himself.

He caught her eye, and as their gazes clashed she stumbled, throwing out her hands to get her balance. She didn't cry out, though, and when she got her footing, she didn't raise her head again.

Yes, whatever was between them, there was no putting it back in the box now.

CHAPTER 3

THE LAST GLOW of dusk lit the rocks in the gorge a radiant red, reflecting off the water and dancing across the wall in the little hollow just above the waterline that Iver had found them.

The tiny cave sat snug beneath the river bank, but the water was low enough to give them a dry place to sit, completely hidden from above.

Quarters were cramped though.

Iver's wet trousers stuck to her bare legs, and Hana shivered as the air cooled. Not for the first time since she'd shimmied out of her fire suit, she wished she hadn't pulled on shorts this morning. There were soft, warm hiking trousers in her pack, but that would mean getting out of her shorts with Iver literally pressed up behind her, which wasn't going to happen. The rushing sound of the stream was probably loud enough to cover most noises they made, but she wasn't prepared to risk unzipping her pack and rustling clothes, or stripping down in front of her boss.

Above them, the sound of people walking and calling to each other was clear, and Hana guessed there were three of them.

There was a fourth man, though. By the sounds of the grumbling above, he was directing proceedings from their runner.

So far, he hadn't bothered to join the search.

"Is he serious there are no bodies in that Sig? How can he tell? It's a ball of flame."

"Don't ask me, man. If they did make it out of there without injuries, then they have a portable sky lane, because they aren't here."

"A portable sky lane? Think there is such a thing?" The first man scoffed.

"Don't know. But if anyone's got one, it'd be Sugotti, right?"

There was silence, and eventually the footsteps moved away.

Hana closed her eyes, waiting, and another shiver ran through her.

Iver made a small sound of . . . impatience? Exasperation? His arms came around her and he pulled her back against him. She stiffened in surprise, then relaxed into his hold as the contact with him warmed her back. Sharing body heat made sense. She just wished it didn't involve her being literally in Iver Sugotti's embrace.

It was still quiet up there, but the searchers had to know the stream was the most likely place she and Sugotti were hiding. They hadn't been tramping up and down here for the last fifteen minutes for fun, but so far they hadn't tried to wade into the stream itself.

Sugotti shifted behind her and she opened her eyes and tilted her head as she turned to look up at him. He was watching her, his face so close to hers she could see each thick dark eyelash framing his dark gray eyes.

She forced her gaze forward.

Iver Sugotti was dangerous.

He noticed things. Things she wanted to keep hidden.

He'd been watching her intently since the first time she'd flown for him.

When she'd worked at HRP, some of the execs had taken her for an automaton, barely registering that she was there. There had been an anonymity to that that had been relaxing.

If only the job hadn't been so boring. And if only the job with Sugotti hadn't come with benefits her new self couldn't easily dismiss.

Now, however, Sugotti was moving from frank admiration to putting his hands on her. And that was breaking the rules.

Something of her frustration must have shown in her body language, because she sensed him give a smile. His hands brushed over hers, and then gripped them.

"Think they're gone?" He whispered directly into her ear, and she jerked in surprise, just narrowly avoiding hitting his jaw with her head.

She shook her head. Leaned back and twisted to whisper: "They aren't gone 'til we hear their runner leaving, and even then, they'll probably hover at high altitude and watch for our heat signatures."

He nodded, his hands still holding hers.

When she tried to pull loose, he wouldn't let her.

"If you do have a portable sky lane, now would be a good time to haul it out." She breathed the words right into his ear and she felt him hold back his laughter.

He dipped his head, his lips brushing her skin. "I wish."

She could feel his arousal now, snug up against her, and automatically started shifting forward, but he tightened his grip.

"So, tell me." He dipped his head again. "Why?"

She was silent for a moment, wondering whether to pretend not to understand him.

"Don't," he said.

She sighed. He was right. That was insulting to them both. "It's complicated."

"You're telling me." His voice was wry. "Why did you pretend you weren't interested?"

"What good would it do?" She hated that she had to whisper so quietly, it came out breathless. "I didn't plan to act on it."

"Humor me."

"No."

She felt him smile against her cheek, the scratchy brush of his chin making her shiver again.

Sounds above them had them both going still and swiveling their heads.

"Get in the water," someone said, and Hana drew in a quick, surprised breath.

"What?" Iver's voice was almost too soft to hear.

She shook her head, listening harder.

"Fuck that. I can't swim, and it looks deep and fast." The person responding was one of the men from earlier. "We've walked along a fair stretch of the stream, and they're not in there."

"Face it, they're dead." Another of the voices from before.

"No. If Hana Farwell is involved, they're alive. She's never met a deadly situation she hasn't walked away from."

Oh, she knew that voice.

Knew that suspicious, backbiting voice.

Sub-lieutenant Linnel.

Hana's mind went blank for a moment in absolute panic, and then Iver's hand was on her back, rubbing in comforting circles, which put a hitch in her breathing.

What did Linnel know?

She forced her lungs to work, trying to be quiet as she drew in air. And the reason for her fear and her survival hummed in her system, doing the job for her, so she was back to normal in a blink.

This really must be a low magfield area.

"There's nothing left of that Sig, and there's no sign of them. No footprints, nothing. They're dead."

"Hana's in the mix, so they're not, but we've run out of time. They'll have to make an appearance sooner or later, whether back at Sugotti's or Touka." Linnel's voice faded as he walked away.

After a minute, she heard a Dynastra lift off. She would recognize that engine sound anywhere. She tracked it as it rose and with the help of her systems upgrade, as she thought of her new self, she could swear she caught a faint hint of it hovering high overhead, just as she guessed Linnel would do.

Maybe she was lying to herself. Maybe she only thought she could hear something, but why take the chance?

She almost gave a shrug, then remembered Sugotti, plastered up against her, and kept herself still.

Finally the sound faded to nothing.

"They're gone," she said, then wished she hadn't opened her mouth.

"I thought they'd gone five minutes ago."

She let herself shrug now. "If they were in a hurry to get away, they might have stayed up high to see if they could catch us, but they'll know someone's coming, so they couldn't do it for long."

"You recognized the boss." Iver didn't make it a question.

She nodded. "Sub-lieutenant Linnel. As you heard, he knows me."

"He still with the military?" Iver asked.

She shook her head slowly. "I don't know. He's not at my old base, but he could have been transferred. Wherever he works now, this isn't a military op. Those other people on his team weren't under military orders or there'd have been none of the backchat. And they'd have gone into the water."

"What did he mean, that you never met a deadly situation you hadn't walked away from?"

She hesitated. "During the war there were plenty of situations where we were lucky to walk away unscathed. Soldiers get weird about luck." She fluttered her hands.

"Weird, how?"

Her lips twisted. "They thought I'd save them. That there was something about me, some twist of fate, that made me indestructible. So they would always try to get me as their pilot. I was their lucky charm."

"You've certainly been mine, so I can see how that would be." He sounded thoughtful. "You're an exceptional pilot. Almost unbelievably so."

She went still. Frowned but said nothing.

"How you evaded the missiles and then got us down was the most amazing flying I've ever seen." Iver ran a hand down her arm. "If that's how you handled yourself in one of those old Dynastras the military were using in the war, I can see why they thought there was something special about you."

She relaxed a little, although not all the way. She didn't know what was normal anymore. That was the fear lurking at the back of her mind since that fateful day she'd crashed in the Spikes and stumbled onto something she still didn't understand. That she'd forget what was normal and what wasn't, and give herself away.

That's why she wanted to go back. Look around where she'd come down and hopefully find some answers.

"I'm a good pilot," she conceded. "That's why Lancaster hired me." She cocked her head. "Speaking of whom, reinforcements should be coming any time now."

Iver shifted behind her again, and her skin prickled in awareness.

Lancaster couldn't come soon enough.

CHAPTER 4

LANCASTER SHOULD BE HERE ALREADY, but he wasn't.

Iver leaned back against cold stone, miserable to the bone.

They'd gone back to Hana sitting between his legs, leaning against his chest. It was the most comfortable position for both of them in the confined space, except it wasn't comfortable at all.

He stared down at the curve where her neck met her shoulder. It called to him. He wanted to put his mouth there and . . .

She shifted, and he closed his eyes briefly, because of course his erection was poking her in the back again.

Fuck it. "You want to go back up? See what the hell's happening?" Because something damn well should be. It had been over an hour since Linnel and his crew had left.

They'd decided it made sense to stay hidden in their little scooped out cave until they heard the Sig Lancaster would most definitely send, but it did them no good if Lancaster couldn't find them.

"Even if Lancaster can't find our heat signatures, he would land, check out the scene." Hana said what they both knew went without saying, but even so, she scooted away from him and jumped into the water, turning to take her pack from him.

She must be at breaking point with their close quarters, too. Although he hoped it was uncomfortable lust, rather than dislike, that had her moving with such alacrity.

He remembered how she'd looked at him when they'd first jumped into the river and calmed down a little.

Lust it was.

He followed her out.

They waded back upstream, the water splashing up his chest as he powered against the current.

It took much longer to get to the point where they'd originally gone in than he would have thought, and he realized the crew sent to kill him hadn't understood how fast the current was, and that's why they hadn't bothered to go into the water. They hadn't believed he and Hana could have gotten to the narrow ravine in the time they'd had.

He said as much.

"Amateurs," Hana agreed. She shielded her eyes against the last light of Faldine's sun, and frowned. "Do we stay and wait?"

"It just isn't possible Lancaster hasn't been able to get any kind of runner since I called him. Even if he couldn't get a Sig and a pilot to fly it, there are other options."

Hana turned to him, and the way she watched him had the hair standing up on the back of his neck.

"What?"

She hesitated, then lifted her shoulders. "If I'm wrong, you'll probably fire me for this."

His mouth fell open, because it was the last thing he expected her to say. "You have my word I won't."

She shook her head. "Doesn't matter, you can do what you think is right. I'll say it anyway."

He didn't think she understood how unlikely it was that he'd do anything that would get her out of his life, but he simply inclined his head.

"It's just something I saw on Lancaster's face when you boarded the Sig today." She worried her bottom lip. "He looked as if he wanted to take out a SAL and shoot you."

Iver's first instinct was to deny it, but she wasn't in the habit of gossiping. He barely got a word out of her, usually, let alone on something personal about his closest member of staff. If she said she had seen something, she had seen something.

"You said you told him to stay behind to deal with an issue. Could this be linked to it?"

He shoved his hands into the pockets of his wet pants and fisted them. "Did you hear the news about what happened on Veltos?"

"Those military officers on the Veltos Trail uncovering some illegal Caruson activity?" She nodded.

"Turns out the Caruson had inside help, from one of the Trail guides. He's from Faldine, which isn't surprising as Veltos is closer to Faldine than any other VSC planet. When he was taken in for questioning, he admitted there was a resurgence of rebel activity here."

"Credible evidence?" She raised her eyebrows.

Iver nodded in sympathy, because there were always rumors that the rebels were reorganizing. "Credible enough they sent me a report about it."

She tilted her head. "And you asked Lancaster to look into it?"

He thought about it. Shook his head. "Not exactly. I asked him to find a person of interest mentioned in the report and question him."

They both considered that for a few minutes.

Iver shifted. "You think Lancaster is involved." It was a stupid thing to say. She wouldn't have told him what she'd seen on Lancaster's face otherwise.

She looked at him with something close to sympathy in her eyes. She reached out as if to touch his arm, then thought better of it and dropped her hand to her side.

"Lancaster, more than anyone, would know you were going to Touka today, and the route we'd take." She shrugged, matter-of-fact. "He also looked ready to kill you himself when he thought you weren't looking, and even though he should be here right now, getting us out, he's nowhere to be found."

There wasn't much more to say about it.

It was just a hard, jagged pill to swallow.

She held out her hand for her pack, which he'd taken from her and hitched over one shoulder as they'd walked up the stream.

He gave her a bland look, and slid his arm through the other strap.

With a barely concealed eye roll, she turned away from him and started walking along the river bank, in an upstream direction toward Touka.

He took one last look in the direction of the downed Sig and the horizon beyond it, still empty of any runners, any sign that help was coming.

Then he turned on his heel and followed Hana.

Sitting beside Iver Sugotti was like flying a Sig at full speed over the worst Faldine magnetic fields.

Hana felt slightly out of control.

She didn't know whether to shift closer or away, unsure how they'd come to be sitting so close beside the fire she'd got going when they'd finally stopped walking.

One of them should probably be on watch, but they'd set a perimeter warning, a standard, off-the-shelf one she'd bought for camping in the Spikes, not the more sensitive, more reliable ones she'd had access to in the military. The low-tech solution should be fine, though. The only thing to really worry about out here other than people trying to kill them was an usinian, and they were so big the alarm would pick one up without a problem.

She scooped up a bite of creamy dyr from the bowl she was holding, which had a sprinkle of sanita in it for crunchy, spicy contrast, and was really glad she'd packed everything she needed to hike the

Spikes before she'd picked Iver up. Her pack would make their walk to Touka much more bearable.

Behind them sat the narrow tunnel tent Iver had set up while she'd gotten the fire going.

Despite its low-slung profile, it seemed to loom.

There would be no room inside it to do anything but curl up against each other.

She tried to shrug the tension at the thought out of her shoulders. "What's wrong?"

She turned her head to look up at him.

The eyes watching her were knowing, with a little uncertainty mixed in.

That didn't compute with what she knew of Iver Sugotti. The head of Verdant String Coalition operations on Faldine was the person in charge of the whole planet.

She'd never seen Iver Sugotti unsure in the six months she'd worked for him.

"It doesn't make sense." She wasn't really avoiding the question-- more than one thing was wrong, and her reaction to Sugotti was only one of them.

He kept his gaze on her steady.

"Even if Lancaster is involved with the rebels, all he had to do was go interview the person you asked him to check out, or tip them off to hide before he could get there. Someone else will follow up on that report eventually, even if they had managed to kill you."

"And you. Don't forget, they tried to kill you, too."

She blinked. Iver sounded pretty pissed about that. More than he was about their attempt on him.

There was a moment of silence before he finally nodded.

"The key word in what you said there is 'eventually'." Iver spooned up some of his dyr.

"You think it's time sensitive?" She considered that. Nodded. "It would explain the amateur hour search team."

"You're being unfair." Iver tipped his head at her. "They didn't think they'd need a search team. They used three missiles against us. They had no idea how good a pilot you are."

"Lancaster did." As she said it, she realized that wasn't quite true. Lancaster knew she was good, but no one really knew how good. She tried hard enough to hide it.

Linnel . . . well, Linnel seemed to know better than anyone.

Iver shook his head. "He didn't fly with you often, and getting a resumé saying you're the best isn't the same as understanding just how talented you are."

She hunched her shoulders. That was true. Even she didn't understand quite how good she was. The line on what was possible had blurred for her in the years since her accident. That's why she'd wanted to go to the Spikes. To find some explanation.

"What is it?" Iver touched her cheek, slowly turning her head to face him full on. "You seem to withdraw whenever your skill comes up."

She closed her eyes. "I don't deserve praise for being able to do what I do."

She had worked hard to be a good pilot, but so had all her colleagues in the war. They'd certainly had enough practice.

The thing that pushed her over the edge to great was nothing but a stumbling, horrifying mistake.

She opened her eyes when Iver dropped his hand, and she turned back to look at the fire.

She cleared her throat. "So you're saying it could be that Lancaster needed to stall the questioning, so he decided to kill you? Don't you think that would bring too much attention on him? After all, we already suspect him. Whoever Arkhor would send to investigate your death would take a hard look at him. He could just as easily have delayed you some other way."

"Unless it was make or break. But you're right." He conceded her point with a nod, stretching out his legs and leaning forward on forearms corded with muscle.

"What else are you involved with right now?"

He glanced at her. "Confidentially, we're about to start a trial of the sky lane between Touka and Permeo. I was going to Touka today to sign off on the construction phase."

She tapped her fingers on her knee. "What happens after you sign off?"

"We announce the project, and surveying in the Spikes starts in a few days."

"And if you were dead and couldn't sign off on anything?"

He leaned back, tilted his head to look at the sky. "Then it would be chaos for a good few months."

"Did Lancaster know about the project?" Unable to resist, Hana leaned back to look at the stars as well.

"In a general sense." Iver looked over at her. "But even I only got the green light for the trial from the VSC yesterday. Because I'd done work setting things up ahead of time, I was able to pull it together right away for a quick start, but Lancaster only found out it was imminent when I asked him to arrange for you to pick me up last night."

"What could he be hiding in the Spikes between Touka and Permeo?" she asked.

He sighed. "I trusted him. I've got no idea what his motivations are."

Suddenly the darkness lit up, dancing with the greens, reds and blues of the aurora, the crazy zigzags like pure, colorful energy. The heartbeat of the sky.

It never got old.

She'd been born on the Verdant String planet of Themis, had spent all her life there until the military had sent her to Faldine to fight, and even the deep green forests of home had nothing on the Faldine aurora.

Whatever had gotten inside her in that terrible accident during the war, whatever was responsible for what she thought of as her upgrade, seemed to respond to the aurora as well, to fizz a little in her blood whenever they appeared. It was both disturbing and exhilarating, a moment when whatever it was made itself known, rather than crouching silently inside her.

She thought of it as tiny organisms in her blood, but couldn't quite remember why she thought that. She didn't remember much of what happened.

The crash, her staggering out of the Dynastra and then collapsing.

She just, at the very edge of her memory, thought she curled her fingers around a short string of metallic beads as she lay on the ground beside her burning runner. Half the time she discounted that out of hand. It just seemed too absurd.

What would beads be doing at her crash site?

She worried--worried a lot--that whatever it was, it wasn't as obvious to her anymore, not because it was fading away, but because she was more integrated with it. That it had become an indistinguishable part of her.

"Where did you go?"

Iver's question forced her to turn to face him.

He had lain back on the grass, but he wasn't looking up as the aurora washed his face in blues and reds, he was looking at her.

"You don't want to know."

"That's the kicker. I do want to know. I want to know everything about you." He made it sound as if he wasn't happy about it, either.

She gave a chuckle at his aggrieved tone. "I really like you too much." She went still as soon as the words were out of her mouth. She hadn't meant to say anything more, let alone tell him the truth.

"And that's a problem because . . .?"

She sighed. "It's complicated."

He gave a snort. "That again? What isn't?"

He went back to looking at the sky and she wriggled down onto her back and pillowed her head with her hands, looking up at the light show.

"You stopped taking women to fancy planetary and city events." She didn't know why she said it.

"Because you were the only woman I wanted to take."

She knew that was what he was saying to her when three weeks into working for him he'd stopped taking anyone to the many dinners and social events he attended as the VSC's head of planet for Faldine.

She was honest enough to know she'd appreciated it. And yet, she'd been a coward and hadn't faced what it meant.

"I . . . I was glad."

He turned to her and grinned. "Now this is progress."

She quirked her lips. "Lancaster noticed what you were doing, and he didn't like it."

"Fuck Lancaster." Iver's tone didn't change, but she read the fury at Lancaster's betrayal in his eyes. "He convinced me you'd walk if I was too obvious, which is the only reason I never pushed." He gave a sudden bark of laughter. "Bet he regrets convincing me to add the guns to the Sig."

Hana grinned. "Yes, that was a poor decision on his part. Probably he never thought he'd take you in the Sig. Maybe he never planned to kill you at all, he hoped you just wouldn't know what he was doing."

Iver gave a slow nod. "He definitely has more access to information where he is, with me in charge and trusting him, than he would with someone new who would want their own people."

"He must have been desperate to organize the hit on you, then." She was uneasy with the resources Lancaster had been able to harness and his escalation to violence.

She suddenly yawned and with a last look at the flickering lights overhead, she forced herself to her feet. They had a day's walk ahead of them tomorrow. "I've got a spare toothbrush," she said, bending over her pack and pulling out the small bag with her toiletries. When she turned, Iver was standing right beside her, crowding into her space.

She handed the toothbrush to him, refusing to back down, and he feathered his fingers over her forehead, tucking her hair behind her ear.

"What would you have done if I hadn't followed Lancaster's advice, if I'd pushed a little harder for a relationship with you?"

Her instinct was to brush off the question with a flippant reply, but she forced herself to consider it. He was putting his cards on the table, waiting patiently for her to respond.

"I don't know. Right at the beginning, when I was new to the job, I'd probably have left. I had turned down three other job offers before I came to work for you, so while I wouldn't have liked leaving, it would have been relatively easy to. But after you stopped taking partners to the dinners . . ." She lifted her shoulders. "I'd have stayed, and worked my way through it with you." She hesitated. "Probably like we're doing now."

He leaned forward, just a little, and brushed his lips where his fingers had just been. "I can deal with that." His voice sounded a little hoarse.

She stepped back, her gaze going to the tent again before she faced the stream, and began walking toward it to clean her teeth and wash her face.

"I can sleep outside, if it worries you." He was suddenly beside her, shoulders brushing hers again.

She was embarrassed that he had read her nerves over sharing such a small space with him, could feel the heat on her cheeks. "I feel like an idiot, and no, I don't want you to sleep outside."

She knelt at the river bank and splashed water on her face, rubbed in some cleanser and then rinsed it off.

He was staring at her in the darkness, but she wondered how much of her expression he could see.

As the magfield wasn't too close to the surface here, her own night vision was enhanced. She could see clearly on his face he was concerned about her.

She was glad of the cool water, because her cheeks felt even hotter.

She held out the toothpaste and he took it from her with a quirk of his lips. They brushed their teeth together in companionable silence, with nothing but the cries of the night birds and the gurgle of the stream around them.

It was quite domestic.

By the time they were snuggled into the tent, Hana had managed to let go of her nerves, grateful to be warm and comfortable. The top of the tent was transparent, so the aurora that still played and danced above them was visible.

"All right?" Iver's voice was a rumble against her ear.

She gave a nod, snuggled in closer to his chest, and unbelievably, fell into a deep sleep.

CHAPTER 5

AS SOON AS HANA MOVED, Iver woke up.

She wriggled under the arm he'd slung over her sometime in the night and crouched at the entrance to the tent. "Someone's coming."

Her voice was low and flat, unlike he'd ever heard her, and then she shook herself, as if coming out of a trance. "I can hear a runner."

Iver moved, sliding out after her and collapsing the tent in seconds.

"Which direction?" He couldn't hear a thing.

She pointed, and at last he heard the faintest of rumbles.

He set aside his interest in her astonishing hearing and put the tiny square the tent had folded into in her pack.

They moved toward the river, leaving nothing behind them.

They'd buried the remains of their fire under sand and rocks before they'd gone to sleep and Lancaster would have to be unusually lucky to find where they'd camped.

They'd already discussed what they'd do if they needed to hide, so there was no talking as Iver slid into the river. Hana slipped in next to him, barely making a sound.

It was freezing. And deeper than he'd expected.

They'd chosen to camp in this spot because the river had a high bank on one side, including another scooped-out cave like the one they'd used before.

This one was narrower and deeper, though.

They barely fit in together, and both of them took the time to go in feet first, so they faced the river. Iver had his SAL out, and Hana took it from him, checking it out.

"You've shot one before?" he asked.

She nodded. "I had to do basic training, like everyone else. I carried one, as standard battle gear, but I never had to use it." She slid the cartridge out, looked at the neat line of tranquilizer cartridges. "I heard they're thinking about using these more broadly within the VSC, because they can't be set to kill, unlike a laz."

Iver hadn't heard that, but it made sense. The SAL had been a necessary alternative to the laz given the dangers the magnetic fields of Faldine posed. Laz fire had a disconcerting tendency to act more like lightning than anything else on Faldine, vacillating wildly.

Shooting a laz, as the first Verdant String settlers had discovered, could be just as deadly for the shooter or the friends beside them as for whoever they were shooting at.

Hana handed the SAL back to him and then went still, a look on her face telling him she was concentrating hard, and he guessed she was listening for the runner.

"They're close." She glanced at him. "Too close."

"As in 'how did they know which direction to choose' close?" There was really only one logical explanation for that.

"Electronic tag," Hana said. "The magfield will be interfering, so they'll have to get closer to get a signal."

He gave a nod of agreement. "If there's one on either one of us, they'd have managed to get a general direction when they were coming in. Now they'll be hunting to refine it."

The aurora had finished hours before, but the lack of it meant the moonlight was useful again, and Iver caught a glimpse of Hana's face. She was worrying her lower lip with her teeth.

"I should have thought of a tag earlier."

"Why?" He hadn't either. "The first team didn't behave as if they had a tag to follow."

"Probably Lancaster didn't think we'd get away. Now he's not sure if we did or not, he's come to check."

The logic of it was undeniable. "And because they're heading right for us, they've been getting an intermittent signal, at the very least. So Lancaster knows we made it. And generally where we are."

"The good news keeps coming." Her voice held a hint of humor, and sudden, unexpected desire flashed through him.

He was plastered up against her, so it was no trouble at all to bend his head and give her a quick, hard kiss.

She went still under him, and then, to his surprise and delight, kissed him back, her lips firm against his.

She cleared her throat delicately, and he thought he saw a flush of color on her cheeks.

Before he could tease her, the sound of a big runner coming closer had him focusing again.

Hana drew in a deep breath. "We need to find that tag."

"I know." It was most likely in his clothing, but unlike Hana, he had nothing spare. His luggage had gone up with the Sig.

Still, if it kept them alive . . . "I'll strip off everything."

She was looking in the direction of the runner, tension in every line of her. "I'm going to trust you with something."

He waited, saying nothing.

She drew in a deep breath. "The magfield is weak enough here that I can find the tag on you, if there is one."

"All right." Of everything he thought she'd say, this was the last thing he'd expected.

She turned to him, reaching out her hands.

He didn't know what he expected. Given her nervousness, he assumed she was about to bring out a banned or modified scanner of some kind. Some illegal equipment he, as the head of planet, would be obliged to report her over. What he didn't expect was for her to run her fingers over him, starting at the top of his head.

"What if the tag is on you?"

"It isn't. I've checked."

He wondered when she'd done that, but said nothing as her fingers ran down his neck, over his shoulders and then down the front of his chest.

She hesitated when she got to his crotch, and he couldn't help leaning in. "It's nothing you haven't felt before." His voice was a husky whisper.

She lifted her gaze to his, and despite the situation, the rising noise of the runner coming their way, he could see the gleam of humor in her gold-brown eyes as she inclined her head. "It's poked me in the back a time or two."

Her lips quirked, but she didn't touch him intimately.

"However good he is, I don't think Lancaster would be able to put a tag on you there."

Her arms came around him, and her hands rose up his back, and then came to a stop on his spine, just between his shoulder blades.

"There." She pressed the spot, and he felt a sudden sharp pain.

"That's quite a gift you have." He said it only to distract himself from the memory of him and Lancaster waking from a night out in the bush. They'd both been stiff and sore after spending a day white-water rafting in the river near his home, and then drinking too much xitin around the campfire.

He remembered how his back had hurt, and Lancaster lifting his shirt to check and giving an easy laugh.

"You must have been sleeping directly on a sharp rock." Lancaster's voice had been teasing. "You've got quite the bruise."

"What is it?" Hana's fingers had lifted off him. "You went somewhere."

"Lancaster did this." He left it at that. Too angry for anything else. "But that doesn't answer how you found it."

"It's too long a story to be told now." She flicked her gaze away and he gave a nod of agreement. But the story would be told. He would make sure of it.

They went silent as the runner came even closer, moving slowly, most likely looking for the tag to light up.

Hana twisted and reached back for her pack, her movements quick and sure, as if she could see what she was doing in the pitch dark at the back of the cave.

She pulled a knife and some anesthetic gel out of a side pocket and then pulled his shirt up at the back.

"Can you roll onto your stomach?" She seemed to plaster herself to the side and ceiling of the cave, giving him a little room to do just that, and then settled on the small of his back, her knees on either side of him, body bent low over him.

The runner was much closer, and he heard the roar as it accelerated.

"They've found us." As he said it, he felt the icy touch of the numbing gel on his skin. When she inserted the knife tip, he was aware of it as it dug in, but the gel had done its work. He felt no pain.

His hands were braced on either side of his head, and she tapped the back of one. He turned it over and she put the bloody tag in his palm.

He heard the crinkle of the wrapping on a healing gel strip, and then felt the warmth of it going on.

As soon as it was in place, he felt her blow out a breath, as if she'd held it in, as if she'd been far more rattled at what she'd had to do than she'd let on.

His hand closed in a fist around the tag, and when she pulled his shirt back down, he rolled carefully to his side to allow Hana to swing one leg over his back and lie down beside him again.

"Do you think it'll float?" He tried to have a good look at the tag, aware that the runner was circling their camp site now.

"No."

He nodded. It would be useless to simply throw it into the water. If it sunk, it'd lead Lancaster's people to right in front of them.

Hana twisted again, rummaging around in her pack, as the roar of the runner's engines seemed to be right on top of them. She pulled out a derpra, the long, smooth-skinned fruit native to Faldine.

"It floats?" he asked.

She nodded. Took the tag from him and pushed it into the soft fruit completely, then dropped it into the water running right below them.

Iver watched it for a moment. It bobbed in the choppy water and then swirled away, disappearing into the darkness.

The runner revved its engine, like a predator after flushed prey, and took off down the river.

"They think we're making a run for it."

She shook her head. "They think you are." Her voice was barely audible. "They don't know whether I'm alive or dead."

He was about to respond when she put a finger to his lips and then pulled herself up on an elbow, head cocked, listening. The runner was still just audible over the sound of the river.

From further downstream, he heard a loud splash, and the drift of voices shouting.

"Time to go or we'll be trapped."

He waited for Hana to pull herself out of the narrow opening first. She maneuvered until she could step down into the water.

He passed her the pack, and she stepped to the side to give him room to get out.

With her and the pack out of the cave, he managed to swing around to come out feet first, but as he pushed out, the bank around him suddenly collapsed.

He landed hard in the water, with rocks and large chunks of clay coming down with him.

A light was suddenly on him from the bank above, someone was shouting, and without looking in Hana's direction, he let the current take him further from her until the loud splash of someone running toward him forced him to find his feet.

"Who's there?" he demanded. "Show yourselves."

There was a sudden pause, as if whoever was chasing him was startled to be challenged. Was startled Iver wasn't behaving like a fugitive.

Time for them to adjust their thinking.

The person running toward him from downstream slipped on a rock, went under and then came up fully drenched and swearing viciously.

Iver vaguely recognized him. Maybe he worked security at VSC headquarters. He had a stocky build and short, spiky hair, and now that he'd regained his feet, he was moving toward Iver with singular focus.

Iver made the choice to ignore him, shading his eyes against the light that blinded him from above. "Is that you, Lancaster?"

The light lowered. "I'd like to say it's nice to see you alive, boss."

He'd expected it, but it was still a shock to hear the voice of a man he'd thought was his friend as well as the best head of security he'd ever had.

"But you can't, is that right?" He tried to keep the bitterness of betrayal out of his voice.

"No." Lancaster had the temerity to sound regretful. "It really would be so much easier for me if you were dead."

CHAPTER 6

"WHERE'S HANA?"

Hana was about to duck under the water to hide when she heard Lancaster's question, and she paused with all but the top half of her head submerged, grateful the moonlight didn't penetrate the shadows beneath the riverbank.

"Hana's dead." Iver's voice sounded flat.

"No, I don't believe you."

Linnel's shout made her suck in a breath. She hadn't thought he'd come back with Lancaster, although why she'd assumed that, she couldn't say. She supposed logically he would have been useful in guiding Lancaster to where their Sig had originally gone down.

"That woman is indestructible." Linnel didn't make the statement sound like a compliment.

"If you don't think she can be killed, why did you try?" Iver stood, legs braced against the current, hands on hips.

"I was told to kill you, asshole. I didn't know Hana was the one flying you until after the first two missiles. How did she supposedly die?"

"She was grabbing gear out of the Sig, and I was off to the side, talking to Lancaster, when the third missile hit."

"No. You asked her what missiles were used, and she answered you." Lancaster spoke slowly.

"I called to her from where I was standing." Iver didn't even blink as he lied.

"She has a way of dodging death." Linnel sounded petulant now. "She came through situations no one could come through, most often with barely a scratch."

"You're saying that she could somehow survive a direct hit with an SD3?" Lancaster's voice was harder to hear, as if he'd turned his head.

"I'm saying she went through a war, with people trying to kill her every day, and walked away unscathed. One time, just to test my theory, I sabotaged her Dynastra's engines, and she not only landed it, she worked out what the problem was and fixed it before flying home."

"You sabotaged a fellow military officer's runner while you were both fighting in a war on the same side?" Lancaster's voice dropped an octave.

Funny. He'd just tried to kill Iver, but he was getting morally outraged at Linnel's sabotage?

Hana had known the damaged engine was Linnel's doing right away. She hadn't reported him, though. There wasn't any evidence, and she knew the fact that she had found it, fixed it, and then never reported it freaked him out.

It was revenge of sorts.

She had never turned her back on him again, though. Nor left her Dynastra unprotected.

"Why the outrage? I thought you were pro-rebel." Linnel's voice was a sneer. "And what are you doing right now but stabbing your fellow colleague in the back?"

Lancaster didn't respond immediately, and Hana saw Iver decide to take the opportunity to start wading toward the river bank.

"Where the hell are you going?" The thug that had been standing in the stream with Iver lunged for him, but Iver had already moved out of reach, and he stumbled.

"The water's too cold to stand around in, listening to you and your friend bicker about who's the bigger traitor." Iver reached the bank and a hand came down to help him up.

Lancaster literally giving him a hand.

Hana didn't understand the dynamic, but for whatever reason, Lancaster hadn't chosen to shoot Iver in the stream where he stood.

Probably scared to leave too much evidence for whoever the VSC sent to investigate Iver's death.

Iver was head of planet and an Arkhoran. The Arkhorans didn't let things like their people being killed slide. There wouldn't just be ripples at his death, there would be tsunamis.

She assumed it would be a lot less trouble for Lancaster if Iver could have been found burned to a crisp in the Sig, but that chance had already pinched to the black and was long gone.

"You want to tell me why?" Iver asked.

"It's complicated." Lancaster sounded genuinely regretful.

Remembering that's just what she'd said to Iver herself earlier that day, Hana's breath hitched.

Lancaster and Iver walked away and the man still standing in the river stared after them. Hana repressed a shiver, and not because of the cold water. Iver had better watch himself around that one.

Lancaster, too, if she was any judge.

He was not happy at being left like a flunky and ignored.

The man made his way angrily to the bank and scrambled up on his own. Linnel had either gone with Lancaster or wasn't prepared to help him.

They were a cohesive, friendly group, all right.

She waited, crouched low in the shallows, until she was convinced they'd moved back to where the runner had landed.

She didn't know if they planned to take Iver away or kill him right here. She couldn't let them do either.

She carefully moved upstream, keeping to the shallows and the dark edges, until she could climb the bank without any fear of being seen.

She was shivering by the time she found a large rock to hide behind. She rubbed herself down with a towel from her pack and changed into dry clothes, feeling immediately better. She ate an energy bar while she dressed to give herself the calories she needed after time in the freezing water, then she hid her pack and stood for a moment, eyes closed, centering herself.

The upgrade, as she called it, the thing that had somehow become part of her since she'd been shot down during the war, stirred inside her. Not at full strength, but the magnetic field was far enough below the ground here not to interfere too much.

These days, it was so much a part of her, she barely thought of it, but when she focused like this, it seemed to amp up her advantage.

She deliberately connected to it, wanting what it had to offer.

The warm, friendly exuberance of it flowed through her. Blowing out the breath she'd held in, she stepped out from the rock and embraced the night.

Hana crept a little closer to the fire burning next to Lancaster's runner, Iver finally in her sights.

"So, how are you going to kill me?" Iver leaned toward the fire as he spoke. He hadn't shaved in over a day, and the shadow on his jaw, illuminated by the dancing flames, gave him a harder, edgier look.

"That's a problem, to be sure." Lancaster's voice was calm. "But whatever the method, I'm afraid it'll have to be soon." He stood up, moving out of Hana's view. "Unfortunately, I can't retroactively burn you in the Sig. Whoever the VSC sends to investigate will see through that in seconds with the kind of equipment they'll have at their disposal, even with the magnetic field issues. I'll have to transport you back to where the Sig went down, have you make hard contact with a rock in the river and then let you float down a little way, making sure you drown."

"Harsh." Iver's tone was slightly amused.

"Shut the fuck up, Iver." Lancaster's sudden venomous hiss made the guard beside Iver jerk a little in fear and surprise. "You don't know how much trouble this has been."

Iver threw back his head and laughed, and Hana heard Lancaster swearing, and then the thud of boots as he stamped off.

She slid a little further to the side, managed to see the silhouette of what she guessed was Lancaster as he disappeared into the Dynastra.

That wouldn't do.

There was no way she and Iver would be safe unless they took the Dynastra and left everyone else behind.

She didn't want anyone's blood on her hands. She'd seen enough killing to last a lifetime, and she'd made a promise to herself when she resigned from the military that she wouldn't do it again.

If it was a choice between life or death for her or Iver then she'd break her vow, but first she would try to find another way.

Leaving them behind would work best.

The hostile guard from the river came into view, no longer in wet clothing. Hana guessed he had been in the Dynastra changing and had been sent back by Lancaster.

"We're all accounted for now except Lunn." He spoke to the guard beside Iver, not looking at Iver at all. "Get him into the Dynastra, ready to go."

He turned away, but instead of going back to the runner, he turned toward the river, his gait impatient and self-important. He'd been tasked with rounding up the last straggler, Hana guessed, and the thought of wielding a little more power than someone else excited him.

She followed him into the darkness, leaving the glow of the campfire behind her.

When she caught up with him, he was standing on top of a rock in the water, an easy jump from the bank. He called to his missing teammate with hands bracketing his mouth.

"Lunn!" There was an anger in the guard's voice now. His mission had gone from being a power trip to being boring.

Life on Faldine, which often had no working comms, gave most Verdant Stringers a newfound appreciation for what they'd taken for granted on their home planets.

And places on Faldine like this one, where the magnetic field wasn't very strong but had enough juice to interfere were the worst. Everything was temperamental, cutting in and out. Working and then not working.

It was something the scientists were still looking into.

A strong magfield wasn't good for whatever was responsible for her upgrade, either, though. She felt much more like her old self, pre-upgrade, when she was in an area with a strong magfield.

It had given her a theory about just what had managed to invade her body, but there was no way she was prepared to get someone to test it for her.

And while the plains around Touka weren't the worst on the magnetic scale, they were strong enough to dampen her advantage.

But only dampen it. She was still more than she had been.

"Lunn!"

Obviously the comms weren't working for Lancaster and his team. Which meant the guard couldn't signal someone for help if she didn't manage to take him down immediately.

At last someone called back, a faint call from downriver, and with a huff of impatience, the guard put his hands on his hips. "We're waiting for you."

He was fully focused on looking downriver, peering into the darkness for a sign of his colleague. It was easy for Hana to jump onto a rock downriver from him undetected.

There were two rocks between them, and she didn't hesitate. She accelerated to full speed, jumping from one to the other, pushing off the last one to get herself airborne and landing right behind him. She shoved him down, her hand going straight to his SAL, holstered on his hip.

She pulled it out as he shouted in rage, and then shot him in the back. He twisted, trying to see who'd attacked him, then collapsed on the rock.

Hana leaped down and started downriver, the guard's SAL still ready in her hand.

Lunn walked toward her in the darkness, making no effort to be quiet or stealthy.

She couldn't blame him. He had his colleague bellowing for him to hurry, as if it were all wrapped up.

These people truly were amateurs. They should never had taken Iver's word that she was dead. Even Linnel, who didn't want to believe it, hadn't carried out even the most perfunctory search for her.

They would pay a price for that.

She considered hiding and waiting for Lunn to pass her, but he was moving too slowly, walking in the river itself rather than making the more dangerous jumps between the rocks sticking above the waterline. She didn't have time.

She ran straight at him, leaping rock to rock. She expected him to react in some way to her speed and the fact that she was clearly a stranger, but he kept his head down, looking at where he was putting his feet on the uneven riverbed.

Sometimes she forgot how well she could see at night. Forgetting things like that would trip her up in the end. It was inevitable.

As she got closer, she could see Lunn was soaking wet and had a bleeding cut on his forehead. He must have slipped and fallen into the river, which was why he was the last one in, and why he was being so careful of his footing now.

"I said I was coming, asshole." Lunn looked up as she made the last jump onto the rock he was about to wade around.

His eyes widened when he realized she wasn't his colleague, and then his hand went to the cartridge she'd just shot into his chest. As soon as his fist closed around it, he lunged forward, trying to grab her.

She jumped straight up, and when she landed back down, he was sprawled over the rock, unconscious.

His feet and lower legs were still in the water, though, and the current was already moving his body from side to side.

He'd fall in if she left him like this.

She stood staring down at him for a moment, wrestling with herself, but in the end, on a sigh, she jumped down beside him and maneuvered him carefully over her shoulder.

She didn't have to go far--the riverbank was close, but it was steep and Lunn was heavy and a good head and shoulders taller than her. With a surge of effort she reached the top and dropped him to the ground.

The night was cool but not cold. And he would wake in two hours.

She gulped in air.

Even with her upgrade, she felt the strain. She ate an energy bar, wriggled her toes in her boots, and commiserated with herself about getting her socks wet again.

She shook out stiff shoulders, and then started back for Lancaster's camp and Iver.

Two down. Four to go.

CHAPTER 7

"WHERE'S NUNESS?" Lancaster asked as the guard pushed Iver into the Dynastra.

The old VSC fighting ships had a larger hold than his Sig, but they didn't maneuver as well. Some of them had been recommissioned after the war for more commercial purposes, but their blades made them an oddity, useful on Faldine only. This one still looked like the troop carrier it had been designed as, and he wondered who owned it.

"Nuness went to get Lunn." The guard prodded Iver deeper into the hold, obviously meaning for him to sit on one of the benches in the back.

Instead, Iver did a slow turn, taking in the whole runner.

"Nice ride. Yours?" he asked Lancaster.

"Sit down and shut up, Iver." Lancaster stood up. "Oniba, go out and kick Lunn and Nuness' asses, they should be back. We need to go."

Iver sat down slowly, suddenly knowing why the two guards weren't back yet.

Hana.

Just the thought of her sent a thrill, a spike of emotion, through him, and he fought a shiver.

Oniba shared a quick glance with Lancaster before he disappeared out the door, and something in the look they exchanged made Iver wonder if they were lovers.

He leaned back against the wall and turned to Lancaster, waving his hand to encompass the runner. "Did you fly it here?"

Lancaster was bent over a screen, and from the irritation in his expression and the way his finger was jabbing, Iver guessed the connection was cutting in and out. The joys of using tech on Faldine.

Lancaster set the screen aside with a vicious thump. "Yes. I flew it here. The fewer people who know about this, the better."

"I recognize Nuness and Oniba. They work for you? For me?" He hadn't seen Oniba together with Lancaster, though, and wondered if their association was new, or if Lancaster had purposely hidden it.

"They used to." Lancaster shrugged. "They resigned from your employ a few months ago."

"To work for you in another capacity, I take it?" Iver shifted on the hard bench.

"I get you want to work out what's going on here, Iver, but I don't have the time or the inclination to tell you. You trusted the wrong person, me, and now you and the VSC are screwed. Accept it and know that's just how it is."

Iver lifted an eyebrow. "The VSC is screwed? That's a pretty big statement. How are you going to bring down the whole system?"

Lancaster lifted a shoulder. "Fine. The VSC's interests here are screwed. The rebels will rise again, and in the time it takes for the VSC to put them back in their place, some people who have offered me a good deal will take what they need from Faldine."

"And by the time we sort it all out, they'll be gone?" Iver wondered again what was hidden between Touka and Permeo.

"Something like that." Lancaster's smile was dry.

"What could the Caruso possibly offer you that's enough to stir up war?" Iver wondered, as he made a guess on who Lancaster was helping. "And where could you even spend what they've promised you? The two breakaway planets are VSC vassals now."

"The Caruso--?" Lancaster shook his head in one quick, violent movement. "It doesn't--"

Oniba stepped inside, his pant legs wet up to the knees. "Nuness is down. I've sent Linnel and Killian out to look for Lunn."

"Down, how?" Lancaster stood.

"Dart in his back." Oniba glanced at Iver with suspicious eyes.

"You think Lunn did it?" Lancaster's question was sharp.

Oniba tipped his head. "Who else?" He looked at Iver again. "Unless you think he's got someone out there."

Linnel stepped inside, crowding Oniba enough to force him to step aside. "We found Lunn, dart in his chest, dumped on the river bank. I told you Hana wasn't dead." He flicked a look at Iver, and Iver had to fight back a smile.

He cultivated a blank stare instead.

"That true, boss?" Lancaster turned to him. "Is Hana out there?"

"I told you, she died in the Sig."

"Sure she did." Linnel shook his head.

"You're frightened of her." Iver said it slowly. "Why are you so frightened of her?"

"Because she's not like the rest of us." Linnel hissed his reply.

Both Lancaster and Oniba looked at him strangely, as if suddenly aware they had someone unhinged in their midst.

Iver's gaze clashed with Lancaster's, and he lifted an eyebrow.

Lancaster turned away in disgust, but Iver could see he was a little rattled by Linnel's fear and obsession.

Then Lancaster turned back, thoughtful. "You'd be more upset if Hana was dead." He pointed a finger at Iver. "I should have realized it earlier. You've been hot for her since the moment I introduced you to her." He tilted his head, as if to look at Iver from a different angle. "If she had really burned up in front of you, you wouldn't be this calm. You'd have tried to attack me."

"Maybe I got over her," Iver said.

Lancaster gave a snort. "No. I saw the looks. The times you sat up front in the Sig, when you usually sit at the back. Even last week you went to that diplomatic dinner and didn't take anyone with you. If you were over it, you would have."

He had him there. Lancaster was good at his job. That he was also a traitorous snake didn't negate that.

Iver simply lifted his shoulders in a shrug. It could be interpreted any way Lancaster wanted to interpret it.

"And even if you were over it," Lancaster spoke slowly, "you'd still be a lot more upset I'd killed her than you are." He jerked his head to the door. "Go get Lunn and Nuness in here, Linnel, and hunt Hana down. And hurry, we're losing time."

"She's probably taken Killian already." Linnel looked out the Dynastra's doors into the darkness. "I haven't heard him since I stepped inside."

Lancaster stared at him for a moment. "Pull yourself together." His bark was sharp and contemptuous. "She's a pilot, not special forces. She's been in a crash, spent the last day with no food or a comfortable place to sleep, and we outnumber her at least three to one."

"You're wrong." Linnel drew himself up. "She's not . . . normal. She gets away with shit no one should. It's like the world doesn't touch her, and no one can fly like she does."

Lancaster's eyes narrowed. "Linnel, how did I miss that you're a crazy bastard?"

"You were desperate for people who were happy to go back to the days of the war. It's been a bit too quiet since it was over." Linnel lifted his shoulders. "But I'm not crazy. There's something wrong with *her*, not me."

Lancaster and Oniba shared a look, and Iver watched Linnel. He had the sincere, focused look of the obsessed.

"What's your end game with Hana?" Iver asked him.

Linnel looked over at him, face strangely, almost obscenely blank.

"I want to expose her. Make her admit the truth."

"The truth about what?" The expression on Lancaster's face was one of distaste.

Iver met his gaze. *Sucks to be taken in by someone, doesn't it?*

"The truth that she's had some kind of enhancement. The military must have experimented on her."

"So after this extremely illegal enhancement procedure, they just let her leave the military?" Iver asked.

Linnel shuffled. "I admit, that doesn't make sense, but she still goes to the base once a month. To check in."

"She volunteers as a mentor to the new trainees," Lancaster said.

Iver looked at him in surprise. He hadn't known that.

"That's what they *say*." Linnel must have heard how crazy that sounded, because he shook his head once, in annoyance. "Don't believe me, then. You'll see. She's out there, and she can't be killed."

"Can you hear yourself?" Oniba asked.

Linnel curled his lip and shook his head, then stepped out into the darkness.

The moment he was gone, Oniba turned an expressive face toward Lancaster.

"I know." Lancaster looked out into the darkness after him. "He's not just a loose end, he's a liability."

"This is the first time I've heard him talk crazy like that." Oniba moved toward the door himself. "You going to be okay watching Sugotti on your own?"

Lancaster grunted a yes, and Oniba stepped out in Linnel's wake.

"So, it's just you and me, now. Is Hana out there?" Lancaster leveled the SAL in his hand at Iver as he moved back to the bench to pick up the screen he'd been working on before.

Iver smiled. "More likely one of your guys decided to take out Nuness. He's enough of an asshole for it."

"And Lunn?" Lancaster's eyes narrowed. "Someone took him out, too."

Iver shrugged. "Maybe you hire a lot of crazy assholes. I know I hired at least one."

"Funny." Lancaster drew back his lips in a parody of a smile, then glanced down at the screen.

Iver saw him scowl at it as if he didn't like what he saw. The expression was so petulant, Iver couldn't hold back the flare of rage.

"So, you must have drugged me that night you tagged me in the back." He regretted the words as soon as they were out of his mouth.

Stupid!

Stupid to be baited into giving important information away.

"I didn't want to do it, but you were getting closer to that sky lane trial, and you wouldn't consider another route, you just had to have it between Permeo and Touka." Lancaster tapped at the screen with hard, irritated jabs.

Iver lifted his shoulders. "You were subtle. I didn't even notice you were pushing for another route."

"I wasn't. I had someone else do it." Lancaster shook his head. "But you always have to be right." He bent his head over his screen, muttering curses beneath his breath. "Yes, we are fucking on our way. Just running the preflight checks." He tapped harder, jabbing at the screen.

Iver went very still. Lancaster wasn't talking to him, or even himself, he was muttering to whoever was communicating with him on the screen.

And he was lying to them.

But that seemed to be how Lancaster rolled.

"The sky lane route isn't a matter of opinion." Iver picked up the conversation as if he hadn't noticed anything. He cast his mind back to the meetings he'd had about the route. About who had tried to argue for a different site. Couldn't think of a single one. "Permeo and Touka are the two biggest cities. The sky lane has to be able to work between them. If it doesn't, I've been wasting my time here."

"Maybe it really is as simple as that." Lancaster rubbed a hand over his short, military cut. "Doesn't matter. It can't go ahead."

"It's going to." Iver looked out through the Dynastra's door, aware that it was very quiet out there. "Whether I'm dead or not. I sent all the plans to the VSC last night."

Lancaster looked up this time, the move jerky. "You didn't."

"I did. I even spoke to Carina personally. She sends her regards to you, by the way."

Lancaster closed his eyes. "I wish you hadn't done that."

"Sorry, I didn't realize you were planning to sell out the VSC in general and me in particular, or I'd have kept it to myself." He realized he was breathing heavily, so enraged he could barely draw in enough air. "What the fuck are you doing, Lancaster? There's nowhere you can run, nowhere you can spend whatever funds the Caruso have promised you. What could you possibly gain from this?"

"That's your problem, Iver. You think everyone follows the rules. There were times when I . . . didn't, and someone found out. Threatened to expose what I'd done, and I am not going to be imprisoned." He shrugged, shuffled backward, and started up the engines. "It sort of spiraled from there. You take one step, and then another, and then before you realize it you are so far down the path, there's no going back."

"We're here, with you about to kill me and the war about to restart because you were *blackmailed*?" Iver stared at him, and Lancaster looked away.

"Doesn't matter, I told you. It is what it is." Lancaster glanced at his screen, and then looked out into the night. "Come on, slackers. We have to go." When he turned, his SAL was steady on Iver. He moved to the doors and glanced out into the night, his foot tapping impatiently. Then he went still. "How did you find the tag?"

That's why Iver had regretted saying anything about it. He knew if Lancaster thought about it for any amount of time, he'd realize there was a big hole in Iver's explanation.

He bluffed it out. "When you came directly toward where I was hiding, I knew I had to be tagged. I remembered the camp trip straight away."

"But you got rid of the tag." Lancaster leaned back against the bulkhead. "How did you get it out? I put it in the one place you would find it hard to even touch, let alone cut out."

Iver said nothing.

"Shit, Hana *is* out there, isn't she?" He shoved the SAL toward Iver as if he wanted to fire it, and there was murder in his eyes. "Shit. We can't just go, we have to round her up, too." He kicked out at the wall and the hand holding the SAL trembled.

"This is--" Lancaster pressed his lips together in a tight line, trying to find control, and then, SAL still pointed at Iver, he moved to where two bags hung from hooks near the door and dug inside one, brought out some restraints.

The end of the road was here, Iver realized. He had gotten as much information out of Lancaster as he was going to get.

His hand closed around the damp towel someone had left on the bench beside him and he threw it at Lancaster's face. Then he launched himself forward, taking Lancaster down hard.

He punched his former friend in the throat and flipped him over, ripping the restraints from his hands and jerking his arms back to slide them on.

When he got to his feet, he stood over Lancaster for a moment, listening to his former friend's gasping attempts to breathe--breathing heavily himself.

A scream of rage from outside galvanized him.

He bent down and grabbed Lancaster's SAL, then jumped out the Dynastra's door.

The shocking, blinding flicker of laz fire made him stumble as he landed on the ground.

Who would be so stupid?

It flickered again, not shooting straight toward where it was aimed, as it would on Arkhor, but leaping and dancing like freed lightning, splitting in two to go left and right.

The light winked out, but Iver had seen Linnel outlined in the laz fire, facing away from Iver and the Dynastra.

He had no problem shooting Linnel in the back.

He fired his SAL and watched the ex-lieutenant fall forward.

"Hana?"

"Here." She walked out of the darkness, the pack on her back, a SAL in her hand. "The others are down."

"Lancaster is tied up in the runner." He held out an arm and after a moment of hesitation she closed the distance between them and he pulled her in close, kissed the top of her head. He felt suddenly weak. The idea of her out here alone, taking on Lancaster's thugs one by one, made him feel a little sick.

She went still beneath him, and then she ran a soothing hand down his back. "I'm glad you're all right."

He tightened his grip for a moment and then turned, arm still around her, to look at Linnel. "We should kill that one," he said. "He's not sane when it comes to you."

The fucker was mad. Using a laz? It was practically suicidal.

Hana turned to look at Linnel, too. "I know."

"Do you know why?"

She lifted a shoulder. "During the war, toward the end, we went out in a squadron of four Dynastras. My runner was the only one that came back. His lover was in one of the others--shot down. I don't think he's been right since then. He thinks there's some kind of conspiracy, although nothing about what he says makes any sense."

Some of it did, though.

Iver remembered her fingers moving over him, looking for the tag.

Now those same fingers suddenly curled into fists, grabbing handfuls of his jacket, and she looked up.

"Something's coming," she said, and there was that flat quality to her voice again.

"What?" He tilted his head.

"A runner." She narrowed her eyes. "Coming in fast and high."

There was a flicker of light high above them, and then Hana pulled him down, face first into the dirt.

He felt the low, hard whump of the SD3 hitting the Dynastra

behind them to the core of his bones. He crawled over Hana's body to shield her as flaming pieces of Lancaster's runner fell around them. One sliced into the ground less than an arm's reach from him.

He lifted himself into a crouch, arms on either side of Hana's back, and turned to look at the inferno.

Lancaster had been in there.

Hana nudged him and he stood, pulling her up with him.

She looked up at the sky. "They're going."

"How do you know that?" He couldn't help the slightly accusing tone.

She lifted a brow when she glanced over at him. "I've got good hearing." Her expression dared him to make something of it. "I suggest we get moving before Lancaster's crew wake up. My guess is they won't be too happy when they do."

He gave a nod. "I think Lancaster foolishly told whoever he was working for that I didn't die in the original hit, and he was going to set something up to make it look like I'd died afterward."

"That would have been difficult to pull off with the caliber of investigators the VSC would have sent in."

Iver gave her a nod. "Guess it was easier to make Lancaster part of the tragedy, which means he wasn't as important as he thought he was."

"You get anything out of Lancaster about what's happening?" Hana adjusted the pack on her back, and he grabbed the back of it, tugging it off her shoulders.

She went still, back turned to him, then shrugged it off and let him take it.

"I got a few things out of him."

"So, can we go back in to headquarters?"

He hesitated. "Someone else was involved. Probably more than one person. But with Lancaster gone, I'm not sure how they'll react."

"So what's the plan, other than getting to Touka?"

"We contact Carina."

She looked over at him, face quizzical.

"Admiral Carina Valerian. Head of the VSC fleet for the Faldine system."

"Oh, that Carina." She gave him a dry look. "My former boss."

"Oh, yes, she would have been." Iver grinned at her as he followed her across the river, jumping from rock to rock to reach the other side. "Guess you'll feel right at home, then."

CHAPTER 8

TOUKA CITY SHIMMERED up out of the haze, a handful of very tall buildings rising up in imitation of the Spikes behind them-- although the soaring majesty and height of the mountains dwarfed them.

Hana stood, feet braced, hands on her hips, and just drank it in for a moment.

Of course, the buildings weren't just constructed as high as possible to mimic the mountains. Like her, VSC tech worked better when it was far from the magfields buried in the ground. Touka would not have been able to communicate with the rest of Faldine if it hadn't gone up.

Her usual view of Touka was from the air, flying in with Iver. This ground-level perspective was wonderful; the city rising up out of the plains, the reflective silver and blue of the buildings a sharper, brighter pop of color in contrast to the soft grays and greens of the mountains behind them.

"You built Touka, didn't you?" She turned to Iver.

His jaw was even darker with stubble than it had been last night, his gray eyes watching her with such intensity she had to fight down a shiver. "I approved some of the plans." At last he turned his gaze away, and it felt like she'd been given a reprieve.

"It's a sight."

He nodded. "And Permeo has a different character, a charming contrast."

She could hear the pride in his voice.

"Did you ever think you'd be head-of-planet?"

He gave a bark of laughter. "No. I'm a scientist and an engineer. I came to Faldine to help the VSC find the least invasive way to extract the minerals we needed, and somehow I ended up running the whole place when the war flared up."

"Do you see yourself staying here?" She couldn't think of anywhere else she wanted to be, but she knew for a fact that was her upgrade talking.

Still, it was an exciting place to live. Full of possibilities.

It had been at least twenty years since Faldine had been discovered, but as it was originally colonized by smugglers, fleeing from the VSC after the crimes they committed during the Halatian disaster, the generally accepted rules for a new planetary discovery hadn't been followed.

The smugglers had stumbled on Faldine and used it as a hideaway, desperate to lay low while the VSC hunted them.

She knew for a fact they had been totally uncaring of the VSC's Do Not Disturb rule for precious livable planets that had no dominant higher sentient species.

When the VSC had caught up to the smugglers and the secret of Faldine's existence was out, the smugglers had tried to turn it into another breakaway planet like Garmen and Lassa.

Hana still thought the VSC was right to have answered that proposition with a hard no, even with the personal price she'd paid for that decision.

The war had only lasted three years--the smugglers turning rebels against the might of the VSC--but it had felt like a lifetime to her. Even without her strange upgrade, she was a different person.

She shook off the thought.

"Nowhere else I'd rather be than here." Iver reached out and touched her cheek.

"I feel the same. Well . . ." She suddenly grinned. "Not here, here. I'd prefer to already be in Touka City."

She was tired, and if she was any judge of distance, they were still at least three hours from Touka, but somehow the fact that Iver wasn't planning on leaving Faldine in a hurry gave her a boost.

There were no paths in the scrubby plains they'd been walking across and the going had been tough since they'd been walking last night. They'd only stopped to rest a few times.

She started walking again and Iver fell into step beside her. She couldn't tell if he was as tired as she was. He didn't look it.

Her own secret well of energy and focus was having to work harder than usual. The magnetic fields under the plains around Touka were obviously a little closer to the surface than the ones under the city itself.

Touka was as good as it got on Faldine as far as magfields went, with the exception of Iver's headquarters and Bero, the small village that serviced it. The city sprawled across a magnetic field buried so deep that it only interfered a little with day to day comms, although it was enough to make reaching up beyond the atmosphere difficult.

Satellites weren't much good here, which was why Iver lived where he did, in the middle of nowhere but with absolutely no magnetic interference at all. The one satellite circling Faldine was solely for him, connecting him to Admiral Carina Valerian, head of the VSC fleet in the Faldine System.

Most would assume that the admiral's job had been pretty easy for the last year and a half, with the war over, but Hana knew the Caruso had been circling, looking for a way to get to the rich resources on Faldine.

When Admiral Valerian had proved too difficult an obstacle to get around, they'd pretended to give up, when in fact they'd turned their attention to the VSC breakaway planets, Garmen and Lassa, and as had just been revealed, to Veltos as well.

The VSC had shut that down and gotten back control of all its vassals, but it was possible the Caruso were making a play for Faldine again.

And using someone like Lancaster to help them.

"You never told me what the Caruso offered Lancaster to make him betray everything he knew."

Iver gave a slight shake of his head. "He never actually confirmed it was the Caruso. Whoever it was, and honestly, the Caruso are the most likely, they were blackmailing him."

"Blackmailing him?" She stopped, her mouth open. "What were they threatening?"

"They were threatening to reveal details that would get him arrested."

"So not money. Freedom." She gave a slow nod. That made so much more sense. Money wasn't the motivator she understood it had been over a century ago, before the VSC restructured its society to be almost completely equal when it came to wealth. The Citizen Dividend had changed the VSC completely. Some earned a little more than others--most likely Iver was paid more for his job as head-of-planet than she was paid for piloting his Sig--but everyone had what they needed. There was no reason to betray their people for material wealth.

"Whatever the reason, I can't believe he was prepared to restart a war to keep his position and his reputation." Iver slid his hands into his pockets, hunching his shoulders.

Hana reached out, hooked a hand around his bicep, interested and not a little flustered to find her hand didn't even cover half of it, and gave a sympathetic squeeze.

"I know he was your friend. I'm sorry he's dead, and that he betrayed you."

He pulled his opposite hand out of his pocket and placed it over hers.

It should have been awkward, walking so close together, linked as they were, over the rough ground, but it didn't feel that way.

Hana felt herself settle a little.

They hadn't touched much since last night. They'd concentrated on getting as far from the wreckage of the Dynastra and Lancaster's crew as they could, pushing themselves through the night.

But this was . . . nice.

Like the moment on the river bank where they'd both been brushing their teeth.

She opened her mouth to say something, and then tightened her grip on Iver's arm and stopped walking.

"What?"

She lifted a finger to her lips, cocked her head. "Land runner." She shouldn't call it that. It was called a lander here on Faldine.

"From?" He didn't ask if she was sure.

She turned toward where the sound was coming from, not directly from the city but to the west of it. She pointed, and he shaded his eyes to look.

She saw movement through the haze a moment or so later, and felt Iver tense a little more when he obviously saw it, too.

She started to move, looking for a good place to hide.

Iver's hand gripped her arm. "They've already seen us," he said. "And we have no reason to assume they're part of this. We could use a lift to Touka."

That was true.

She gave a nod and they stood side by side, watching. Hana took a step away from Iver, putting a little distance between them. She didn't like how hard it was to do.

He flicked her a look.

"They'll recognize you. Best we keep things uncomplicated." She didn't know if she said it because it was a good idea, or because it kept what was between them secret a little longer, and after a moment staring into her eyes, Iver gave a tiny nod.

The lander was clearly in view now, and coming straight toward them; a small, open vehicle.

A man and a woman sat in the front seats, both wearing dark eye protectors, so Hana couldn't read their expressions well. The lander rocked and bucked as it hit rocks and small bushes.

"Hello!" The woman, who had been sitting in the passenger seat, half-stood as they came within hailing distance, and swayed alarmingly as she waved. To Hana's surprise, Iver lifted a hand and waved back.

The driver, the man with her, focused on negotiating the rough ground, weaving the vehicle around as many obstacles as he could.

They came to a stop with a creak and a shudder.

Hana would never get used to these wheel-based vehicles. They seemed so clunky and impractical compared to the hovers in every other part of the VSC, but then, Faldine wasn't friendly to VSC tech.

"You're Iver Sugotti." The woman stood and lifted her eye protectors to peer at them. She turned her head to her companion. "Si, it's Iver Sugotti!" She swung back to look at them. "What are you doing out here?"

"Our runner went down," Iver said.

The woman turned to look at Hana, but the man kept his eyes on Iver, Hana noted. Even while pretending he wasn't.

"I didn't think the magnetic field was that strong around here." She looked beyond them, as if looking for the downed runner. "You the pilot?"

"Yes." Hana tried to smile. "We'd be grateful for a lift to Touka, if you're going that way."

"Oh, sure!" The woman turned again to the driver, a little too bright and cheerful. "We can definitely give you a lift."

"Of course." The driver spoke his first words. "Where is your runner?"

Hana felt the tingle at the back of her neck, the flash of cold down her arms and spine. Her warning system going into full alert mode. It flared and then shut down, reacting to the magnetic field beneath her feet, but it had given her enough before it fizzled. "More than a day's walk away. We'd appreciate a lift. We've come a long way on foot." She kept her voice light, her face neutral.

Iver must have sensed something in her tone. He sent her a quick, worried look.

"It's lucky you weren't hurt," the woman said as Hana and Iver walked toward the lander.

Iver reached the back first, and before she understood what he planned to do, he put his hands on Hanna's hips and lifted her up, swinging her into the seat.

She slid over to give him room to climb in himself without looking at him, her heart knocking in her chest.

She liked his hands on her. A lot.

It was a pity they were in the presence of their enemies.

"Luck had nothing to do with our being in one piece," Iver said as he pulled himself up. "Hana is just that good a pilot."

"Oh." The woman twisted in her seat to look at them. "Well, that's good. I'm Vannie. This is Simon. It was such a nice day, we thought we'd come out looking for saspri to use for decoration for the Dancing Lights Festival, but then we saw you and came over to see if you needed help. Not a lot of people this far out of Touka. Not on foot."

"We're glad you did." Iver leaned back in his seat, stretching his arm behind Hana's shoulder.

She kept her hands on her thighs, her whole body alert and ready.

She wasn't anywhere close to her full capacity with this strength of magfield, but at least she'd been forewarned. She concentrated on their rescuers.

The driver turned the lander around in a series of jerky movements, reversing and then going forward a few times until he was facing the city.

"I wish normal runners worked here." Vannie hung on to the dash in front of her with white knuckles. "Aren't you working on that?"

She flicked what Hana realized was a flirtatious look at Iver. "The sky lane, right?"

He gave a nod. "Trying to." He gave her a polite smile. "You're Raxian?"

"Yes, what a clever guess!" Vannie smiled at Iver again.

Hana barely resisted a little snort. Vannie was clearly Raxian. From her style of clothes, to the way she spoke the common tongue.

When they'd first encountered each other, the inhabitants of what was now the Verdant String had been shocked and surprised by the fact that they shared the same origins, even the same root language. It had changed their knowledge of where they'd come from, what their history had been. But in spite of the real, undeniable common root each group had, the different planets they'd settled on had imprinted an indelible mark on them. They hadn't been separated as a species for long enough for clear genetic differences to present themselves, but the regional differences in the language and culture of each planet was unmistakable, and differences in food and minerals had made some subtle differences in physiology.

"And you, Simon?" Hana asked.

"Si is from Bodivas." Vannie glanced at her companion. "We're quite the mixing pot here on Faldine, aren't we?"

Hana hummed in agreement.

Interesting that Simon let Vannie do the talking for him. She wondered what he was hiding.

Plenty, if she were any judge.

And she didn't think either she or Iver would like it when they finally revealed their secrets.

CHAPTER 9

TOUKA CITY DIDN'T REALLY HAVE outskirts.

It wasn't because it hadn't been in existence long enough, although it hadn't. It was because it had been engineered in advance.

It always felt to Hana as if it had risen out of the plains fully formed--sleek and perfect and complete. It was built in concentric circles, and each time the population increased, a new ring road and accompanying buildings were added.

There were less than ten thousand people on the whole planet and most of them lived in either Touka City or Permeo, so there weren't that many rings radiating out from the skyscrapers at Touka's center, but the potential was there. Each new circle's buildings were a story lower than the ones closer to the center, so Touka looked like another mountain in the Spikes.

It never failed to delight her.

Still, the stark change from open plains to built-up city surprised her every time.

The lander bounced from uneven dirt, dust flying behind it, onto smooth road, as if leaping from one world into another.

Simon slowed the lander as soon as they hit the surfaced road, and Hana tensed.

Since they'd moved onto city ground, all her senses had improved, stretching awake. She used to feel an overwhelming sense of gratitude from whatever had invaded her when she reached a place with a weaker magnetic field, but as it had become less alien, more fundamentally part of her, she experienced the feeling as more a sense of deep satisfaction.

Nothing, however, was like the feeling she got when she flew high enough in a runner that she was completely free of the magnetic pull of Faldine. That was when she knew she was as strong, as smart, as capable as she could ever be.

And she knew she needed to understand why.

But that was a mission for another time, now.

"Where can we take you?" Vannie asked.

Even going as slow as he was, Simon had driven through a few junctions, where the concentric circles of the ring roads intersected with the spokes, the roads running from the center of the city to its outer circumference.

He didn't turn down any of them, keeping them on the outer ring road, where the population was sparse.

No one was visible, although there were a few landers parked along the street, and Hana heard music coming from a top floor window.

It felt to her like Simon was marking time, waiting for a signal of some sort.

"Just drop us off wherever you like. You've already saved us a lot of trouble." Iver straightened in his seat.

So he'd noticed it, too.

The leap and sparkle of the afternoon sun off the Indura River caught her eye, and she glimpsed it up ahead.

They were approaching the bridge that curved over the deep, fast-running water, in perfect alignment with the other bridges lined up all the way to the city center. Simon slowed even more, almost coming to a stop as he reached the bridge.

Hana jumped down just as Vannie turned to look at them.

She saw the Raxian's face register surprise as Hana kept her hand on the lander, walking beside it as it rolled forward.

Iver started to rise. To follow her off.

"No, don't rush off. We could take you to your hotel." Vannie's voice was as friendly as ever as she lifted her hand and shot Iver in the chest with a dart from such a tiny SAL, Hana almost stumbled as she stared at it in surprise.

She could run, but she couldn't leave Iver, and her hesitation cost her. She caught the hint of movement from the corner of her eye and jerked her gaze to Simon, but he'd already taken his shot. She felt the sting as a dart lodged in her throat, and then she let go of her hold on the side of the lander and fell.

Her last view was of the lander's wheel, covered in the brown-red dust of the plains, passing a whisper from her head as she landed on the ground.

From above her, she heard Vannie's voice.

"Did you see her face? She's one scary--"

The world went black.

"So what do we do with them now?"

Hana heard the nerves in Vannie's voice as she came to on a cold floor. She suppressed a shiver of relief at the word 'them'. Iver was still alive. Hopefully he was lying near her.

She wondered why they hadn't already killed them both.

Just over a day ago, they'd clearly wanted both Iver and her dead. They hadn't been messing with those SD3s.

Then again, Vannie and Simon could have shot and killed them on the plain and left their bodies out there. There had been no benefit to them in bringing her and Iver into Touka only to kill them in the city--it only increased their risk.

Something had changed, something that was keeping them alive. Either that, or Vannie and Simon were not Lancaster's lackeys at all.

What were the chances there was more than one group of people who meant them harm?

She cracked her eyes open just a little and caught sight of the feet and lower legs of five people.

There were stacks of containers against the walls, and a strange, sweet smell in the air, a little like rotting fruit, that made her think she was in a warehouse.

The ground she was lying on was smooth and cool, and her hands were bound with metal shackles with electronic locks. She wondered why they'd used them, because the restraints didn't always work on Faldine--the magfields interfered with the locks--but they were standard VSC issue, and maybe they didn't have access to anything else.

She felt strangely relaxed about getting out of them. A deep-seated confidence infused her thoughts, and she realized with a jolt of shock that the feeling was coming from her upgrade.

She hadn't felt it as so distinct from her for a while. Not since around the first six months of their forced acquaintance.

She shoved the thought aside. It wasn't important right now.

She needed to concentrate. To find out what they planned.

"How long until they come round?" Simon nudged her shoulder with the toe of his boot.

"Iver should come out of it first, he's a lot bigger than the pilot. Maybe half an hour?"

She recognized the voice as one of Lancaster's people who'd come after them in the now-destroyed Dynastra--Oniba.

So this *was* part of Lancaster's operation. Oniba was definitely one of the guards she'd shot just before Linnel tried to kill himself, along with her, by using an actual laz--before Iver had tranqed him in the back.

She needed more information to understand why killing Iver was no longer top priority.

"Half an hour is too long." A man whose voice she didn't recognize snapped in annoyance. "I need to leave in fifteen."

She risked cracking her eyelids again, and noticed boots directly in front of her.

She kept her body relaxed and closed her eyes again.

"Don't assume Hana won't come out of it quickly."

Her heart lurched. Linnel. He was the one staring at her.

She felt afraid of him for the first time. Lying within kicking distance of his feet.

"You're still on this bullshit story that she's special in some way?" Oniba sounded vicious.

"She doesn't react the same way as the rest of us, and she literally can't be killed." Linnel sounded completely reasonable as he spoke.

The sad thing for him was, he was more or less right. Although not about the killing thing. She was sure she could be killed. But it would take a bit of trouble from whoever planned to do the deed.

"We've got her lying at our feet, unconscious. She can be killed in seconds, right now." The stranger, the one she didn't know, stepped closer, and she felt boots against her leg.

"Go on, then, Banyon," Linnel challenged him. "Go ahead and kill her. Or try to. I dare you."

"You are not just worrying me, Linnel, you are pissing me off. Get outside with the others and make sure no one is snooping around." The man Linnel called Banyon's voice dropped low.

There was a moment of silence.

"And she lives again," Linnel said, a sense of vindication in his voice. He turned to go, and Hana heard him take a few steps.

"Linnel." Oniba's voice was low and mean. From the thin slit of her barely-open eyelids, Hana saw him take a step closer, one foot back, and her blood was suddenly fizzing, her body flooded with adrenaline.

"What?" Linnel's sneer was evident.

"She's not invincible. Watch." He swung his boot at Hana's ribs, and with an almost fatalistic sense of what was about to happen, against her wishes, because Iver was somewhere behind her, still unconscious and restrained, she felt her restraints give, unlocking.

She rolled, so Oniba overextended his kick, stumbling forward.

She was on her feet, swinging the solid metal restraints. They connected with Oniba's temple and without waiting to see the results, she spun hard right, arm extended to hit Banyon.

As she turned, she glimpsed Vannie and Simon's faces, slack with shock, as blood sprayed from Banyon's face where the metal restraints had connected with his nose.

The way to the door, the only exit she could see, was open except for Linnel, who was staring at her with a mix of horror and excitement.

She ran at him, arm back to strike, and with a squeal of fear, he ducked, so she passed him without any resistance.

Beyond the warehouse was a loading dock.

There was one person standing with his back to her, loading a lander, and a guard facing the street.

Oniba had told Linnel to go stand watch with the others, so there might be more, but Hana couldn't see them.

Hana ran toward the guard, her mind calculating how fast she was moving, what her next moves should be, and then she jumped to get the height she needed to hit him on the back of the head.

He went down without a sound, and then she was on the street, looking right and left.

No one was in sight.

She spun, looking up at the roof of the warehouse, and saw someone scrambling down the pitched surface to get to the ground to chase her.

Right at that moment, there were no eyes on her.

She needed to find a way back into the warehouse so she could rescue Iver.

A lander turned the corner near the warehouse, engine roaring, heading right toward her, killing any hope of getting back unseen.

Furious, she ran toward it.

And who knew? Maybe not everyone in Touka City was in on this.

As she neared the vehicle, she saw the driver was wearing the same uniform as the guard she'd just dropped outside the warehouse and it looked like he was driving the lander Vannie and Simon had picked them up in, roof still lowered.

So no help there.

She was committed, though. There was no other option.

The driver blinked at her in surprise and braked, uncertain.

Hana put her hands up. "Help me." She didn't slow down, reaching the driver's side, and jumping onto the running board.

The lander was still moving, and the driver's hands tightened reflexively on the steering wheel.

He looked around him, to make sure there were no witnesses, Hana guessed. He thought he was the dangerous one in this situation.

As soon as he brought the lander to a stop, she dropped down to the ground, and as she hoped he would, he opened the door and slid down after her.

"Take it easy--"

She'd held the restraints out of sight against her thigh, and as soon as he was down, she jumped back on the running board and lashed out, striking him just above the ear.

He went down with a moan.

Up ahead, Vannie, Simon and Linnel ran out onto the street, and Hana got into the driver's seat and reversed, speeding backward.

She twisted, looking behind her, and there, at the junction with the next road, she saw traffic, people walking, businesses that were open.

She spun the lander, and accelerated away.

CHAPTER 10

A DOOR SLAMMED, jerking Iver all the way awake.

"Shit. She's gone. And we can't chase her in the open." Simon's voice sounded right next to him.

He'd risen to consciousness in quick, jerky steps, with the vague knowledge that something big was happening around him.

There had been shouting and running.

It had jumped his heart into a hard rhythm as he struggled to make sense of what was going on.

"I told you about her. Didn't I tell you?" Linnel was hissing at someone.

"All I saw was a woman who took us by surprise. Simon obviously didn't get enough sedative into her. She had to have been waiting to make her move for a while."

The voice he heard was familiar, and Iver tried to place it, but the speaker stood behind him.

Wherever he'd heard it before, it seemed out of place here.

"I shot her directly in the throat." Simon's voice was bitter.

"Then there was problem with the dart. And a bigger problem is we don't know how much she heard, and that she saw my face."

"There wasn't a problem with the dart," Linnel said. "She isn't normal. She obviously metabolizes the sedative faster."

"Linnel." Simon sounded like he'd reached the end of his patience.

"What? Oniba was going to show me how she's just as breakable as anyone else. He couldn't even get a kick in to her ribs." The sneer was evident in Linnel's voice.

Oniba had tried to kick Hana to make a point to Linnel?

Iver had to breathe through the rage that rose up in him.

It had the benefit of clearing the last fuzziness from his head.

"Linnel, just get out there, see if we can get an idea of which direction she went in." Oniba spoke for the first time, weary, by the sound of it.

Iver opened his eyes in time to see Linnel turn and stalk out of the room.

"Do you believe that guy?" Simon asked when the door had closed behind him.

"I see him as barely useful at this point. He's got to go." Oniba moved restlessly. "Lancaster called him a liability, and I have to agree."

Vannie made a sound of exasperation, as if she was tired of the whole situation. She started to pace. "She'll run straight to the safety officers. We need to move."

"I'll make sure she doesn't get in touch with anyone in authority." The familiar voice was still behind him, and Iver heard tapping, as if he was communicating on a screen. "I can't afford to have any fingers pointed my way. As it is, I've got to get back right now and deal with this bloody nose she's given me."

"And if whoever you're sending after her doesn't succeed?" Simon shook his head. "We still have to move, just in case."

"Fine, run and hide, but you'll have to deal with the logistics. I've got to leave now. I've cut it too close as it is."

"Where will we go?" Oniba asked, aggrieved.

"I don't know. I don't have time to think about it. And now I have the added weight of worrying over being recognized. Because someone else didn't do their job properly." Whoever they were, they were more than just annoyed. Iver thought he heard the shiver of fear in his voice.

Good. And if Hana had bloodied his nose, even better.

"*I* did my job properly." Simon took an aggressive step forward.

The stranger walked away, and Iver heard a door opening. "Let me know if you do move, and I'll keep in touch when my people grab the pilot."

"*If* they grab the pilot," Vannie said.

"Now you're sounding like Linnel," the man said. "She's alone and she's not from Touka City. I'll get her. I shouldn't have to, but I'll clean up your mess."

"She just escaped VSC restraints and managed to attack four people. How did she get out of those restraints, anyway?" Vannie's voice rose with every word.

"I don't know and I don't have time to work it out. Probably a magfield glitch. That shouldn't be a surprise, especially when you're using VSC tech here." There was some serious anger in that voice. "Just get what information you can from Sugotti, dump his body, and clear out of here. As you say, it's burned now. There's no coming back."

The door closed sharply behind him.

"There's no coming back?" Simon suddenly kicked a container hard. "Fucker. This warehouse is my business. Questions are going to be asked, and this property is registered to me."

"I've been left hanging out to dry, too, if you hadn't noticed." Oniba's voice was soft. "With Lancaster dead, there's no way I can go back onto Sugotti's payroll. The point of no return has come and gone."

"No shit." Vannie turned, eyes widening when she saw Iver was awake. "Well, well, well. Look who's back among the living."

Simon and Oniba spun toward him.

Iver didn't like the look on Simon's face. A need to cause pain, to lash out, was clear in his eyes and in the twist of his lips.

At least Hana got away.

Oniba crouched in front of him and Iver narrowed his eyes as he saw a rivulet of dried blood on the side of his face.

"What do you think I can tell you? Just yesterday you tried to kill me more than once. Why the interest in what I have to say now?"

"Do you know who blew up the Dynastra?"

"No. Obviously no one friendly to me, or they'd have picked me and Hana up. And they'd have checked first to see if I was in the runner before they vaporized it."

"True." Oniba blinked and rose to look at the others. He rubbed at his temple as if he was in pain, and judging by the blow he'd taken, he was. "It can't be the VSC."

"Then who?" Vannie asked, exasperated.

"Either someone in our little group has decided to cut out as many of the top layer of management as possible to maximize their own profit, or . . ."

"No." Vannie shook her head. "A common goal holds us together. There's no betrayal."

"I think you're thinking of a time long before the war." Simon's voice was soft, and not unsympathetic.

"I won't believe that. Who else could it be?" Vannie put her hands on her hips. "The Caruso?"

"Why not? We were planning to see if they were interested in what we had to offer anyway."

"Eventually, when we knew what we were dealing with. How did they find out about us?"

"Maybe someone in the group put out a feeler? Thought they were doing us all a favor." Oniba scrubbed at his face.

"And the Caruso pricked up their ears and came looking to muscle us out?" Vannie's voice was heavy with skepticism.

"It isn't their thing, I agree." Simon nodded toward her. "They're after minerals. Every time they've been caught out recently, it's been mining-related."

"Maybe it's primarily mining," Oniba conceded. "But the VSC has shut them down three times in a row. Maybe they're looking for whatever they can get."

"Shit." Simon spoke with feeling. "That sounds all too plausible."

There was silence as they digested the idea.

Oniba suddenly straightened. "We'll have to think about the implications of this later. Right now we need to move."

"One more thing." Simon moved back in front of Iver. "What happened just before the Dynastra was hit? Did Lancaster say something to you? Did he notice the incoming?"

"I was already out of the Dynastra before they approached." Iver didn't see a reason to keep quiet about that part of it. He was learning a lot from their back and forth. No need to interrupt the flow. "I'd already shot him with his SAL and left him inside. I stepped out the runner and saw that imbecile Linnel trying to shoot Hana with a laz. I dropped him with a dart and was running to Hana when the Dynastra was hit."

There was a moment of silence.

"Linnel shot at her with a laz?" Simon asked carefully.

"Yes. He's lucky it didn't hit either him or her. I shot him in the back before he could get off another blast."

"I'll get the laz off him." Oniba and Simon exchanged a look.

"It looks like your usefulness is over." Simon glanced down at him. "Time to kill you and dump--"

The high-pitched whine of a dru-dru approaching had him biting off his words.

The dru-dru was an agile, two-wheeled vehicle used by everyone in Touka, but Iver saw all their minds went to the possibility this was a visit from the Protection Unit, who definitely used them.

Vannie lunged for the lights, and plunged the warehouse into darkness.

It was still daytime, but there were very few windows in the warehouse and they were high up.

Iver had been gearing up to fight, to make killing him as difficult as possible, so he was up on his feet and running for cover before anyone's eyesight adjusted to the almost complete darkness.

Half-blind himself, he ran into a stack of containers, but they held steady, and he ducked behind them, standing still to get his bearings.

"We should have left straight away." Vannie's voice came from near the door. "Let's go now. There's only one of them out there."

"That we know of. And we can't leave Sugotti alive." Oniba sounded like he was moving through the warehouse, coming closer to where Iver was standing.

"We don't have time to kill him."

"And if we get caught? What happens to our plans then?" Vannie's voice was soft.

Oniba swore. His footsteps retreated.

"How were you going to kill him, anyway?" Vannie asked. "With your bare hands?"

Because they only had SALs, Iver realized, which would knock him out, but not kill him.

"I was going to slit his throat," Simon said, voice cold. "But I won't risk getting caught."

The door banged closed, their voices cut off, but Iver didn't move. It could be a trap.

Or he could be wasting time.

The minutes ran together, until he couldn't tell how long he'd been standing in the darkness.

Now or never.

He ran toward the door, and Oniba stepped out of the shadows, SAL in his hand.

Iver jinked to the right, then snapped his leg, hitting Oniba's wrist.

The SAL went flying, and Oniba howled in pain.

With his hands still behind his back, Iver used his shoulder on the door, muscling his way out into an empty loading dock.

A dru-dru was parked near the entrance, and as he ran toward it, Linnel stepped out--the helmet from driving the dru-dru still on his head--and leveled his laz at Iver's chest.

"You're not going anywhere. As long as I have you, she won't be far behind."

The smirk on Linnel's face snapped something inside Iver. He was usually even-tempered, but everyone had a limit. He'd just reached his.

With a roar, he charged, jumping just as he reached Linnel and spinning, swinging his elbow as far forward as the restraints allowed, to deliver a vicious blow to his cheek.

The laz went off, flickering and leaping and Oniba screamed behind him.

Iver stumbled, off-balance from the spin, and saw Oniba was down, and Linnel was on one knee.

He kicked out at Linnel's head, the jolt of impact with the helmet vibrating up his leg, and then he ran.

Pity he didn't know where to.

CHAPTER 11

IVER WAS GONE.

Hana lay on the warehouse roof, looking down through the small skylight near the entrance.

There was no one here.

A soft grunt and then low, sustained cursing from the loading bay had her inching forward face down until she could see over the edge of the roof.

Linnel was dragging a limp Oniba toward a small, brightly colored dru-dru. An enclosed trailer was attached to the back of the colorful scooter with a tow hitch.

Linnel dumped Oniba's body beside the dru-dru and opened the lid of the trailer.

He looked around, laz in hand, and then bent down and pulled Oniba up by the arms to stuff him in the trailer. By the sound of the grunts and swearing, it wasn't an easy task.

Hana tried to work out how Oniba had come to be dead or unconscious.

Her only guess was Linnel had shot him with the laz, either deliberately or by mistake. But it was very difficult to shoot someone on purpose with a laz on Faldine.

Maybe he'd been aiming at Iver and had gotten Oniba instead.

Hana was fine with that. Very fine with that.

As soon as he'd gotten Oniba inside the trailer and had closed the lid, Linnel moved out of sight, disappearing into a small structure next to the loading bay. The security booth, Hana guessed.

The dru-dru looked cute, sitting there. They were ubiquitous in Touka City, and like everything on Faldine, they had wheels. They'd become the symbol of Verdant String courage and empathy in the face of adversity during the Faldine War. Civilians had rescued people from bombing raids in dru-drus and dru-drus had been used to transport the wounded to medbays.

Their appeal was more than the strangeness of having wheels in a culture used to hovers, though. They were small and colorful, coming in a range of colors too many to count.

The one Linnel was using was a strange green-yellow, and he strode out from the small hut, swung into the seat, and rode away.

What to do?

Had Vannie and Simon had already taken Iver away? It seemed likely.

Which meant she was too late, had taken too long to get back.

Iver wasn't just gone. He was likely dead. At the bottom of the river, just as Simon promised.

She felt hollowed out, disoriented, as if she had lost her grip on the roof and was tumbling through the air.

"He's gone."

The voice came from just beneath her, and she went very still.

Vannie.

Fury swept through her. This woman had killed--

"We're going to have to go after Sugotti." Simon stepped into view, out from under the roof's eaves on the far side of the loading bay.

Go after him? Hana had to make herself listen over the roaring in her ears.

"Linnel just took out Oniba with a laz, and all you have to say is we have to go after Sugotti?" Vannie's voice sounded thin and brittle.

Simon sighed. "I don't think Oniba's dead. I'm guessing Linnel is taking him to a medbay. Linnel may be behaving strangely, but he's not suicidal. He wouldn't have risked himself with that laz. He probably had it on the lowest setting."

Hope began to bloom inside Hana's chest. She'd come here to rescue Iver, but it looked like he'd rescued himself.

Vannie was shaking her head. "Even so, it can kill in the right--"

"I know, Van. What do you think this is? People are getting killed all the time. Lancaster is dead. We've killed others indirectly. Just because we haven't pulled the trigger ourselves yet doesn't mean we weren't involved. And what were we going to do to Sugotti and his pilot? We were going to kill them."

She was silent. "I don't like this anymore. It sounded like such a great idea in the beginning. But now--"

"Bit too real for you?" Simon's voice was derisive.

"Yes." She stepped out to join him. "And now we've got our own people turning on us. We've lost the advantage. Sugotti isn't just not dead. He's on the loose. I don't think he saw Banyon's face, but the pilot did, and Sugotti has certainly seen ours. We have to go underground now. No more hiding in plain sight."

"That was always going to happen. It just came up a bit sooner on the schedule."

"But Linnel--"

"At least it wasn't the Protection Unit. I can deal with Linnel." He lifted a comm device. "It's me. Sugotti got away." He held the device away from his head for a beat or two, a dark look on his face. "Blame Linnel. He had a fucking laz, and he tried to shoot Sugotti with it. Took out Oniba instead, and Sugotti got away. Sugotti's still in restraints, and he's on foot. Vannie and I are going after him now."

He widened his stance, looked down at the ground as he listened. "Linnel got away on a dru-dru, not sure where he's going, but he's got Oniba with him. He's probably taking him for medical help. Get one of those people you were going to call to stop the pilot and have them grab him. They'll have enough to lock him away, what with the unconscious body in his trailer and the laz in his possession, and all."

He paused, then lifted the comms device away from his ear and looked at it. "Fuck you, too, Banyon."

The sound of a vehicle coming up the street had Hana turning her head, but instead of looking nervous, Vannie moved past Simon toward the sound.

"Cribo's got a lander for us." She didn't check to see if Simon was following her.

He stared after her for a beat, then headed for the lander himself.

Hana waited for them to disappear and then wriggled down the side of the building and stood in the darkening alley between Simon's warehouse and the one next to it, thinking about where to go next.

Where would Iver go?

Her heart caught a little just thinking about the question, because he was alive and she had been so sure he was dead.

Relief washed over her, not in one big wave, but smaller, choppy slaps of emotion.

She leaned against the wall to collect herself.

Vannie and Simon didn't know where he was any more than she did, so following them would be a waste of time. She needed to use what she knew of him to work out his next move.

The council offices were a good guess, but Vannie and Simon would probably think so, too. And if Banyon had come through with his promise to have people in place to stop them both, Iver would need her help if he went there.

It was as good a starting point as any.

She'd already started moving through the shadows before she noticed the man blocking the end of the alleyway.

She couldn't see his face, but his shape was outlined in the fading light, and she felt a prickle of awareness down her spine.

Iver.

He took a step toward her and something too big for her body unfurled in her chest as she ran, full-tilt, toward him.

His hands were behind his back, so it was she who gathered him in her arms, her hands running over his wrists so the restraints fell away.

Then his arms were around her, his mouth on hers, and she felt the tears she hadn't cried at the thought of his death earlier run down her cheeks.

"Shh." He nuzzled her neck. "What's wrong?"

"I thought they'd killed you. That I was too late."

"No. And I knew you'd come back for me. I realized a few minutes into my escape that I was running away from where I needed to be."

She tried to laugh, but it came out garbled. "Good thinking."

He pulled back a little, brushing the tears from her cheeks with his thumbs. "I'm full of good ideas."

She leaned on his chest and his hands came up to tangle in the hair at her nape.

He tugged a little. "So are you going to tell me how you can release restraints with just a touch of your hands?"

She went still, then gave a sigh.

"And can come out of a SAL sedative well before anyone else? Or hear a runner from miles away? Or find a tracker under someone's skin also with just a touch of your hands?"

She buried her face deeper in his chest. "I'd rather not."

He gave a chuckle. "Linnel says you're the product of an illegal army experiment. That they conducted banned genetic engineering on you."

"Did he?" She lifted her head, surprised. "That's actually not a bad guess."

She saw his face and shook her head. "It's wrong, but it's not as strange as I thought he would get."

"And what is the truth?"

"Do we have to do it here, in an alleyway next to our enemies' headquarters?"

He narrowed his eyes at her. "You keep putting this off."

"People keep trying to kill me." She shrugged, unrepentant.

He shook his head. "You have me there." He let her go, and she suddenly wondered if she should tell him, just to keep his arms around her a little longer.

"Coming?" he asked, putting out his hand.

She put her hand in his and followed him through the shadows.

***

The sun had sunk down behind the Spikes, and the lights of Touka City were coming on in their usual kaleidoscope of colors.

The bridges lit up first, the warm colors playing across the water, and then the buildings began their nightly display, images and patterns swirling from one high rise to the other, jumping streets and climbing towers to end in a spectacular finale, only to start again elsewhere.

Iver moved a little closer to the edge of the ledge that gave them a view of the council building at the heart of the city. It was Iver's favorite design in Touka. He had personally overseen the plans and he knew the building inside and out.

Hana was pressed against his side, her head resting against his shoulder. She seemed reluctant to be out of touching distance, and he was fine with that.

They still hadn't had their talk, but even he knew now wasn't the time. She'd need time and safety to talk about whatever secret she seemed to carry like a load around with her.

He would make sure there was time later, though. They would not sleep tonight until she shared that burden.

"Looks like the whole city is down there." Her voice was weary, and he realized he felt the same.

They had been on the run for nearly three days straight.

The lights in the city suddenly stopped moving, dribbling down to the ground as if a sprinkler had been turned off and then they winked out.

A projection of the head administrator of Touka City, Moiri Tanek, standing on the council building's steps, blossomed on the front of the building.

The crowd standing in the street at the foot of the stairs stepped closer.

"I can confirm the runner bringing Iver Sugotti to Touka City was shot down. I can also confirm a second runner, potentially containing Sam Lancaster--Sugotti's head of security--was also destroyed. We do not know if anyone perished in the blasts. We are waiting for the VSC fleet to send down specialist forensic investigators, and we are doing everything we can to look for survivors, although the strength of the magnetic fields beneath both points of impact mean our runners are forced to fly high to scan for life. We're sending wheel-based vehicles to any thermal signatures they see. We will update citizens as soon as we know anything more." Moiri sounded rattled, Iver noticed. She was usually a little cool with him, a little withdrawn, but she sounded as if she were genuinely upset he was missing.

"Who's behind this?" Someone called. "The rebels?"

"We don't know who's behind it. It would be premature to say this is the rebels, or some new start to the war." Moiri's lips firmed and she leaned forward. "Former rebels live peacefully in Touka City right now. They are your friends and neighbors. One thing I will promise, though. Whoever is behind this, we will find them, and hand them over to the VSC fleet commander to deal with."

There was a beat of silence at that.

"This isn't considered an in-planet matter?" A member of the media asked.

"Considering it involves the head-of-planet, no." Moiri drew herself up. "Now, I'm sure you will understand how much I have to do right now. I'll make an announcement as soon as we learn something substantial that will shed light on what's happening." She turned on her heel and walked back up the stairs, an assistant on either side of her. One leaned closer to whisper in her ear, and she gave a nod and sped up, disappearing through the front entrance.

"We need to talk to her," Hana said.

Iver grunted in agreement. The crowd was slowly dispersing, some standing in groups to talk, others drifting away in small huddles, heads together.

There was a nervous tension in the air.

A worry.

"They're scared the war is about to start again," Hana said. "*I'm* scared the war is about to start again."

Iver didn't like the bleakness he heard in her voice. Because she was thinking she would have to go back to flying runners, and he didn't like that thought. Not at all.

"It's not going to start again." He would make sure of it. No matter what he had to do.

CHAPTER 12

"THAT'S the dru-dru Linnel escaped in." Hana crouched against the council building wall and stared at the bright green-yellow of the scooter parked near the back door in the fine, misty rain. She wiped rain drops off her forehead and rubbed her cheek against a sleeve.

"You're right." The rain had caught in Iver's dark hair, forming tiny droplets that gleamed like crystals in the diffuse up-lights set in the flowerbeds. "Looks like he just rode up and parked in the most convenient spot."

Iver leaned against her, shoulder and thigh against her own. She liked the solid feel of him. Liked the way the fabric of his clothes stretched over his muscles.

"Simon told Banyon to point whoever is cooperating with him in the Protection Unit at Linnel, that it would be easy to arrest him because Oniba was in the trailer." A trailer, she noted, that was no longer attached to the scooter. "Would the Protection officers bring the dru-dru here if they had arrested him?"

Iver shook his head. "It would have been taken to Protection Central. It looks like he ditched the trailer somewhere."

"So either he escaped the net Banyon threw out, or he has

contacts of his own." As she said that, Hana rejected the idea. Linnel was too obsessed, too focused on his own agenda to make contacts and connections outside the army. He was almost incapable of doing even that. She'd noticed how appalled his colleagues were with his obsession with her, and she didn't think he would be accepted back into the group now that he'd shot Oniba.

"So he's got a friend in the building?" Iver said.

Hana shrugged. "Or he thinks he does. Or more likely he has someone he has some leverage over. I don't think Linnel has friends. Not any more."

Iver gave a nod. "Well, this doesn't change our plan to sneak in quietly and talk to Moiri when she's alone."

"But if Linnel sees me . . . " Hana thought it through. What would he do? He wanted her for something--she wasn't sure what--but attention of any kind probably wouldn't suit him.

"He'll slink away and wait for another opportunity to get you," Iver said.

She nodded.

They approached the door, and Iver put his fingers into the gene sniffer to get in. The laz locks more commonly used through the VSC were another piece of tech that didn't work here. Unless you were fine with being accidentally shocked every time you opened a door.

"You're coded in here, too," he told her.

She hadn't known that. "Why?"

"Just in case you needed to come in to fetch me. Lancaster set it up."

"He never told me. I'm surprised he thought it was necessary."

"I told him to do it."

She grinned. "Bet he didn't like that."

"But couldn't find a good enough reason to disagree." Iver grinned back.

They stepped into a cool, double-height atrium that gave the impression of space and light, even in the early evening gloom.

The sound of the rain on the high windows made Hana think of cozy evenings and comfortable chairs, and she was suddenly bone tired.

At least there was no one around, which made sense for this time of day, although clearly Moiri and some of her staff had remained at work to deal with Iver's disappearance.

Iver moved confidently toward the spiral lift, old tech that had found a new life here on Faldine, where newer innovations didn't do as well.

"They had one of these spirals on Kalastoni's moon, Cepi, you know," he said, as he grabbed a handhold.

She took the next one, enjoying the sensation of being spun around as the spiral twirled her around and up.

"Is that where the tech originated?"

"Maybe. They've worked out the Cepi ruins are too old to have been built by our own ancestors, but our ancestors might have stopped at Cepi on their way to populate the Verdant String and studied the tech. One group obviously settled on Kalastoni and the rest carried on, taking the idea of the spiral lift with them."

It was a fascinating idea. Hana hadn't spent much time thinking about the origins of the Verdant String until her upgrade. She was very interested in it now, though.

Iver stepped smoothly off the spiral many floors up, and Hana followed him.

She'd never been in the council building, although she'd walked past it many times while walking the streets on the days she was here waiting for Iver, shopping or attending the live theater that flourished on Faldine.

Touka City had at least four theaters, running shows every night, despite it's relatively tiny size from a Verdant String perspective.

Comms screens didn't always work that well here, so live theater came into its own.

She went to a play every night she'd ever spent in Touka.

Had the war done that, she wondered? Did it make the soul

hunger for fun, laughter and stories, in a way that made you truly part of the emotion, as live theater did?

Iver slowed in front of her, and she realized the low murmur of voices she'd heard since she'd stepped off the spiral was coming from behind a door at the far end of a walkway.

The walkway was flush against the wall on one side, open to an atrium on the other, with a view to the right of the council building's entrance, where Moiri Tanek had given her speech only half an hour earlier.

They stopped in front on an office and Iver leaned against the door, listening.

"There's no one in there," Hana told him.

He accepted her word with a nod and opened the door, holding it for her. She slipped inside and he followed her, closing the door behind him.

"What's the plan?"

"This is Moiri's office."

She'd forgotten he must be very familiar with the building and where everything was.

He walked to the desk and touched the comm unit.

"Pollard? We're in the conference room." Moiri's voice sounded irritated.

"It's Iver. Pretend I'm Pollard. I'm in your office. Make an excuse, and come over."

"I'll be right there." The comm cut off immediately.

Hana hadn't moved far from the door, and she slid up against the wall beside it, listening to Moiri's footsteps.

The administrator had come alone, as requested.

The door burst open, and Moiri strode in.

"Iver!" She quivered in outrage.

Moiri hadn't even noticed her, Hana realized as she flicked the door shut, content to let it stay that way, at least for a while longer.

"Moiri."

The administrator stumbled to a stop, and Hana suddenly realized how disreputable Iver looked.

His jaw was dark with stubble, and his hair was wild, sticking up a little above his forehead. His clothes were streaked with dirt, crumpled and even a little ripped.

Her heart gave a little gallop in her chest. He was magnificent.

At that moment, he lifted his gaze to her, and she caught the flare of something in his eyes.

Moiri spun as she realized there was someone behind her, and openly gaped at Hana.

She assumed she looked as bedraggled as Iver did.

"The pilot?" Moiri asked.

Hana inclined her head.

Iver made a sound, and she saw his eyes narrow.

He didn't like that people thought of her as simply his pilot, rather than a person in her own right.

She, on the other hand, liked it a lot. The more anonymous she was, the better.

It was one of the reasons she'd tried to steer clear of Iver from the start. But that spaceship had pinched to the black, as the saying went. It was too late now. Iver was stuck with her.

She was struck with an urge to smile at the thought.

"Her name is Hana Farwell," Iver said, voice cold.

Moiri sent him a quick, curious glance. "I've heard of you, of course. The most decorated pilot of the war. I thought you were older."

Hana lifted her shoulders in answer.

"We've got problems, Moiri." Iver's words had the administrator turning back to face him.

"I'm aware." The dry humor in her voice made Hana warm to her.

Iver's lips twitched. "Lancaster arranged for Hana and I to be shot down. Then he was double-crossed by someone else, who shot *him* down."

"Lancaster?" Moiri drew in a sharp breath. "I thought he was trying to find you when he--"

Iver shook his head. "And he isn't the only traitor. There's someone on the council who's involved, too."

"Who?"

Hana thought Banyon would probably wince at the fury in Moiri's voice.

"His name is Banyon," Iver said. "I haven't seen him, but Hana has."

Moiri shook her head. "No one of that name is on the council."

"It may not be the name he uses except with his fellow conspirators," Hana said. "And he might be in the Protection Unit, not the council."

Moiri grimaced and tapped her foot as if thinking, then strode to her desk. "First thing I need to do is let Admiral Valerian know you're safe. She's sent three special forces runners down to look for you."

She'd just reached the comm unit when Hana heard the quick click of footsteps coming toward the office.

She stepped to the side in two quick steps, getting into place beside the door.

She caught Iver's gaze, signaled with her hand for him to shift out of the line of sight of anyone opening the door.

He moved, and Moiri looked up at him, frown creasing her brow, as she waited for the comms to connect with the head of fleet.

The door burst open, too hard and fast to be normal.

Moiri lifted her head, and Hana saw her eyebrows lift as a young man strode into the room.

"Moiri, there's an urgent message--" He stumbled to a stop. "Oh, you're on the comms." He had left the door open, and Hana took a step toward it to close it.

Before she reached it, a flash of laz fire flickered through the room.

It struck the young administrator, danced up to the ceiling and then a thin tendril shot down to touch Iver.

Hana just managed to suppress a cry. She would have to get across the door to reach Iver, and that would expose her to Linnel, who was the only one who seemed insane enough to use a laz on Faldine.

She was about to run across in a burst of speed when Moiri raised her arm from in her desk and shot at the open door with the SAL in her hand.

Linnel made a sound of frustrated anger and Hana used the distraction to leap across the opening, rolling to her feet near Iver, and crouching beside him.

"Just my arm." He was holding his left arm close to his side, struggling to stand, and Hana helped him up.

"We need to go."

Linnel was lying in the doorway in a crumpled heap, but he might not be the only danger out there.

Moiri was bending over her staffer, and she glanced over at them. "He's out. He needs help."

"Your boy there set it up for our attacker. There's no way it was a coincidence that he came in just before an attack, and I notice he kept the door open. There was also a little too much melodrama in his entrance. We don't know how deep this goes. Who in your office is compromised."

Moiri winced, and Hana guessed she was also suspicious of her employee.

"What will you do?" Moiri straightened up.

"Tell Carina that we'll be in touch with her people as soon as we're somewhere safe. When are they expected to get here?"

"I don't know. Not before tomorrow, given where the space fleet was when you disappeared. How will you be in touch?"

"I'll find a way." Iver gritted his teeth as he moved to the doorway and looked down at Linnel, lying unconscious across the doorway.

"Fine. Do you know who that is?" Moiri gestured to Linnel.

"A sub-lieutenant in the Faldine Military, Vic Linnel. I'm not sure if he's resigned, or if he's still active. And he's not all that . . . reasonable when it comes to me." Hana's lips twisted.

"He's obsessed," Iver's voice was flat. "He's after Hana for somehow surviving the war when his fiancé didn't, and he's working with the people who shot us down."

"There's more than one motive going on here?" Moiri looked at them in astonishment.

"I think there may even be more than one player." Hana stepped over Linnel's crumpled form.

"What the hell is going on? And why now?" Moiri asked.

Iver joined Hana in the passageway. "That's something we are going to try to find out."

CHAPTER 13

THE RAIN WAS BLOWING in thick, lazy sheets now instead of the misty stuff that had fallen before they went into the building.

Hana bit her lip and glanced at Iver. His arm was still tight against his body, and his skin looked ashy in the uplights from the flower bed outside the back entrance.

They stood under the narrow awning above the door and she realized she was swaying on her feet.

Iver put his uninjured arm around her, hand cupping her shoulder, and pulled her closer. "We aren't going to find out anything unless we get some sleep."

She hesitated, second-guessing their decision to leave Moiri and go their own way. They didn't have anyone they could trust, and Iver was right, they needed a safe place to rest for a bit.

"It was the right move." Iver leaned back against the door, pulling her with him so she was slightly off-balance, resting against the length of his body. "We weren't safe there."

"You reading minds, now?" she asked, surprised she could smile.

He gave a snort. "I wish."

She straightened, looking at his arm. "You need a medkit at the very least, and the one I had is sitting in my pack in that warehouse."

"We'll buy another one, and hole up somewhere for a little bit."

That made as much sense as anything she could have come up with, and Hana knew neither of them could go on much longer.

She closed her eyes and leaned back against Iver, putting her arms around him. They were dry, warm, and resting.

It was hard to step out of the moment and force herself to move.

With a groan, she pulled them both straight and slipped out from under his arm. "Banyon's friends are still wandering around out there, and Simon and Vannie are looking for us, too." She stepped out from the shadows under the awning, face lifted against the icy needles of rain, and swept the area at the back of the building for any sign of danger.

The moment she emerged, a man stepped out from the shadows of the next building, and in a sudden, blinding instant of clarity, she saw a SAL dart flying toward her.

She shifted, instinctively lifting her hand and batting the dart away with the back of her fingers as it flew toward her face.

Escape.

The word seemed to reverberate in her skull.

"Iver." She shouted his name, because no other word would convey the urgency as well. She meant he should step back into the building. Get to safety.

She felt his hand on her shoulder, pushing her down into a crouch as a second dart skimmed past.

"Stay down." Iver's shout came as he ran past her, and with a jerk of shock she realized there was a tight, thin line of pain along her shoulder.

She looked up, in time to see Iver running straight for their shooter, who, in a sudden fit of panic, ran.

Iver pulled up short as he disappeared around a corner. "He's spooked, but he'll be back." Iver turned to her, rimmed in light from the nearby building, the rain glittering as it fell around him.

She shook her head. She was losing her grip on reality.

"Is that a lander?" Iver was frowning, looking at the narrow access road on the side of the building, and at last she heard it, too, the low rumble unmistakable.

How had she missed it? Had she ever not heard something that close and clear since her upgrade?

She lifted curled fingers to her shoulder, and they came away bloody.

The SAL dart had grazed her.

She wouldn't go down for long, but she would go down. Some of the tranquilizer was in her system.

And they didn't have time for that.

She ran toward the side of the building, but Iver got there first, so she was forced to crouch behind him as they peered around for a look.

A lander, one that had a separate front cab and a sleek, enclosed rear compartment, was idling outside a side entrance, the door of which suddenly opened. A man ran to the driver's side but the light above the side entrance threw shadows across his face, rather than illuminating him.

Hana managed to tap Iver's shoulder. "I think that's Banyon."

She tried to keep her eyes open as Banyon gesticulated in a heated conversation with the driver.

"I thought I recognized his voice in the warehouse, but in the gloom, and only in profile, I can't say where I know him from. They don't look happy with each other." Iver glanced at her, and then his eyes widened. "What's wrong?"

She had slumped a little, she realized.

"Just a scrape," she managed to get out, waving a hand at her shoulder.

"You were shot." He pulled at her shirt, and then swore.

She didn't have the energy to answer, and gave in to temptation and let her head rest against his arm.

From somewhere nearby, she heard shouting, and a door being flung open.

Iver swore again, low and vicious. Then nothing.

Iver saw the spark of consciousness wink out of Hana's eyes, and then she went under.

Not for long, if her recovery before on a full dose was any indication, but long enough that she was helpless.

And he wasn't much better.

She was resting on his uninjured side, and he maneuvered her so she was hanging over his shoulder.

He stood slowly, amazed at how light she was. How insubstantial.

She didn't seem that way when she was awake.

Banyon had moved from the driver's side and had walked to the back of the lander, which looked like some kind of supply vehicle. He threw the back doors open, but his back was to Iver now, and Iver still hadn't managed to get a clear view of his face. He was a big man, although he was hunched over in the pounding rain.

He was shouting at the driver, his full attention on what was in the back.

Aware there was still a very real threat behind them, Iver looked back to where the shooter had been only minutes earlier.

Their attacker hadn't expected to be attacked in turn, and he'd run in panic, but it wouldn't take long for him to calm down and realize he was the one with the SAL.

And if he wasn't alone, he'd most likely find his friends and bring them along.

The memory of Hana flicking a SAL dart away like an annoying insect flashed into his head, and he wondered if he had imagined that, or if it had really happened.

Banyon's shouting suddenly cut off, and Iver looked around the corner again.

Banyon had left the back of the lander open, and was back at the driver's door, leaning in and speaking in a low, intense tone.

From behind him, Iver heard a shout and the pounding of feet, and suddenly out of options, exposed to anyone who stepped into the small area at the back of the building, he ducked into the narrow alleyway and headed for the open lander.

His arm was on fire where it had been hit by the laz.

He got a better grip on the back of Hana's legs, and started to move along the wall, keeping out of Banyon's line of sight.

He heard another shout behind him, and the sound of the council building door slamming.

The lander's doors were still open.

It took only a few steps to reach them. Iver hesitated for a moment, but the sound of running from the small parking lot spurred him on. He eased inside, careful to distribute his weight evenly.

He slid forward, each step as light as he could make it, until he reached the far back of the space and was able to squeeze behind a stack of crates.

He felt the lander rock slightly from the front, as if the driver had jumped out.

The rear doors were suddenly closed, plunging them into a thick gloom, and then the front rocked a little again, and the vehicle began to move.

Iver stood, feet braced as the lander rocked him from side to side, wondering if he'd just made a massive mistake.

They were out of the rain and no one knew where they were.

But when those doors opened again, they'd have nowhere to run.

CHAPTER 14

HANA WOKE UP SLOWLY.

There was no sense of danger, no quick, sudden leap of fear.

Beneath her cheek she felt the rumble of an engine, and she registered that she was cocooned in warmth.

She opened her eyes, found herself staring at a shadowy stack of crates, the light diffuse and coming from above. She turned slowly.

Iver shifted, his arm curling around her to bring her closer to him so her head rested on his bicep, and she spent a moment looking up at him.

A spike of hard, sweaty desire swept through her.

She'd been attracted to him since she'd met him, but now . . . The change in their relationship was enough to give a girl vertigo.

He smiled at her, and she did another free fall flip.

"How long have I been out?" Her voice was rough and cracked.

"Eight hours." He lifted up, careful to ease her head down onto the blankets beneath them, and reached for a bottle of water.

She took it gratefully, gulping down at least half of it.

"Eight? But . . ."

She stared at him blankly. She had barely been scraped by the SAL.

"I think you needed the sleep. Probably most of it was exhaustion."

She thought about it. Gave a nod. "We're in the lander?" she asked, handing the water back to him.

He set it beside him, and lay back down with her, giving a quick nod.

"And your arm?" She levered up on her elbow, lips tight, to check it.

He held it out, the movement much easier than before.

"There are about a hundred medkits in here. I found an advanced one and was able to repair the damage. Resting helped, too."

She flopped back in relief. "Do you know where we're going?"

He shook his head, his expression more serious than she'd ever seen it. "No windows, only light vents at the top of the roof, so I haven't been able to look out, and as we've mainly been traveling in the dark, I haven't been able to see inside much, either. I've been second-guessing myself for getting us onboard almost since the doors closed."

She shook her head, but he held up a hand.

"I know. You were unconscious, I was injured, and I could hear the shooter coming back with at least one other person. The doors were open, and I made a split-second decision. And still . . ."

"If you hadn't, we might already be back in that warehouse. Or at the bottom of the river."

She didn't doubt that for a moment.

She knew the hard way there were seldom perfect choices. You did the best with what you had.

He gave a nod, but she wasn't sure he was completely convinced.

"Thank you." She leaned in close, brushed her lips against his.

"Hold off on the thanks until we're sure we're going to get out of this." His voice was a rumble against her throat as he nuzzled her just under her chin, and she didn't hide her shiver of delight. The last few days had been nothing but a fight for their lives. A relentless slog. And before that … she was very far from the pilot who'd signed up to help fight the Faldine War.

For the moment she was safe and warm, with dawn breaking through the thin light vents above. She clutched what she had now tight, a moment as bright as sunlight.

It was a rare feeling.

Within her, her upgrade stirred in worry, and she found herself sending soothing reassurance. They, in and of themselves, didn't make her life worse. Had saved her life many times.

It gave her pause that she could sense their disquiet, though. She hadn't felt them as such separate entities within her for at least eight months or more.

"What is it?" Iver was looking down at her, a crease between his eyebrows. He brushed her hair back with the tip of a finger.

She caught it, gave it a squeeze. "You found us a place to rest and recover, and you probably also helped us get a step closer to finding out what's going on. Thank you."

She slid an arm around him, under his shirt, and slowly traced the muscles of his back. "Do you know why Banyon was so excited about what was in the lander? Why he was shouting at the driver?"

Iver lifted his head, and she swiped a nervous tongue over her bottom lip at what she saw in his eyes. Her fingertips pressed into the skin of his back and he closed his eyes and shook his head in a sharp movement, as if to clear it.

"I heard Banyon shouting about inventory. I'm guessing whatever's in the back here has been taken without being officially accounted for, and Banyon is afraid it's going to come back on him. The driver wanted him to sign something, and I'm betting it was an inventory approval."

"You think the driver's making a supply run to whatever is happening out in the Spikes? The place Lancaster was afraid you'd find when you started the sky lane route survey?"

"We've been off a sealed road for some time, so yes." He lay back down, ran a bold hand over her breast, down her side. "I wish we had time and the guarantee of privacy."

She smiled against his cheek, even scratchier after three days of scruff. "Me, too." She wanted to rub herself against him, resisted the urge with difficulty. He was right. This was not a safe place for what they wanted to do.

He sighed and lifted up reluctantly. "Are you hungry?"

She nodded, and he rose to a crouch, reaching for a small stack nearby and taking two boxes with intertwined letters on the front.

"R-Meals." She gave a resigned shrug as she took one. "Nothing I haven't eaten before."

"They aren't good," he agreed. "We should really do something to fix that."

She smiled. "Tell the admiral that you'll solve the transportation problem on Faldine only after you've managed to create delicious army food."

"As food science is not my area, why don't I just get someone else to do that at the same time as I'm building the sky lane?"

She pointed the spoon that she'd unclipped from the side of the box at him. "Of course. I sometimes forget you're head-of-planet."

He raised his brows and grinned at her. "I'd like to forget it, most days. It was a hard lesson on deferring my public service obligations. By the time my deferment had expired, they needed a head-of-planet."

She cocked her head. "Isn't head-of-planet one of the few voted roles?"

"Yes, but that's on a full VSC planet. Faldine is technically still a vassal, so the VSC decided who got the job. They picked me, and generously decided to count it as my public service duty."

"Poor baby." She leaned across and kissed his cheek.

"You say that, but I don't think you mean it."

She grinned and shrugged. Forced herself to swallow some more of the congealed food on the disposable tray.

Beneath them, the engine sound changed, from a steady rumble to a sudden, higher whine. The whole vehicle lurched.

Hana exchanged a look with Iver and packed away her food. He had been busy while she slept, she saw. There were two packs stacked against one of the crates and he rose to his feet and lifted them off the floor.

He must have put them together from the supplies in the back.

She took the one he offered her, testing the weight of it before she strapped it on.

The lander had slowed and Iver moved to the doors. "It's going slow enough now that it should be safe to jump out."

She nodded. Better escape while they could than stay and possibly be trapped inside in an enemy camp later.

Iver opened the doors, and she saw they were traveling over rocky ground, the vehicle battling with the uneven terrain.

The whole vehicle suddenly slowed further and tipped upward, and Iver jumped out, the ground just an easy step down.

He turned for her, hand outstretched, and she took it, hopped out, and carefully closed the doors behind her.

They both crouched down at what she saw was the foot of a rocky outcrop, and the lander disappeared from sight above them.

"Follow it?" Hana asked.

Iver nodded. "The speed it's going, I think we can keep up easily."

Hana smiled at him. "That's because the head-of-planet hasn't fixed the transport problem yet."

She heard his laughter behind her as she hauled herself up the rock.

CHAPTER 15

THIS DEEP IN THE SPIKES, the mid-morning sun was muted as it reached down to the valley floor.

Iver looked up to see searing blue skies above while they walked in the shadow of the mountain.

"There's something about this place." Hana looked over her shoulder at him. "My warning systems are on full alert."

He thought she looked genuinely worried, as if there was more to it than just a feeling.

"It's the strange effect of the light." He agreed with her, though, it felt like more than that. The back of his neck prickled. "I've had a few submissions regarding bringing VSC tourists here to experience the atmosphere."

She muttered something under her breath, which sounded like 'good luck to them'.

Despite the eerie sense of something watching them with ill-intent, he grinned.

She delighted him.

Up ahead, the lander's engine changed pitch, and he slowed, just as Hana did, waiting for it to negotiate whatever obstacle was in its way.

It stopped moving, and they heard a shout, and then the sound of raised voices.

Hana turned her head to look at him, then pointed to one of the boulders that lined the sides of the valley like a row of sentinels. He followed her as she jogged toward it. He dropped his pack beside hers, giving her a boost up the side of the rock and then pulled himself up after her.

"Anything?" He settled in beside her, keeping his voice to a soft murmur.

She shook her head. "Whatever's happening, its just over the rise." She pointed and he saw the top of the lander was just visible up ahead but nothing else.

The shouting grew a little louder.

"We need to get closer." He pointed to a spot up ahead, a cluster of bushes that might give them enough cover.

She nodded and turned, sliding down the rock to land in a graceful crouch. She had their packs in her hand by the time he'd jumped down beside her.

They moved silently, weaving between boulders and staying low. The ground was covered with a thick, lush vegetation Iver wasn't familiar with, but it was good for muffling the sound of their footsteps.

"We just want to know what's going on." The first voice Iver could hear clearly was an annoying whine.

They had reached the bushes, and he lowered himself to the ground, hoping he'd be able to see through the branches to whatever was happening beyond.

Hana crouched beside him, head cocked to listen, her face intent.

"Given you set a trap for me, I'm not likely to tell you, am I?" A hand moved, just a flash through the leaves, but enough to give Iver the location of the driver.

He seemed to be out of the lander.

"We only did that because we knew you wouldn't stop if we tried to flag you down." A woman spoke. Iver just made out her silhouette through the leaves.

"Well, now you've had your chance to say what you want, let me be on my way." The driver's voice had an edge to it.

"Sure." A third voice spoke up, another man. "We're not going to stop you, but consider things from our point of view. I've seen a few of your friends coming and going, and some of them I recognize from the war. Made me curious, that's all. There's talk about a resurgence, and we were just wondering--"

"We are not planning a resurgence." The driver cut him off, tone flat and angry.

"That's what you say, but you're on a supply run, unless I'm mistaken, and as I said before, there are people I recognize from way back, from the havens. And I want in on what's going on. Especially as we've been living in this part of the Spikes since the war ended, and I still haven't found the camp you're headed for. Some trickery going on here, is my guess."

"This deal is invitation only." The driver moved his hand again, a cutting motion. "If you didn't get an invite, that's the end of it."

"Well, now, I'm sure our invitation was just an oversight." The woman put a little lilt into her voice, shifted again. "As Craven said, we live out here, and we have a right--"

"Not any right we recognize." The driver moved; Iver could hear from his voice that he was bending down. He heard a rock hit the ground, as if the driver had thrown it. "You going to move your obstacles, or not?"

"Given you haven't been very polite, why should we?" The first man, the whiner, asked.

There was a beat of silence.

The driver sighed. "How about I promise to raise your issues with the top tier? That's all I can do, anyway."

Maybe he'd spent too long in the thick of politics, but Iver heard the insincerity in the driver's voice. He was saying what he thought they wanted to hear to get out of there.

"Proper old style hierarchy." The third person in the group's voice was approving. "None of this VSC flat structure nonsense." The man spat.

"You were in the havens, you said?" the driver asked.

"I was. We all were."

"I'll tell them. It'll mean something to them."

There was another beat of silence, and then the sound of rocks being rolled away.

From behind them and up the hill, Iver heard the long, lonely cry of a druf.

Hana turned at the sound, frowning.

"You can tell your two colleagues to come out, now that we're all friends here," the woman said.

Iver went still, and his gaze clashed with Hana's, wide with shock.

"Two colleagues?" the driver asked.

"The two you dropped off a little way down the valley. The ones who've been trailing behind you."

The driver made a sharp sound, and Iver saw a ripple of movement.

"You saw two people climb out my lander?"

"Yes." The words were choked out, as if the driver had grabbed the woman by her throat.

There was a scuffle and heavy breathing.

"Easy. You didn't know about the two people?" One of the men said slowly. "They were stowaways?"

"Apparently." The answer was gritted out between teeth. "What do they look like?"

"Why don't we just go get them? Last I saw, they were just over the rise."

"They're definitely watching us," the other man agreed. He gave a whistle and Iver heard the sound of rocks dislodging down the side of the valley. He turned his head to see two women and a man running down the slope toward him and Hana.

Smugglers, Iver realized as he rose up. These were smugglers, hiding in the Spikes. Their clothing was tattered and dusty, their hair wild, but one was holding a SAL, and it looked just as efficient as anyone else's.

Hana had her feet under her, crouching as she also took stock of who was coming at them.

"The ones who're with the driver can't see us, that bird call earlier was the signal. Either they don't have comms, or comms don't work out here." She shrugged on her pack.

He gauged how long they had before the three smugglers reached them. "We need to move."

Hana straightened up. "There." She made a small movement with her hand, pointing to the other side of the valley, where the rocks were bigger and there were more hiding places.

Iver agreed. "Go."

He ran with her, pack banging against his back. They made themselves difficult targets, weaving around bushes and rocks, jumping the narrow stream that ran along the valley floor.

The three chasing them shouted something Iver couldn't hear. It didn't matter--they'd made it to the stone sentinels on the other side, tall boulders standing in a drunken line down the length of the valley.

Hana turned as soon as they reached the first one, looking back with a quick glance.

She swore.

"They're fast. They're making good time."

"And I heard the lander start up. They're going to turn it around and try to run us down." Iver could hear the three people who'd stopped the driver shouting questions about his and Hana's location to their friends.

"Then we go up, where the lander can't reach us." Hana took off at an angle, cutting left and up the side of the mountain.

Iver followed, head pounding with exhaustion, boots slipping on the loose scree that covered the valley slope.

He hadn't slept in at least two days, and while he'd rested in the lander, he'd been too afraid to sleep while Hana was unconscious. He'd dozed a few times, but hadn't let himself truly rest.

He didn't think he could manage this pace for much longer.

Up ahead, Hana gave a sudden cry of pain, and he found he hadn't reached the end of his resources after all.

He sped toward the rock that was blocking her from view, and then had to grab her as he rounded the corner so he didn't bowl her over.

"You're hurt?" He ran his hands down her shoulders and arms.

"Trapped." She pointed to her foot.

It was caught in a nasty serrated metal device that had closed over her boot.

Rage, blinding white and just as hot, seared him. This was . . . unacceptable.

He crouched down, saw it had punctured the fabric of her boot and blood was welling beneath it.

"Go." She half-crouched herself, balancing awkwardly with her trapped foot.

"What?" He stared at her, incredulous.

"I'm not going anywhere. You don't have time to free me now, but if you hide, you'll have the chance to rescue me later."

"No."

The shouts of the smugglers were getting louder, and then they were drowned out by the lander's engine.

"Please, Iver. Hide. Come for me on your own terms. If we're both prisoners, or dead, what good will that do?" Her face was ashy with pain, her lips almost bloodless.

"I don't want to leave you." He slid his palm over her cheek.

"I don't want that, either." She leaned into his hand. "But I don't want us both caught even more."

Iver could hear the clink and crack of boots on scree now. He rose up, torn by the most difficult decision he'd ever had to make.

"Now," she whispered. "Now, before it's too late. And watch out for more of these traps."

He leaned forward, kissed her hard on the lips and then darted behind the next rock, taking an angle that would make him invisible. He reached the next one, and then slid under the first bush he came to.

He wasn't leaving her alone, he was just hiding. If they tried to kill her, he planned to stop it, no matter the consequences.

No matter what.

CHAPTER 16

HANA TRIED TO TURN, to face the smugglers racing up the hill-side toward her, but the metal trap was fixed in place, and when she moved, pain shot up her leg in white hot agony.

Her upgrade had deadened the pain until she tried to move, then it had let the pain loose again--an admonishment to keep still or she'd do more damage. And even with the deadening, it was still a throb, like a hammer hitting her with every beat of her heart.

She steeled herself for the arrival of the smugglers, throwing her arms out to make herself bigger and easier to see, so they wouldn't slam into her.

A woman rounded the rock first, backpedaling as soon as she saw Hana. She was jostled by the man who was right behind her, and he swore at her before he understood the situation, jerking her roughly aside.

The woman sent him a look of deep dislike, almost malice, and then elbowed him in retaliation.

The third woman arrived a few moments later, panting, her steps far slower. She was young--Hana guessed not yet in her twenties.

She skidded to a halt at the sight of them. "She's caught in the trap?" Her eyes went wide with horror.

"Run down and let Craven know," the first woman said, her eyes never leaving Hana.

"What about the man with her?" The other woman asked.

"Don't worry about him now, Lia." The woman was impatient. "Craven needs to know we have her."

Lia's mouth formed a stubborn line, then she took a step back, turned, and disappeared.

"Lia's right, though. We need both of them. We should keep up the chase. She's not going anywhere." The man's gaze lifted higher up the mountain side.

"Well, go on then, Barre." The woman crossed her arms over her chest. "He's got quite a lead by now."

Barre turned on her, snarling, and Hana felt genuinely afraid for the first time. This man was feral.

"Fuck you, Brynja."

The woman must have been used to him, though, because she stood her ground, head slightly cocked. She stared him down, and with a curse he turned and stalked past Hana, although his speed indicated he'd all but given up on the chase.

As soon as he was gone, Brynja relaxed slightly and straightened. "Your friend left you, did he?"

Hana stared past her, ignoring her. She wondered if it would be better if they knew they were chasing the head-of-planet, or not.

Smugglers were unpredictable.

The information could make them back away, or they could think it was a great opportunity to blackmail the VSC.

On balance, she decided no information was the best route.

She wondered where Iver had hidden.

Close, she would bet.

She could only hope he'd left no trail for the feral Barre to follow.

The sound of footsteps coming up the hill snapped Brynja's

attention from Hana and she was standing straight as a group arrived. Hana guessed the first three were the ones who'd stopped the lander, then came Lia, and then came the driver himself.

The gang was all there.

The driver winced at the sight of the trap. "That's . . ." Words failed him. He looked at the smugglers in a side-long glance that spoke of disgust.

"You try living out here without access to the perks of a VSC city, and you'd be setting traps, too." One of the men who'd blocked the lander narrowed his eyes at the driver's reaction. It was the one with the whining voice.

"Your choice to live out here." The driver stood a little apart from them. "The VSC doesn't discriminate on the citizenship dividend, and since the war ended, they've actively encouraged everyone to join Faldine society as equals."

Brynja spat. "What choice is that? Bow to the empire? Take their blood money? No thank you."

"Here." Lia tossed Brynja a small metal lever and she caught it automatically, looked at it, and then stepped close to Hana.

"This will hurt." She crouched down beside the trap, and then hesitated. Looked up. "Well, hurt more than it already does."

She stared at Hana for a beat, and Hana guessed she was looking for signs of pain in Hana's face.

Maybe she wasn't showing enough.

She kept her face blank. Inappropriate behavior would give her away. *Had* given her away, somehow, to Linnel.

To cover herself, Hana closed her eyes, and took a deep breath.

With a sudden creak of unoiled metal, the two serrated jaws fell open, and a wave of pain had Hana turning away to vomit.

She bit back a cry.

Iver would come running if she made too much noise, she was sure of it.

"Stoic little thing, isn't she?" The man who seemed to be the leader of the group shuffled closer. Hana remembered he'd told the driver his name was Craven.

She was bent at the waist, her body turned away from him, and she felt the hot spike of anger lodged in her chest cool to something more dangerous than simple temper at his words.

"Where's your friend?" The driver asked her.

She straightened, digging in a pocket for a tissue, and carefully wiped her mouth. "Gone."

Her foot throbbed, but the pain had receded. Her upgrade going back to work.

She hadn't had many injuries since her accident, but she'd bounced back suspiciously quickly when she had been hurt. She'd also noticed small childhood scars on her legs and arms were fading and a few of the smallest ones were gone completely.

She shrugged off her pack and found a small rock to sit down on.

"Hey!" The whiner exclaimed. "What are you doing?"

"I'm hardly going anywhere." Hana suffused as much disdain in her voice as she could. "I don't want an infection."

She lifted out the medkit Iver had put in the pack for her, and then carefully eased her boot off.

When she peeled off her sock, the driver sucked in a breath.

It *did* look bad. But it would look much better soon, so she wanted them to see it at its worst, for them to underestimate her mobility and her pain level.

She'd take any advantage she could.

She used a steri-wipe and then ran a small wand over the deep gouges in her skin. She pulled out a clean sock and carefully worked it on.

When she'd finished gingerly putting her boot back on, she lifted her head to find them all staring at her.

"What?"

"Very stoic." Craven nodded. "Military?"

Hana stared at him blankly. A yes would make her most definitely this man's enemy. The smugglers had been part of the rebel corps. There would be no quarter given if she admitted to fighting for the VSC.

The silence extended.

"Stoic and silent."

"We going to kill her, or what?" the whiner asked.

The driver rounded on him. "Kill her? Are you being serious?"

"Now, now." Craven glanced at the whiner, and gave a tiny shake of his head. "Tillis here was just messing around."

The driver gave a disbelieving laugh. "Like that's better?"

"You'll have to excuse us," Lia said. "We've gone a little feral out here. No social niceties, you understand."

Brynja turned her head and stared at her, and the smile Lia gave her was more of a grimace.

"Where's Barre?" Tillis asked.

"He went after the other one," Brynja waved up the hillside.

The driver turned to look, and then shifted, as if he was eager to leave. "What were you doing in my lander?"

Hana shook her head and leaned back against the boulder behind her. She closed her eyes, suddenly exhausted. She didn't have the energy to make up a story, and nothing she said would be believed anyway.

"I can't wait around here. They're expecting me at camp. If you get the other one, all good. You can let me know you have him when I come back this way. I'll take this one with me now." The driver stood between Hana and the others, as if worried they wouldn't let him take her.

Hana didn't smile, but she wanted to.

Tillis had frightened the driver. The talk of murder had shocked him and he was truly outraged by the trap.

This one wasn't as cold-blooded as Vannie and Simon, or even Banyon.

It was hard to find good sociopaths these days.

"Just to get it straight, you want us to find the other one?" Craven asked.

"I'm not saying go out of your way. But if you do find him, I know they'll want to question him at the camp, so you can leave a message and we'll reach out to you." The driver spoke carefully.

"And if we don't find him? Are we still invited?" Craven leaned back a little, arms crossed over his chest.

The driver had been walking a fine line since he realized he wasn't going to get away without some give and take, and he lifted his shoulders. "I told you, I'm not top of the chain. I'll tell them what you've said, and I'll leave their answer where you stopped my lander. But if you have the one who got away, that would certainly facilitate your welcome."

Craven gave a slow nod. "Stopping at the same place we put the stones across the road is a good place to leave a message. Someone will be watching."

The driver's mouth tightened.

Hana couldn't blame him. Craven was not-so-subtly letting him know that the route in and out of the camp was being watched, and that if things turned sour, there could be more ambushes.

He gave a sharp nod, and then took her pack.

"Can you walk?"

Hana pushed herself slowly to her feet and tried to put a little weight on her foot. She sucked in a breath. "Is there something I can use as a walking stick?"

Lia turned and disappeared into the bushes, came back with a short stick that was better than nothing. Hana took it with a murmur of thanks.

"We'll be seeing you soon," Craven said. There was a hint of amusement in his voice, as if he was aware that he'd played a strong hand against the driver.

"Looking forward to it." The driver's smile was as fake as his jocular tone.

He indicated that she go first, and Hana gave a nod, took one last look at the smugglers standing in a semi-circle around them, and then limped away.

She hoped that Iver had been close enough to hear what had been said.

She was about to find out about the camp first hand.

CHAPTER 17

"SIT UP FRONT." The driver, who'd introduced himself as Fraen, opened the passenger door, and Hana clambered up awkwardly, hauling herself into the seat using her arms.

She kept the stick Lia had given her tucked against her side. Fraen said nothing about it, and she wondered if he understood it could be a weapon.

Maybe he did, because he clamped restraints on her.

Unfortunately for him, they were standard VSC restraints with electronic locks.

She settled in, trying to work out what her plan of escape would be.

She couldn't walk right now, not on her foot in its current state, but she didn't need to if she took the lander by force.

The driver closed her door and then moved around the front of the vehicle. He looked angry, and she understood why when he lifted a large rock and tossed it to the side. He kicked out a few times at smaller rocks also in the way, and finally got into the driver's seat.

He was breathing hard, and there was a sheen of sweat on his face.

"Those fuckers will pay for this." He started up the engine.

"They seemed to think they'd got one over on you," Hana said.

"Let them keep thinking that." With a sneer, Fraen maneuvered the lander around the last remaining rocks and then picked up a bit of speed.

"You're not worried they'll follow you to wherever you're going?"

He gave her a quick look, mouth open as if to say something, and then shut it with a snap.

Interesting.

The smugglers who'd stopped him were definitely deeply embedded in this part of the Spikes. Their clothing and general state of dishevelment told a story of living rough for a while, but however well they were ensconced in this valley, they hadn't found the camp.

And they had clearly been looking.

Which meant it was extremely difficult to find.

"Do you think they ambushed you to steal your supplies?" she asked. It occurred to her that that might have been the real reason for the ambush. "They look like they're living pretty close to the bone."

With a low, vicious curse, Fraen smacked the steering wheel, then checked the dash display.

They had left the smugglers behind, and there didn't seem to be anyone around.

He braked, hard, and jumped out, disappearing around the back. Hana heard the rear doors open.

She leaned over to the display. Touched it to see if she could short it out.

Her upgrade had been working on her foot, but the further they'd driven from the ambush spot, the more sluggish the repairs had felt.

The magfield was strong here.

As it was through most of the Spikes.

Her runner had come down here during the war, had crashed, because of exactly this reason.

This was not a place that was kind to tech of any kind and she had long believed her upgrade to be tech of the most sophisticated kind imaginable.

It was struggling.

She felt a surge in her fingertips, but while the screen went fuzzy for a few seconds, it did not die.

She leaned back in her seat as Fraen came storming back.

"Assholes! They took a couple of boxes." He hit the wheel with an open palm, even harder than before. "Must have done it when they led me up to where they'd caught you."

Hana said nothing. There was nothing he could have done to stop them. Not on his own. And as she had some of his stuff herself resting inside the pack balancing against her left leg, she couldn't really criticize.

"Did you see how many more of them there were?" Fraen's eyes were narrowed when he looked at her.

She shook her head. "Just the three who stopped you and the three who ran after me. So either there were more of them I couldn't see who stole your supplies, or that one who supposedly went after my friend doubled back to do it."

The driver paused, tapped a finger to his lips. "You're right, he was out of sight the whole time."

"If he did, he did it without the others knowing. Brynja thought he was on a fool's errand, but she seemed to genuinely think he was chasing my friend down."

The driver started the lander moving again. "It would explain why so little was taken. If it was one person, there is only so much they could carry."

"Especially if they were also hiding it from their own people." Hana looked down at the restraints on her wrists, and wondered for the first time if her upgrade was capable of getting them off her.

The valley floor fell away suddenly, the lander's gears grinding down to accommodate the sudden change in angle.

She couldn't see the ground in front of them, the slope was so steep, but she could see the vista ahead.

The valley flattened up ahead, forming a wide plain that curved and wound its way through the heart of the Spikes, almost like a road dividing the Spikes into two.

She had seen this from the air, she remembered, but it didn't look so wide and smooth from above. She could see why Iver and his people had thought it would be the perfect route for the sky lane.

The lander reached the bottom and instead of driving straight ahead, the driver made a hard right, turning toward what looked like a side valley, wedged between two of the high, pointed mountains that gave the range its name.

They had traveled for ten minutes or so when she felt her skin prickle, and her energy begin to sap. She went still, her breathing labored, her limbs useless, alone in her body as she hadn't been in nearly two years.

She slumped to the side, her head hitting the window with a thunk.

"You in pain from your foot?" The driver glanced at her, then turned his attention back to the path ahead. "We're almost at the camp."

"Yes." She forced the word out between clenched teeth.

"I've never seen anything like that trap. It was disgusting. What kind of people would leave something like that out in the open?"

She made a sound, and he must have taken it for assent, because he kept going, fingers tapping the screen on the dash in front of him.

Was he signaling that he was coming in?

She could barely put the thought together.

She thought she'd already be free by now.

That she would be able to get back to Iver.

And here she was . . . caught.

She was on her own in a way she hadn't been for a long time. It was a revelation.

She'd come to depend on her new self. Her upgrade.

Linnel would get his wish if he met up with her now.

She was no longer impossible to kill.

Iver came out of his hiding place the moment he realized Barre had no intention of looking for him.

He watched as the smuggler glanced over his shoulder a few times in the direction of Hana and the others as he worked his way back toward the lander, making sure to keep out of sight.

Interesting twist.

He wondered what Barre was up to. Whatever it was, it was to Iver's benefit.

He moved silently, getting close to Hana again, so he could hear every word spoken.

When the driver insisted she come back to the lander with him, he took a parallel path to Barre, just in case the smuggler decided to come back the same way he'd gone down.

He reached the vehicle much quicker than Hana and the driver, to find Barre unloading things from the back.

Stealing.

Well, well.

He hefted his own, stolen pack. He and Hana didn't have much room to point fingers, although they'd taken only what they needed.

Barre had a big pile of items at his feet, and it looked like he was being discerning about what he was taking.

Still, if he didn't leave soon, Iver wouldn't be able to stow away inside the back again.

Time to hurry him along.

Iver crouched behind one of the boulders and found a stone that fitted in his hand. He aimed at another boulder near where Hana and the driver would be coming out and threw the stone as hard as he could toward it.

The loud crack of rock on rock had Barre freezing in place. He closed the doors quietly and then gathered up what he had.

As he moved away, heading toward the bushes and rocks on the other side of the valley, a few items dropped and Iver could hear him swear as he bent to pick them up.

He didn't wait for Barre to get out of sight.

He didn't have time for that.

He ran to the lander, slid inside again, and moved right to the back, to the little nook he and Hana had hidden in before.

It was only a few minutes later that he heard a low conversation between Hana and the driver. The vehicle creaked as Hana got in the passenger seat, and he relaxed a little when the tone between her and the driver seemed calm and non-confrontational.

It took longer than he thought it would to get going, but then he remembered there were still rocks rolled in the way.

The driver must be moving them himself.

It gave him time to change out of his clothes and pull on the items he'd taken earlier from the crates. He'd added them to his pack as a clean set of clothes to change into, but if he was going to get out of this lander without being noticed and rescue Hana, it would help to look like everyone else in the camp.

Depending on how many were at the camp, of course.

If there were only a few, then he would stand out, no matter what he was wearing.

As he pulled them on, he noticed the clothing belonged to the Faldine security services.

Someone was stealing uniforms, or misappropriating them.

Iver tamped down a flare of anger at the thought.

This was his planet, damn it, and someone was corrupting it.

It would be his pleasure to get to the bottom of it.

He'd just finished getting his boots back on when the lander started to move, slowly at first and then gaining speed.

Suddenly, the driver slammed on brakes. The lander slid a little to the side, came to a stop and then rocked as the driver threw himself out of his seat. Iver could hear his stamping footsteps as he came around to the back.

He was sure he hadn't given himself away.

He would have to trust this was something else.

The doors opened, flooding even Iver's hiding place with light.

"Shit." The driver must have seen immediate signs of Barre's theft. "Shit." It sounded as if he was kicking the rear tires.

He didn't step inside the back of the lander. Instead, he slammed the doors with another curse, and Iver leaned back in relief as he heard him storm back to the front.

They moved off again, a jerky hop of a start that told Iver the driver still wasn't in full control of his temper. They gained more and more speed as they went, and then the whole vehicle tipped forward, as if flying down a steep hill.

The hard right when they reached the bottom caught Iver by surprise, straining the straps holding the crates in place, dislodging everything that wasn't tied down.

Evasive maneuvers?

They drove on, the ground much smoother than before, and at least ten minutes passed before they slowed to a stop.

Iver lifted his restocked pack and stood in the far corner, out of sight, with a bulky but light box he'd chosen to blend in as someone unloading the supplies.

He heard a shout and then the low murmur of conversation, before the vehicle started moving again, much slower this time.

It rolled up a ramp and down the other side, then drove for longer than he was expecting, which told him the entry to the camp was a good distance from the camp itself.

Eventually the lander rocked to a stop, and he heard the driver's door open and then slam shut.

There was a conversation just beyond his ability to hear clearly, and then the passenger door was opened.

"Careful." He recognized the driver's voice, and felt a prickle of fear run down his spine. The man sounded concerned.

Hana's foot had been badly hurt, but she'd seemed to be coping fine when she'd walked down the path to the lander.

She'd wanted him safe, though. Had wanted him to hide, and he could see her downplaying the pain to get him to comply.

Rescuing her might be a little more difficult than he thought, he realized. And the odds were already not ideal.

He'd spent a considerable part of the journey looking through the crates again, but he had yet to find a weapon.

They were obviously a lot harder to steal than food or clothing.

It made him feel like at least some parts of the system were working.

Not everyone they'd encountered who was part of this plot had had a weapon and there was no reason to assume it wasn't the same here.

They might even specifically not want the camp workers to have any. Just in case someone decided to take over from what the driver had called the top tier.

Or maybe he had it all wrong, and everyone here had a SAL in a hip holster.

He needed to stop speculating and get outside.

Find Hana and get out of here.

The doors to the back opened.

"I need to tell you something, Bret," the driver said.

"Yeah?"

"We were robbed." The driver's voice was loud enough that Iver could hear him clearly, and he thought there might have been a sudden quiet, all conversational buzz cut off.

"By whom?"

"Smugglers. They ambushed me in the valley. Set rocks across the road. Made it look like a rockfall. As soon as I stopped, they surrounded me."

"That woman in the front have something to do with this?" Bret asked.

"Partly. I was negotiating my way out of it, trying to promise as little as possible while getting them to let me go, when they told me I had two stowaways who'd climbed out the back of the lander at the part of the road where you have to almost stop to get over the rocks, and that they were watching us."

"And?" Bret didn't sound as dismissive as before.

"When they realized I didn't know about the two who'd been hiding in the back, they chased them down for me. They caught the woman in some kind of nasty metal trap. The man with her got away. While I was questioning the woman, one of the smugglers doubled back around, took what he could from the lander."

"How do you know it was just him?"

"I don't, but he was the only one who wasn't with me when I was questioning the women."

"So there could be more of them?"

"Could be." The driver was standing right outside the door, now. "But if there were more of them, my guess is we would have lost even more stuff. I think he could only carry so much, and needed to hide it quickly. Either from me, or from his own friends, or both."

Bret gave a snort. "So what did you promise them to get away?"

"That I'd let you know they wanted in on the action. Their parting shot was a threat that I could stop where they ambushed me and pass along any message you had for them. Because someone would be watching."

"Shit." Bret started moving away. "Who were they? Did you get names?"

The driver's answer was hard to hear as he moved away with the camp leader.

Iver picked up the box he'd chosen and carefully moved out from behind the crates, down the narrow pathway between the supplies, to the open doors.

There was no one that he could see in front of the lander, and he jumped down lightly and looked around.

Two men were ambling toward the lander from the left, coming out of what looked like a semi-permanent structure made of wood and plasti-cast. The driver and the man he'd called Bret were walking toward them. They stopped to talk and Iver turned away from them, grateful for the distraction.

He'd been holding the box up, using it to hide most of his face, but he lowered it slightly to better see what lay in the other direction and stumbled a little as he took in a massive ruin.

If he hadn't been so focused on the threat of being seen by the driver and his companion, he'd have noticed it immediately.

It rose up, four or five stories high, made of a dull gray material that looked metallic. The roofline was haphazard, as was the facade, as if five or six buildings of different heights and sizes had been joined together. All the buildings had a similar architectural style, but they looked like they should be set apart, rather than put together to form a single unit. Two of the roofs had collapsed, and one wall had a gaping hole in it.

A crescent of twelve windowless huts formed a semi-circle to one side of it, and guessing they were the camp accommodations, Iver headed toward them, still reeling at the sight of the ruin.

Faldine was a rare, habitable planet with no upper-level sentient life to claim it as theirs.

Even so, it should still be subject to a VSC Do Not Disturb order, but the smugglers had shot that to hell when they'd settled in, using Faldine as one of their hiding places while the VSC hunted them down after the Halatian disaster.

By the time the VSC had tracked them to Faldine, the damage had already been done. Every Do Not Disturb protocol had been smashed.

He'd come to Faldine specifically to make sure the smugglers and the VSC's impact on the planet was as low as possible, and still, he knew it had been changed irreversibly.

What he also knew, though, was every thou of ground on the planet had been mapped and nowhere--absolutely nowhere--did an ancient ruin appear.

A shout from behind him pulled him out of his shock, and he glanced around, keeping the move casual, keeping his pace steady.

One of the men he'd seen approaching the lander was hailing him, and he simply lifted an arm in a wave and vaguely indicated toward one of the huts.

When he reached the small dwelling he was headed for, he put the box down in front of the door and then moved around the side, keeping his pace steady until he was completely out of sight.

The man hadn't called again, so he still had a small window of time to hide.

Behind the huts was a low wall made of the same material as the ruin, and then beyond that stood an energy array that looked like it was harnessing power from a fast moving stream, the wind and the sun.

A cable ran from the array, over the wall, and disappeared into a power unit, in what had to be one of the most ancient tech solutions Iver had seen for a long time.

They were either making do with whatever they could find, or nothing else worked out here.

He wondered if they were sitting on an extra strong magnetic field.

He looked along the curve created by the layout of the huts, toward the ruin, and turned from it with regret.

Hana was here somewhere, and she was hurt and in danger.

He realized his hands were trembling, and he gripped the straps of his pack tighter to still them.

He'd caught a glimpse of a few people through the crumbling wall of the ruin--so there were people inside it. Looting it, studying it, whatever it was they were doing, they had tried to kill him to prevent him from finding this place.

Whoever these people were, they hadn't declared their profession when they'd arrived on planet, and they would not be reputable experts.

He forced himself to let go of the fury he felt at the deception involved to hide this from him and his VSC superiors, and instead hunkered down to get a better view of the lander and the buildings on the other side of the camp.

There were actually three buildings, much larger than the huts, and all made of plasti-cast. He guessed they comprised the canteen, the common areas, as well as whatever management offices this operation needed.

The two men unloading the lander had been joined by two other people, and they were carrying crates to the middle of the three buildings.

There was no hover cart here, and they were carrying boxes by hand between them.

His suspicion about the high magnetic field seemed to be accurate.

No one seemed interested in coming after him, and from their body language and the way they were joking with each other as they carried the supplies, they didn't seem to be on alert.

Even when the lander had arrived at the camp's entry point, no one had looked in the back.

Things might change a bit since the smugglers had issued a challenge, but for now, their complacency made Iver's life a lot easier.

He needed to use the time wisely.

He hadn't been able to see where they'd taken Hana, and now that he was tucked behind the huts, he guessed she was on the other side of the large central space where the lander was parked, in one of the big communal buildings.

It would make sense their medbay was on that side.

Darkness came early in the Spikes. The steep sides of the mountains made it difficult for the sunlight to penetrate.

He would have to wait until the light was lost, and he could move about easier, without being seen.

Every moment he waited, he risked something happening to Hana, so he would keep watch, as well as he could.

He looked for a good spot to hunker down, turning to the low wall that seemed a strange barrier to erect. It was useless in terms of protection, unless he was missing something, and he wondered why someone would take the time and effort to put it up.

If he got on the other side of it, he could keep low, move around the ruins, and approach the three communal buildings from behind.

He made sure the hut behind him blocked him from view, and then jogged to the wall and vaulted over it.

He felt a strange sense of vertigo as he swung over, and he landed hard on the other side.

He peered over the wall to check he hadn't been seen and a chill ran over him, pinpricks of cold starting at the top of his scalp, running down his neck and along his arms.

The camp had disappeared.

There was nothing in front of him but rocky ground, with the sharp incline of a mountain in the near distance.

He put both hands on the top of what was now an invisible wall and jumped over it again.

The camp emerged from what seemed like hazy air on a hot day.

He didn't waste time staring. He jumped back again and then leaned against the wall in shock.

Nothing he knew about VSC tech came close to this, except perhaps pinching to the black.

This seemed to be a shield that rendered the area it surrounded completely invisible--not just to scans, but also to the naked eye. It distorted reality, not just making the ruin and the other structures disappear, along with the people, but making the mountain slope look closer, the ground in front of it rockier and harder to traverse.

No wonder the smugglers hadn't found the camp. They'd probably looked right at it and moved on.

And no wonder Lancaster and his friends had tried so hard to stop the progress of the sky lane.

It would have been almost impossible to hide this with the construction teams and surveyors moving all through the area.

As for the reason they were hiding it . . . Iver could understand the massive importance of this. A shield this effective?

The technological implications were staggering.

These people, Lancaster among them, had tried to keep this to themselves. To steal it. And it would be Iver's pleasure to ruin their plans.

Ruin them utterly.

CHAPTER 18

HANA HAD the sense they didn't know what to do with her.

There was no place in the camp to hold her prisoner, and she ended up in the infirmary with a nervy medic who kept looking at the man in charge, Bret, as if he couldn't quite believe what was happening.

"Her foot's a mess." The medic glanced at her as soon as the words were out of his mouth and winced. "I mean . . ."

"Get to the point, Vras. What's the problem?" Bret was staring at her, and unlike the flustered Vras, he seemed to be taking her arrival in stride.

He looked at her with the calm, focused look of a predator sizing up its prey.

She hadn't felt like prey for a long time, but she wasn't herself at the moment.

She would be working on a way to get out of this, if only she didn't feel so weak. So drained.

Her upgrade could no longer make her a faster, sharper version of herself. Not only had it shut down, but something was affecting it.

There was a pulse, like a heartbeat, somewhere outside this room and to the left.

It thrummed through her, each thump vibrating in her chest.

She just wanted it to stop, and yet, she didn't dare ask about it. No one else seemed in the least bit affected, and she had the very real sense the less she spoke right now, the better.

If she was lucky, the injury to her foot was causing some of this feeling of debilitation. She didn't want to believe that her current weakness was from having her upgrade neutralized. If this had been what she considered normal before the crash in the Spikes two years ago . . . No. She couldn't have been this weak.

This had to be the cumulative effect of the damage to her foot, the pain, and the lack of sleep and food, the multiple hits from the SAL tranquilizers. And that cursed thump, thump, thump from some machine outside.

The conversation swirled around her, and she was peripherally aware she'd zoned out.

She should be grateful, she supposed.

She'd wanted to come to the Spikes, find out more about what had happened to her, and while this current situation wasn't what she'd had in mind, the loss of her upgrade told her more than anything else could how far she'd drifted from what she'd been before.

Living a new life since her accident had given her exactly what she'd feared it had. A completely skewed view of what was normal.

No wonder Linnel had sensed something was off.

"What's going on in that head?"

Bret stepped closer to her bed and she snapped back to the present.

"Who are you?" His eyes were cold.

Her injured foot was stretched out in front of her and she was leaning back against some pillows. Her heart beat faster at her vulnerability.

She stared up at him. Said nothing.

"She's in pain. She fainted in the lander." The driver was looking at Bret, looking like he regretted his decision to bring her here.

"What was it that did this?" Vras bent over her foot. "Looks like something bit her."

"It was some kind of metal trap." The driver shook his head. "They're living like animals out there."

"The smugglers did this?" Vras had already given her an injection to stave off infection and he began bandaging her up.

"They're a problem," Bret conceded. "Where are they camped?"

He seemed to be asking her.

She shrugged.

"She's not with them. She probably got in the lander in Touka City." The driver made an impatient chop with his hand. "Why, I don't know. But the smugglers didn't know her, that I can promise."

"Can you?" Bret turned to look at him.

"Yes." He was unequivocal. "You didn't see how they ran her down. How they dealt with her when they found her. One of them is totally off the rails. Tillis. I couldn't get away from him fast enough. He was talking about killing her, and I believed him. The others tried to cover for him, make it sound like Tillis was joking when they saw my reaction, but he wasn't."

"And the one who robbed us?" Bret leaned back a little, arms crossed over his chest.

"I didn't interact with him at all. He was part of the team that ran her down, then he supposedly ran off after her friend, but he must have seen the opportunity to steal some supplies, so he doubled back. I never even spoke to him."

"You did, though?" Bret turned to her.

Hana nodded. "Briefly."

"And?"

She wondered why he thought she would be helpful, but Vras had done a good job on her foot, so she decided she owed them something. "He's feral. The woman who chased after me with him, Brynja, she's wary of him. Doesn't trust him."

"Brynja?" Bret went still. "I know that name."

"They said they were in the rebel corps. Some of them are still wearing parts of the uniform." The driver, Fraen, narrowed his eyes. "They're not trustworthy."

Bret gave a bark of laughter. "I know that." It took a while for his chuckles to die away. "What I don't know is where you fit in." His gaze was back on Hana's face, hard and mean.

"Boss, we got those parts we wanted." A man stepped into the room, one of the two who'd carried her here when she'd arrived.

"Good." Bret turned to the driver. "You did good, Fraen. I assume Banyon isn't happy with you?"

"He just about burst a blood vessel. I wouldn't be surprised if he didn't come out here, scream at you, too."

"Huh." Bret tapped a finger to his lips. "He screamed at you? In public?"

Fraen tilted his head. "In an alley. We were the only ones there. But out in the open, yes."

"Risky."

Fraen nodded. "That's the only reason he reined it in in the end. We could hear people coming."

"He's getting more and more excited. I suppose having the head-of-planet dead is causing him some grief."

"Especially as they didn't kill Sugotti as planned. He survived the first attack. They eventually caught up with him and his pilot. Had them locked down in Touka." Fraen spoke matter-of-factly, and Hana wondered how he could talk like that about her and Iver's death, yet take such offense when Tillis had threatened to do exactly the same.

"I wish you'd led with that." Bret visibly reeled at the news. "Iver Sugotti is alive?"

"No." Fraen shook his head, then shrugged. "Why would they keep him alive? He survived the hit on the Sig, but he and his pilot made it to Touka on foot and Vannie and Si rounded them up before they reached the city itself. They were holding them at Si's warehouse. I left with the supplies before they came round after being tranqed, but the plan was to put them at the bottom of the river."

"How the hell did they survive being hit by SD_3s?"

"The pilot was some hotshot in the war, apparently." Fraen shrugged.

"And Lancaster? What does he have to say about this?"

Fraen blinked at him. "I keep forgetting. I keep forgetting you can't get transmissions here. Lancaster is dead. Someone shot his runner down while he was out looking for Sugotti."

There was dead silence. Hana looked up to see the man in the doorway who'd given the message about spare parts was visibly shocked.

"Who did it?" Bret croaked the words out.

"No one knows. Rumor is the Caruso."

Silence descended again.

"And how would they know anything about this?" Bret's voice was soft.

Fraen shrugged. "Someone reached out to them, tried to see if they might be interested in buying in, maybe?"

"I'd like to know who that person is. Teach them the error of their ways."

Hana saw Vras swallow hard at Bret's tone.

"And you? Where do you come in?" Bret rounded on her, jabbing a finger at her.

She shook her head. "I don't know what's going on. I just want to go home."

"And where's that?"

"Touka City." She lied without compunction. There was only one reason anyone lived in Bero. The small village was built in the one spot on Faldine where the magnetic fields were buried so deep they were almost undetectable, and everyone who lived there either worked for the head-of-planet, or someone they lived with did.

Bero was her personal paradise; where her upgrade could be

everything it was meant to be. The only other place she felt as free was when she was flying high above the ground.

"You got into the lander at Touka?"

"It was a mistake, okay? I didn't know I'd end up here, and I certainly haven't had a good time of it." She pointed at her foot then looked at Fraen. "I'd be grateful for a lift home when you leave."

Bret gave a snort of laughter. "That's not going to happen. Whatever you're doing here, I'm not having anyone telling tales about this place anywhere on Faldine, but certainly not in Touka City. You're stuck here until this is finished, so get your head around your new reality."

She clenched her fists, although his answer wasn't exactly a surprise. They'd tried to kill Iver to keep this place secret, they weren't going to let someone they didn't know or trust out of their sight to spread the news.

"When *will* it be finished?" She spoke through gritted teeth.

"Not sure. A while." Bret looked over at Vras. "Does she need to stay in the medbay tonight?"

Vras gave a slow nod. "It'd be better."

"Then Grimms will have a day to clear out half of her hut, and make space for this one." He walked toward the door.

The man who'd come to tell him about the spare parts was still there, Hana realized, blocking the way.

"Luki, make sure someone has their eye on her at all times." Bret gave the order as the man stepped out of his way. "She won't get far on that foot so no need to put a guard on her full time, but someone needs to have an idea of where she is throughout the day, and Grimms can have the pleasure of keeping an eye on her at night."

Luki winced, as if he didn't like to think about how Grimms was going to take that news, and Hana lay back on the bed and closed her eyes.

She couldn't do anything right now except get some rest. And she would. If only that steady engine thrum would quieten down.

"She has a fever."

She felt the touch of a med wand on her face.

"Good. Then she'll be nice and compliant."

"What if it turns into something serious? We don't know what was on those metal teeth." Vras sounded like he was wringing his hands, but Hana didn't have the energy to open her eyes and look.

"Then she shouldn't have climbed into Fraen's lander. Whatever happens, she'll have to make do with what we've got in camp."

"What about her friend?" Fraen called out after Bret as his footsteps moved away, and Hana felt like kicking out at him.

She'd been hoping they'd forgotten about Iver.

"The smugglers are looking for him. Brynja's relentless. If she's the same soldier I remember from the war, if anyone can find him, she will. I'll send someone to that ambush spot tomorrow, see what they have for us."

He disappeared.

"Get her what she needs, and then lock her in here for now." Luki was probably talking to Vras, but Hana didn't open her eyes to look.

"I'll need to check on her from time to time."

"I didn't say you couldn't. Just make sure she's secure in this room while I make arrangements for someone to keep an eye on her."

Vras must have nodded, because she heard Luki walk away.

"Luki seems a little tense." Fraen lowered his voice.

"They all are. And now they know Iver Sugotti wasn't killed outright, I'm guessing they'll be even more tense." Vras began removing her other boot, and Hana let him, keeping her body relaxed.

"Still having difficulty finding the generator?"

"It's like the shield has sprung up out of thin air. And the scanners you brought in last time to help look for it don't work in here. Nothing works. We only have power because we set up an energy array outside the perimeter and are bringing it in with an insulated cable. It's lights out by 10pm every night to prevent us draining the system too much."

Fraen made a sound of disgust. "Pity someone started shopping this around before they actually had it in hand, then, isn't it?"

"You know how it is." Vras put a blanket over her. "They wanted to be ready to go as soon as they had it. They knew the sky lane was coming this way, and even with Sugotti gone, it's eventually going to go ahead."

Fraen said nothing.

"Do you really think someone brought in the Caruso, and they killed Lancaster?" Vras moved away to his workbench.

"That's what Simon thinks. Who else could it be? The Caruso've been in the VSC's face for months now. They'd love to get shielding tech like this. It's a game changer. Imagine it covering a battle cruiser?"

Vras sighed. "Well, I'm done here. Let's go."

"She unconscious or something?" Fraen's voice was suddenly louder, like he was leaning right over her.

"Just deeply asleep." Vras touched a wand to her face again. "Her body's trying to cope with whatever bacteria was on those teeth. Who do you think she is?"

"No idea. And by the way she keeps her mouth shut, I'm guessing she won't be telling us any time soon."

The door closed and Hana heard the click of a lock.

That was fine.

She didn't mind a little privacy. A little time to recover and catch up on her sleep.

Then she would work out how to escape.

She had to believe that however good Bret thought the smugglers were at tracking, Iver would be one step ahead of them. And she would find him again. Soon.

CHAPTER 19

NIGHT CAME SWIFTLY in the Spikes.

Iver knew it, but the reality of it was always a surprise.

As he watched from the thin line of trees near the camp's entrance, he caught the moment when gloom descended almost between one breath and the next.

The people who lived in the small villages at the mining sites deep within the Spikes called it the shadow fold, where you could look up at the dark blue, sunlit, sky far above, but be standing in darkness. Darkness folded below, light above.

"The shadow fold is one of the best things about this place," one of the guards at the camp's entrance said to her companion, pointing upward. She was stretched out on top of the ramp that sat on the camp side of the wall, one arm folded behind her head. The ramp was set right up against the wall, ready to be swung over and tipped down to allow access from one side of the camp to the other.

"Speak for yourself." Her fellow guard's voice was a low rumble. "I miss the lights of Touka City, and the theater. This place is too quiet."

"What you miss is your lover," she answered, her tone amused.

"Did he believe your explanation in the end about why he couldn't come for a visit?"

"He said he did." The guard's voice lowered even further and Iver finally made out where he was standing. He was leaning against the ramp, his head a little higher than his colleague's prone form.

"You don't believe him?" She sat up, leaning back with arms extended behind her.

"He's intelligent enough to have some doubts. A secret mine in a society where secrets are almost always considered illegal or suspicious?" The big man shrugged. "I blamed the need for secrecy on Sugotti, and now he's dead--"

"Didn't you hear the news from Luki?" The woman swung her legs over the side of the ramp. "Sugotti lived through the first assassination attempt, but Luki said Simon got hold of him before he could make it into Touka City."

"Shit." The guard turned, and Iver could just make out his beard and the bulge of his massive arms as he crossed them over his chest. "He's dead now, though?"

His colleague shrugged. "So Fraen says, but he wasn't there for it. That was just the plan he heard before he left Touka to come here with the supplies."

"Damn." The second curse was drawn out and soft. "This is not good, Grimms."

"I'm sure it'll be--" She stopped talking suddenly, and beside her, the other guard went still, arms dropping and then coming up again, this time with a SAL in hand.

They were staring over the wall, in the direction the lander had come in from earlier, and eventually Iver heard the sound of two men talking.

"We've been this way." The whine in the voice that floated over to him told Iver the speaker was Tillis.

He shifted from his spot against the tree trunk to get a better look and went still at the sight of two small handlights pointed at the ramp from the outside of the shield. The backwash of light lit up two faces.

Tillis and Barre.

They stood on the other side of the wall, looking straight at the guards.

"There's something about this place." Barre seemed to lean forward a little, staring straight at the guards as if he was looking right at them, then turned away without another word.

"Let's go right. We've only looked at the river about a hundred times." Tillis turned away more slowly, and then started off across the rock-strewn ground. "I'm sure that's not enough."

"Fuck you, Tillis." Barre stood for another moment and then turned to follow him. "All you do is whine."

They disappeared into the darkness, and after a minute had passed, the guards blew out a breath in unison.

"Close," Grimms said, voice very low.

"Too close. They'll hit the wall one day soon, just stumble into it. I'm not sure why they haven't already." The guard shook out his shoulders.

"Bret thinks it's because there's something in the shield that repels people. Like a vibration or sound wave that's too high or low to hear, but warns you off."

The guard glanced at her. "Then how did he find it?"

"Don't know. Maybe it doesn't work if you're..." She made a gesture with her hand, as if to imply Bret was crazy.

That was good to know.

"It's not just us, you know, not talking when they come by, even though Bret says they can't hear us on this side of the wall. Jeera and Luki don't talk, either. I asked them."

The man snorted out a laugh, shaking his head. "I'll track them as far as I can on this side of the wall. You keep watch here."

She nodded and the guard headed straight toward Iver, then veered off through the trees.

Iver waited for the sound of him moving through the undergrowth to fade, then took a last look at Grimms, who was standing on the ramp to give herself some height, looking out toward the valley.

He melted into the darkness created by the trees and headed back to the camp along the rough road the lander had used.

He wouldn't need to worry about the guards behind him for a while at least, they were too shook up by their near-miss. The fact that there was only two of them also told him Bret was keeping things very tight when it came to his crew.

Either Bret couldn't find the right people, or he was trying to keep the number of people who knew about this place to a minimum to stop leaks.

Given what had happened to Lancaster, it looked like someone already had leaked. Iver thought it likely that person was Lancaster himself, though. The double-crosser had had the bad luck of being double-crossed.

Lights bloomed out of the darkness up ahead, and Iver could make out the three big camp buildings by their lit windows. Small lights lined a path from the middle building to the huts on the other side of the open space, with the ruins sitting dark and forbidding in between.

Someone laughed, a low chuckle that told Iver whoever it was was relaxed, and from how clear the sound was, they were sitting outside. Someone murmured in response, and the chuckle came again, along with the clink of a glass.

He eased around the side of the building closest to the low wall and saw what he hadn't noticed earlier that afternoon, that there were tables and chairs set outside the middle building.

The sky suddenly lit up, and the aurora blazed in an arc over the Spikes.

There were at least five people sitting outside, and Iver heard some gasp, others cheer.

Suddenly the lights cut out, and the only illumination was the aurora in the sky, washing the mountains in blues, greens and purples.

Then, as if in tune with what was happening below, it winked out as well, plunging the world into absolute darkness.

"It's not ten," someone grumbled.

"No, but Baxter and I were trying to make those repairs with the parts Fraen brought in today, so we used up more power than usual." The person who spoke had a similar depth and rumble to his voice as the guard at the gate.

Someone sighed. "Then I'm going to bed."

Most of them broke up and went their separate ways, but Iver could hear two sets of footsteps coming toward the door of the building he was leaning against.

"Doing a last check for the night, Vras?" The man with the rumbling voice asked, something slightly mocking in his tone.

"Yes." The answer was short and irritated. "You coming to check on her as well, Luki?"

"Might as well. She still asleep?"

Iver hadn't realized he'd straightened up and tensed, but when he looked down at his hands, he saw they were clenched.

"Last time I checked."

"Could she be faking it?" Luki's voice was so similar to the guard at the gate that Iver guessed they were related.

"Maybe," Vras sounded unworried. "But she's not faking her fever, so I doubt it."

Luki didn't answer, and they disappeared into the building.

Iver waited, heart beating too loudly in his ears.

Luki came out first, and Iver noted his physical build was similar to the gate guard's as well.

Vras made his way out a few minutes later. "You waiting for me?" He sounded surprised.

"Just making sure you get out safe and sound. We don't know what she's capable of." The tone was mocking again.

"Whatever, Luki." Vras walked away.

"You locked her in?" Luki's voice was soft, but Iver heard it clearly enough.

"Bret told me to, didn't he?" Vras didn't even look back.

"I'll take the key. I'll need to check on her later tonight."

Vras turned at that, the handlight he was using to light his way giving his face a ghoulish cast. His lips were formed in a thin line. "I also have to check on her later. I need the key."

"Come ask me for it, then."

"No. You ask me." Vras turned again and Iver caught the bob of his handlight as he walked at a fast clip toward the huts, not quite running away, but close.

Luki stood staring after him, shoulders hunched a little. Iver heard him swear softly, and then he stalked toward the building on the far end of the row.

He disappeared into the darkness, and Iver waited until he heard a door open and then close in the distance before trying the door they'd just come out of.

Whatever fight they'd had over the key to the room Hana was in, they hadn't locked the front entrance.

Sloppy.

This whole operation was sloppy.

He stepped into the building, closing the door silently behind him. The room he stepped into felt big and empty. Iver switched on the handlight he'd had in his pack, pointing it at the ground and shielding it with his hand to lessen the glow.

He was in what looked like a medbay reception area, but there were desks with papers on them and he wondered why it looked strange until he realized there were no comm units anywhere.

They didn't work here, obviously.

To his left was a long conference table, and he guessed this was most likely the administration building as well as the medbay.

He moved to the far end of the room and found himself in a narrow passageway. There were three doors, the one directly opposite him looked like a private office, a bathroom to the right, and the door to the left was closed.

He tried the handle but just as Vras had confirmed, it was locked.

"Hana." He knocked softly and called as loudly as he dared.

He heard the sound of movement beyond, and then the handle

rattled.

"Iver?"

She didn't sound herself, and the tension in him ramped up with worry for her.

"Yes. Can you open the door?"

There was silence for a moment, and then he heard a thump, as if she'd hit the door with her fist. "No."

Her tone was anguished. As if she had somehow failed.

"It's all right. I'll get you out. Stand back."

The door had a mechanical lock, a DNA sniffer or electronic system probably wouldn't work here, so he would have to find something to lever it open, and he didn't think there was anything like that in the main room.

Besides, they didn't have time.

He kicked out, hitting the door just under the handle, and heard a crack as part of the door gave way.

He kicked again, and with a pop it opened.

In the muted glow of the handlight, he could see Hana leaning against a bed, her dark hair sticking to her damp forehead, face flushed, eyes too wide and glassy.

"You came." She took a limping step toward him, and he closed the distance between them and held her close for a moment.

He could feel the heat of her fever.

"Any medication we should take with?"

She nodded and stepped out of his arms. He handed the light to her and moved back toward the broken door while she searched.

Kicking the door in had sounded over-loud to him, and he strained to hear any noise from the main room.

"Ready." She was shoving medication into her pack, which they must have allowed her to keep with her.

Sloppy, sloppy, sloppy.

"Can you walk on your own?"

When she nodded, he took her pack and the light from her, and moved out into the passage.

She limped after him, holding onto the doorway for support.

He didn't miss the sound of her quick intake of breath as she followed him out into the reception area.

"Do you need me to carry you?" He moved back toward her, tried to scrutinize her face in the gloom.

"I'll tell you if I do. I promise."

Her eyes glittered in the light, and she shivered.

He gave a reluctant nod, but if she could manage on her own, that would leave him free to fight if they were discovered.

He waited a moment beside the entrance, listening, and then looked at her.

"Not at my usual level of hearing," she said, voice trembling a little.

He gave a nod, took another moment to listen, and then eased the door open.

The cool night air blew in, and he stepped out, holding the door for Hana.

"This way." He headed toward the wall, waiting for Hana on the camp side and then lifting her over.

Her skin was hot to the touch and for a moment he wondered if he was doing the right thing taking her away from medical help.

"Did I tell you how happy I am to see you?" she whispered as he swung over to join her.

He pulled her closer, just for a single beat of time, brushing a kiss on her sweat-damp hair, and then swung their packs onto his shoulders. "I guessed."

"Let's get as far from here as we can." Her voice sounded a little stronger now, as if leaving the camp had lent her strength. She looked back, but there was nothing to see but darkness, and Iver didn't explain about the shield.

There'd be time for that later.

He took her hand and led her toward the river, deeper into the Spikes.

Hopefully, Tillis and Barre were long gone.

CHAPTER 20

HANA WOKE in Iver's arms again.

She could get used to this, although if she were honest, she'd prefer a soft bed inside four walls, rather than rocky ground under an overhang.

The sun was just rising, lighting the sky above them with pinks, oranges and reds--another type of shadow fold, a mirror of dusk the day before, although not quite as spectacular, with the sun coming from the opposite direction.

She moved her foot carefully, wriggling her toes, and felt a sharp pain run up her leg, but it wasn't as bad as it had been.

She was better now she was away from the camp. Much better.

The first gentle fizz in her blood happened as soon as Iver had lifted her over the wall. She'd felt her upgrade wake up, sluggish but thankfully still there, with every step she'd taken.

There was also the relief of having the deep, thrumming beat of the invisible engine fade behind her.

For a while there, lying in the medbay, she'd been terrified her upgrade had been permanently damaged.

She'd suddenly realized she did not want that.

After nearly two years, and plenty of anguish, she'd accepted her new self. She didn't want to lose it.

Right now, she wasn't anywhere near her peak--the magnetic fields here were too strong--but she never was anyway unless she was in Bero or flying high. She could live with the weak response she felt now. It was way better than the dead feeling she'd had before.

"You awake?" Iver nuzzled the top of her head.

"Just about."

She lifted her hand and covered his own where it splayed just under her breasts. Squeezed.

"Thank you for getting me out of there."

"You know I wouldn't leave you." He drew her back against him and she tightened her grip on his hand.

"How did you get in?"

"Hitched a ride in the back of the lander right from the start."

Hana drew in a quick breath. "Were you the one who took the supplies?"

"No. That was Barre. I was lucky to get in before you arrived."

"The leader at the camp is angry about the theft. I think Barre is going to regret doing that."

"Now that you're gone, they may decide I'm to blame." Iver brushed a finger down her cheek and tucked a strand of hair behind her ear.

"Did anyone see you at the camp?" She turned in his arms and looked up at him.

"They saw the back of me, carrying a box toward the accommodation huts. I don't know if they worked out later that I wasn't one of their crew, but they didn't at the time."

"Don't you think they'll assume I escaped on my own?"

He lifted a shoulder. "I kicked the door in from the outside. And you weren't in a good state last night."

He was right about that.

Iver had half-carried her after they got beyond the river. She'd run out of energy and couldn't go on.

"How close are we to the camp?" She rolled back onto her side, looking out at the view from the overhang.

They were on a hillside, and she could hear the river below, but from her position on the ground, she couldn't see it. She couldn't see the camp, either.

The valley below curved to the left, open and wide between the mountains, and she could see why Iver's surveyors had chosen it as the best route for the sky lane.

"We're close to the camp. Too close, but in the dark, with you still injured, we didn't have any choice about getting further away. If the camp wasn't shielded, we'd see it if we sat up."

She narrowed her eyes, lifted up on an elbow, and looked out, but there was nowhere the camp could be that she could see. There was a rocky field to one side, and then the river, glittering gold where the sunlight managed to touch it, frothing white around the large rocks that were embedded in it.

"Where?"

He had risen up behind her, and he pointed over her shoulder, but when she followed his finger, all she saw was the rock-strewn field.

"What did you hear at the camp about the shield?"

"The shield?" She tried to think, but she hadn't been at her most focused while she'd been there. "They might have said something about it while Vras was dealing with my foot, but I wasn't paying much attention."

"There's a shield around the camp. That wall that I lifted you over, that's the shield boundary. When you're on the outside of it, you can't see the ruins, can't see the camp, can't see anything except some visual trickery that makes the area look like a stony field right up against the mountain."

Hana turned to look at him over her shoulder. "Some kind of advanced tech?"

He nodded. "Or very old tech, something we haven't encountered before. There's a ramp they extend over the wall to let the lander in at the entrance. Once you're on the inside, you're invisible to the outside world."

"And when you're on the inside of the wall, looking out? What do you see?"

"Everything as normal. Full visibility."

She stared down the mountain at where the camp should be. "That's what they were trying to hide from the sky lane construction crews."

Iver nodded. More sunlight had begun to angle through the Spikes, sweeping the valley floor, and when she lay back down and turned to him, the planes and lines of his face above her were etched in a golden glow.

"Anyone who discovers how this shielding works has a significant advantage, obviously for military purposes, but for illegal operations, as well. And if the rebels do want to start up the war again, imagine if they could hide their bases from view?"

"And smugglers could hide their ships."

Iver turned to her. "And the Caruso could hide theirs. Or any mining operations they have in mind. That's what they were doing on Veltos, right under the nose of the VSC, and that was without any shielding."

She nodded slowly. "If the Caruso are involved, this is why. They want this for themselves."

"My guess is Lancaster had already given whoever he was dealing with enough to find the camp without his help, so they decided he was better dead than alive and being questioned by the VSC. If I'm right about that, the Caruso, or whoever his co-conspirators are, will be sending someone, or coming themselves, and soon, to take what Lancaster promised them."

"Except . . ." Hana frowned. "Bret told me I needed to accept I wasn't going anywhere, because they weren't letting me go until they were finished at the camp. And when I asked when that would be, he didn't know. He said 'a while'."

"You know what I keep thinking about with this shielding thing?" Iver was looking at one of Faldine's small moons when Hana turned to look at him. "I think about Cepi."

"The Kalastoni moon they blew up less than a year ago?" Hana remembered that. Remembered there had been a lot of fuss about the mysterious gravity and atmosphere generator that had encased the tiny moon. Her eyes opened wide at the implication. "You think this shield is similar to the ancient tech on Cepi?"

Iver shrugged. "There's a ruin here. There was a ruin on Cepi. A ruin that wasn't built by anyone from the Verdant String, or our space-traveling ancestors. The ruins are way older than that. And while the shields aren't exactly the same--this one's an invisibility shield, the other was an environmental generator--there are similarities."

She nodded. Rested her chin on her hands. "At the very least, knowing there was a physical engine to steal on Cepi might have inspired Bret to find out if there was a similar shield engine here."

"And there were definitely smugglers involved in what happened on Cepi. Bret seems to have fought on the rebel side in the war, so it's possible he even knew some of the people who tried to steal the engine from Cepi."

"You think one of them might have given him information to help him in what he's trying to do here?" she asked.

Iver shook his head. "Everyone involved in that attempted theft died on Cepi before the Kalastoni blew it up. They were killed by the people who'd employed them."

"So maybe he just saw the parallels, like you." She closed her eyes, let the heat of Iver's body beside her warm her through.

After a while, Iver sat up, and she joined him, leaning back against him in a way that reminded her of their positions hiding from Linnel after the missile had brought down her Sig.

It was peaceful, sitting in the gloom of the overhang, watching the sunlight slowly gild the mountains and valley in gold.

Iver leaned to the side and grabbed one of the packs, handed her some water and an instant meal.

She didn't realize how hungry she was until she had the spoon in her hand. It shook as she scooped the mixed fruit into her mouth.

She glanced at Iver, saw he was eating just as fast. She gave a wry smile. "I take back what I said about these the other night. They're not that bad."

He grinned. "Yes, they are."

"Okay. They are." She drank her water and leaned back again, eyes half-closed. It was the most calm and safe she'd felt in days.

Iver picked up the pack again and brought out two sweet nut bars, and she took one with a quiet whoop of joy. She kissed his cheek before she opened hers and bit in.

When he didn't do the same, she turned her head to look at him, saw he was watching her with the kind of attention that had her cheeks flushing.

Then he leaned closer and covered her lips with his.

She groaned at the feel of his mouth against hers and twisted in his arms. He lifted her up onto his lap in a move that was so easy she didn't realize it had happened until she was straddling him.

She rocked against him where their bodies joined and it was his turn to groan into her mouth.

"Should we take a risk?" she whispered.

"It's probably not wise." His hands slid under her shirt and jacket and kneaded her back. "And you're injured."

Then his mouth moved down her neck and she tilted it, giving him access.

"Not that injured." Guess she wasn't feeling all that wise and neither was he, because it seemed like moments later she was naked, back in Iver's lap, sliding down inch by delicious inch onto the hard length of him.

She arched back in his hold as they moved together, undulating in a smooth, slow dance that sped up when he latched on to the tip of her breast and sucked.

She shuddered as she came, held him when he did the same, and then sat quietly with her head on his shoulder, enclosed in the loop of his arms, and slowly got her breath back.

His fingers began a lazy, light stroke from the top of her spine, down to the small of her back, and she hummed in contentment.

The sound of shouting voices from down the valley drifted up on the gentle breeze, and for a moment she ignored them, shut them out.

"Guess they discovered you're missing." Iver's grip on her hips tightened, and with a soft curse he lifted her off him.

She leaned forward, resting her forehead against his for a moment, and then forced herself to move.

She looked down the hill as she struggled back into her clothes, trying to work out where her searchers were headed.

"They must have decided to wait until it got light before coming to look for me."

Iver was crouched beside her, both packs in hand, all their debris put away. He ran a finger down her neck as if he couldn't help touching her and she shivered.

"They're down by the river." His voice was deeper than usual, a little rough.

"Hopefully that's just them being thorough. Maybe they'll think I headed for Touka City."

Iver shrugged. "That would be helpful, but they won't want to go that way looking for you. Now they know the smugglers are watching for them, they won't want to give them a chance to follow them back to camp."

"It's surprising the smugglers haven't found them before now." She'd wondered about that. Brynja, Craven and their friends had looked like they'd been in the Spikes for a lot longer than Bret and his crew had been at the camp.

"My guess is the smugglers don't live in this valley usually. They probably saw the lander come through by chance, but were too far away to follow it. Maybe they saw it from afar a few times and tried to narrow down where it was going until they set up a watch for it."

That would explain their unkempt appearance. If they were far from their usual camp, making do while they waited for the lander to show up, they'd look a little rough.

"Come on, let's move. Hopefully they're just checking the river for obvious signs of you, but it doesn't hurt to take precautions."

She looked over at him, frowning. "Where are we going?"

He pointed upward, to the ceiling of the overhang. "This is a large rock embedded in the hill. Up top there's been enough of a soil buildup that long grasses have gotten a foothold. It's a good place to hide and see out over the valley."

He must have found that after he'd carried her up here last night.

She could barely remember getting much further than the river, and she gripped his wrist as he started moving.

"Thank you. I'd still be in that medbay without you."

"And I'd be nothing but charred bone in a burned out Sig without you." He held her gaze. "There's no tally here, Hana. I'll protect you, and rescue you, and have your back whenever you need it."

She nodded, her throat too tight to answer, and then she followed him up the steep slope of the hill on one side of the overhang, and crawled next to him through the long grass to the edge of the flat piece of rock.

The view, as Iver had said, was excellent. If the camp wasn't shielded, they would be looking down on it, but as it was, all she could see was two women walking along the river bank, looking all around them.

"One of them is probably Grimms," Hana said.

"She is." Iver pointed to the one at the back, a tall woman with a tangle of dark hair pulled back from her face.

"I was supposed to share a hut with her tonight." Hana watched

Grimms kick a rock into the fast-moving water, and then put her hands on her hips.

She turned slowly, looking up the hill at where they lay hidden, and then toward the camp, and then up the valley.

A waterfall, just a thin ribbon of water far in the distance, fell from the juncture where two of the mountains met. It gleamed golden red in the morning light, as if molten.

Grimms called to her companion, and after what appeared to be the back-and-forth of conversation, they both turned and headed toward the camp.

"Well, well, well." Hana saw the flash of movement a moment later, and focused on the spot on the other side of the river.

"What is it?" Iver looked over at her.

"Someone's watching them. Following them. Look."

Two people moved out from behind the low trees that squatted close to the river bank. Both of them were in dark clothing, with hooded jackets pulled up.

One crossed the river, almost directly opposite where she and Iver were lying, while the other kept to the other side.

"They're hedging their bets, taking both sides of the river, which means they don't know where Grimms and her friend are going," Iver murmured. "They look like smugglers."

"Not as tattered as the others, but yes. Same general uniform."

"If they're part of the same group, that ambush was more coordinated than it appeared." Iver leaned closer to her as they followed the progress of the smugglers as they trailed the two camp crew.

"They're keeping well back. They don't intend to grab them." Hana knew intellectually that the camp, which she'd seen from the inside, was in the field to their left, but when Grimms seemed to jump into the air and disappear, she couldn't help the gasp of surprise that escaped.

The two following Grimms were obviously just as shocked.

The person on the camp side of the river was clearly a woman, although with the hood up on her jacket, Hana couldn't make out her face. The woman crouched down in surprise, and the man, following on a parallel path on the other side of the river, froze.

They glanced across at each other, and then turned in time to see Grimms' friend disappear the same way.

The two smugglers stayed where they were for what felt like a long time, and then the woman crept along the path to the general area where the camp crew had jumped into invisibility.

She touched the wall, her hand coming back in shock to find something she could feel but couldn't see. Hana saw her take a deep breath and then pat her way up the wall until she found the top, then slowly lift up and lean over.

Half her body disappeared, and she drew back so fast she fell on her backside.

She moved clumsily into a crouch and then ran, bent low, back the way she'd come.

Her friend across the river gave up being quiet and shouted something at her, a warning, and when Hana looked over, she saw Grimms and a huge man were racing down the path.

The man leaped to the riverbank as the woman began to cross, and lifted both hands as the two camp guards came into range.

"He's got a SAL." Hana realized her whole body was tense, just watching what was happening below.

The dart must have hit Grimms, because she went down, and her partner leaped over her and then jumped down the bank, but the woman had made it to the other side by then.

Her friend shot again, much closer this time, and the man fell back.

Hana held her breath as he fell, but he landed mostly on the river bank, not in the water.

There was another shout as three more people came racing down the track, and she relaxed.

They'd at least make sure their friend didn't drown.

The two smugglers ran up the hill and disappeared.

Hana rested her chin on her folded hands and watched the

guards from the camp haul the big man out of the river, and then cross to the other side for signs of the smugglers. After fifteen minutes, all three of them came back empty-handed.

"Guess the smugglers know where the camp is, now." Iver handed Hana a nut bar and she chewed thoughtfully as the camp crew dragged their friends back behind the shield.

Everything looked the same as it had half an hour before, but it wasn't. Things had changed completely.

The camp was discovered, and Bret had some decisions to make--

A whoosh from the other side of the valley made her freeze, and she leaned closer to the edge, gaze sweeping the landscape for where it was coming from.

"What--?"

She held up a hand to quiet Iver's question and used her elbows to lever herself even further out.

There.

A vapor trail was just visible, and she pointed to it, then just caught the quick glint of silver metal as it shot up toward the sky.

"A TellTale." The implications rocked her. She turned her head, met Iver's gaze. "Who can be waiting in nearspace to receive it?"

Iver looked upward, and Hana saw the TellTale give a final wink as it disappeared above the clouds.

"There shouldn't be anyone up there but the VSC battleships. And from what the head administrator of Touka City said to us, there are VSC special forces on their way to look into my disappearance, which means smaller military runners coming in from wherever the fleet is stationed. Whoever is lurking up there is taking a huge risk."

"The Caruso wouldn't dare, would they? The VSC has to be on high alert after what happened on Veltos last month. I can't imagine they could get through the VSC security net. It's not like Faldine is undefended."

"No." Iver tapped a fist into his open palm. "I agree, they have to know any sign of a Caruso ship in Faldine nearspace would have the VSC mobilizing."

"So, what?" Hana asked. "It's not the Caruso? Or it is them, but they're using a VSC ship?"

"Maybe." Iver's lips were in a tight line. "Whatever it is, whoever is up there, now they've been given the location of the camp, we can expect company."

CHAPTER 21

"SO, WHAT NOW?" Hana slowly worked her way back from the edge of the rock, and then stretched out as if her muscles were stiff.

They'd slept on hard ground, and she was still injured, but she hadn't spoken a single word of complaint.

"I wish you weren't caught up in this." The sudden spike of rage that erupted in him had him clenching his fists.

She looked over at him, surprised, and then frowned. "You're not feeling guilty, are you? This is on Lancaster and everyone who's involved in the camp."

It was more fury than guilt, but there was a lot of that in the mix, too.

When the VSC had more or less bribed him into taking the head-of-planet position, he'd been pleased with the challenge. He'd never thought his position would endanger someone he cared about.

"Listen." She reached out and grabbed his jacket, so she had his full attention. "I fought for four years so Faldine would have a fair chance, so the VSC didn't have another Garmen or Lassa on their hands. And if these assholes think they can plunge us back into that so they can . . . what? Go back to their secretive havens that allow them to steal and ambush traders at will? That's against everything I risked my life for. This is not on you. Put the blame where it belongs."

She took a deep, shaking breath in, and Iver realized her anger was almost at the same level as his.

He closed his hands over hers where they still gripped his jacket and she looked down in surprise, and then her lips quirked up in a smile.

"Guess it fires me up a little."

He leaned forward, brushing a kiss on her forehead, and was hit by a yearning to have her naked and in his lap again, rocking away the trouble and the discomfort and the danger, until it was just her and him, in a world of their own.

"I don't want to, but I think I have to go over the river to where that TellTale was set off, see who's there and what they're up to." As he said it, he realized how reluctant he was. He didn't want to leave her, even though finding out what he could from the scouts who'd found the camp was his duty as head-of-planet.

She closed her eyes, opened them again. "I'd say I'll come with you, watch your back, but my foot isn't healed enough yet."

He gave a snort. "It's only been a day since you were injured, there's no way you should expect it to be healed already."

She stared at him, almost blank-faced for a second, then shrugged. "I heal fast."

"No one heals that fast." But he had a sense she really believed she should be up and active again. He ran a hand down her arm. "Give yourself a break, Hana. You're not invincible."

"Not according to Linnel." She shot him a wry grin.

He shrugged. "Linnel is delusional and under arrest in Touka City." He looked back over the river, knew he needed to get moving in case whoever was out there decided to go to ground.

"I'll be fine. I'll stay here, use the overhang as a place to sleep again tonight if you're not back yet."

He wanted to say of course he'd be back by then, but he couldn't be sure. "I'll see you soon. Stay safe."

She gripped his jacket again, drew him in, and he kissed her hard, marveling that he had her in his arms at all, after months of accepting that he never would.

He pulled back reluctantly, grabbing his pack as he slid backward. He kept low until he found enough cover, and then he ran down the side of the hill to the river.

He looked back when he reached the bank, up to the rock embedded in the hillside, and thought he saw movement--the wave of a hand. It was a good position. Hana was hidden but had a good view of everything.

She would be fine. Absolutely fine.

He forced himself to turn away and drop down onto the narrow strip of rocks below the bank.

When he was across, with boots only a little wet, he found the path the two scouts had taken.

They had chosen speed over covering their tracks, leaving crushed vegetation and broken branches to show the way they'd taken, as well as some boot prints in the mud.

If he could follow it easily, so would the guards from the camp-- and they would be coming back this way to search, no doubt about it.

Once they had their people in the medbay, Bret would send more than a few of them out. Secrecy was everything to the camp, and it had just been breached. They'd want to find and silence whoever they could find. And if they'd seen the TellTale launch . . .

He couldn't see how the camp leader would be happy with that.

Iver increased his pace.

When the camp guards came, he wanted to be well ahead of them.

He followed the path around a stand of trees and slowed to a stop as he smelled the throat catching stink of a solid fuel cell from up ahead.

There was no sound, no voices to be heard, but he carefully stepped off the path, and winced as dry leaves crackled beneath his boots.

He went still, waiting for a reaction, but when none came, he looked around, and then up.

The trees were close together, forming a small copse, with entangled roots and low branches.

He jumped, grabbing hold of a branch and swinging himself into a tree.

The trees were so close together he was able to move easily from one to the other until he could see around the curve in the path, to a small clearing on the other side.

The TellTale had definitely been launched here.

The thick green ground covering was scorched, and when he rubbed one of the leaves hanging near his face between his finger and thumb, he felt the slightly oily residue typical of a burn-up.

Maybe they'd launched and run.

Although he hadn't seen any evidence they'd run back toward the camp. He and Hana would have seen them. Maybe they'd gone to fetch their friends.

If so, they'd chosen to send the TellTale first. Presumably giving the camp's location to whoever they were working for was paramount. He wondered again who could be up in Faldine nearspace, waiting for information from below.

He was head-of-planet, and he knew the VSC battleships did a regular scan for unidentified vessels, as well as patrols.

Whoever was up there, they were either using tech the VSC didn't know about, or it was avoiding scrutiny in some other way.

"It still stinks." A woman coughed suddenly, so close to where Iver sat hunched over on his branch, his grip slipped for a moment in shock.

"Yeah. It's better than it was--bearable--but still not good. When some of those guards from the camp follow our trail here, they'll know something was launched, if they didn't see it lift off." The man cleared his throat, hacked a cough himself.

Iver tried to see where they'd come from, noticed a narrow gap in the undergrowth just to the left of his tree.

"We couldn't help that, the TellTale had to be sent." The woman moved out into the center of the clearing, looked toward the river. "Wish they'd warned us about the smell." She lifted her arm and covered her nose and mouth. She took a few breaths, looking around. "We need to find a good place to hide before the camp guards get here."

"We're only to attack if there's one of them, Craven said. We stay put if there are more." Her companion coughed again.

"Sure." There was a slightly derisive laugh in the woman's voice. "We play it safe, got it."

The man sighed, then the fumes must have got to him again, because he coughed for a minute. "There aren't enough of us to risk being hurt or captured, Lia." There was a more aggressive edge to his voice now.

Iver recognized the name. He hadn't gotten a good look at the woman who'd been part of the group that had chased Hana into the steel trap, but he'd heard her name mentioned. There couldn't be two women with the same name in the area.

So these two *were* part of the smugglers' group.

Iver had gotten a good look at all three men who'd been part of the ambush team back in the valley, and the man with Lia now wasn't one of them.

So there were others in the group. How many would be interesting to find out.

"I said sure." Lia snapped out the response.

"You say a lot of things, and then just go your own way."

"I found the camp, didn't I?" Lia's tone was sharp.

"You did. But you also let them see you. So now we have to bring the plans forward." There was a nastiness in his voice.

"You ever get tired of being Craven's little sycophant, Roj? Because that's all you do. You toe the line."

Roj turned to her, aggression in his stance. "Why did you join up if you don't want to toe the line? No one forced you to come out here."

"Fuck you." Lia sneered, hands on hips. "I fought in the war as soon as I was old enough to join, and I lost big. I'm not losing out again because someone's scared of acting."

"It's called being strategic." Roj's hands were fisted at his sides, then he went still, his gaze snapping to the path.

He signaled to Lia, pointing back the way they'd entered the clearing and then ran silently to the bushes opposite to where Iver was hiding.

Lia hesitated, then followed Roj's directions, slipping back the way they'd come.

Iver hadn't heard whatever had alerted Roj, and the silence dragged out. The camp guards had either smelled the burn of the TellTale, or they'd heard Roj and Lia talking. Either way, they'd gone silent.

As time stretched out, with nothing happening, Iver decided the other option was that Roj had been overcautious, that there hadn't been anyone there in the first place.

He heard the rustle of foliage to his left, where he knew Lia had gone to ground.

She was getting twitchy. Or tired of waiting.

There was a sudden shout, coming from Roj's hiding place, and two men burst out into the clearing, fighting.

It was ugly.

There were vicious blows and hard knocks, the men grunting and grappling as they rolled around on the blackened ground.

Iver recalled Roj had had a SAL earlier, when he'd shot Grimms and her fellow guard, but there was no sign of it now.

Both men started coughing as they picked up the grit and residue of the TellTale, so their labored breath became part of the ugliness of the fight.

Iver recognized the man from the night before. He'd accompanied the medic to check on Hana in the medbay--Luki.

His face was smudged with black residue, which made the pale blue of his eyes even more intense in his face.

He looked lost in the violence of the fight. There was no strategy, it had devolved to a desperate struggle for survival, and Roj was outclassed, not because he didn't have the skills, but because he wasn't trying to kill his opponent.

And Luki looked like he was prepared to do murder.

Iver couldn't just sit in his tree and watch. He looped his pack over his shoulders, moved close to the edge of the branch, and looked below to check the ground where he would land.

As he committed to the leap, two more people burst into the clearing, coming around the trees from the direction of the river.

It distracted Iver and he landed hard, falling to his knees on the twisted, uneven roots.

One of the newcomers was the woman who'd been with Grimms earlier, searching the river for Hana, the other was a man Iver didn't recognize.

The man must have seen him jump, because his attention was fixed on Iver.

The woman had a SAL, and she was trying to get a clear shot at Roj as he rolled around with Luki. She was shouting at Luki to move, but he seemed not to hear her.

The man turned briefly as she screamed Luki's name but then swung straight back to focus on Iver.

The shouting seemed to be the final straw for Lia. Iver saw her burst out of her hiding place with a shout of her own.

She had nothing but a thick stick in her hand, raised above her head and she took a swing at the man who had started in Iver's direction.

He wasn't looking her way, his focus was fully on Iver, and the stick connected against the side of his head with a crack.

He went down without a sound, and Lia turned in a single, smooth move and brought the stick down again, this time on Luki's back.

He roared in pain and fury, striking back at her with one arm and kicking out with his closest foot.

The move lifted him off Roj, who used the brief reprieve to pull something out of the side pocket in his military pants. As Luki turned back to him, Roj stabbed upward.

Luki bellowed in pain again, and Roj heaved him off.

As soon as he was free of Luki, the woman used her clear shot, and Roj looked down with a frown at the SAL dart sticking out just below his collarbone.

"Shit." He coughed as he looked over at the woman, seeing her for the first time, and then fell back down, and lay still.

The woman was breathing hard, and she sneezed as the after-burn irritated her nasal passages. She turned the SAL on Lia, but Lia was already moving, stick raised up, and the camp guard missed as she was forced to leap back and shoot at the same time.

"That's got, what? One or two more darts?" Lia swung the stick again, leaning forward to extend her reach.

The stick struck the woman's hand, and the SAL flew out of her grip and landed amongst the tree roots, near Iver's feet.

He scrambled over and picked it up, saw neither woman had noticed him yet.

Lia was swinging the stick again, the camp guard dancing out of reach with the hand that had been hit tucked up against her stomach.

Enough of this.

Iver stepped out of the copse and shot Lia in the back.

For a moment she went still, then tried to look over her shoulder before she fell face first onto the ground.

The woman from the camp stared at Lia in shock, unsure what had happened, and then finally lifted her gaze and saw him.

"Who are--?"

Iver shot her as well.

He checked the SAL as she collapsed. Lia had been right. There were no darts left.

Someone made an animalistic sound, and Iver turned to find Luki staring at him, both hands at the wound in his side.

As Iver took a step toward him, Luki started to cough, a heaving, hacking sound, and then he passed out.

Iver started coughing himself.

TellTale after-burn was foul.

It should be banned.

Iver decided it *would* be banned. As soon as he got back to his job of running the fucking planet.

Which these fuckers had tried to stop him from doing.

He vaguely realized he was about to kick Luki, that his boot was going back so he could really put one in, and he stumbled away, back into the trees and turned from the clearing, breathing the clearer air.

Then he staggered to the path and stood for a few minutes taking deep lungfuls, head bent, hands on his knees.

There was something in the after-burn chemicals that triggered violence.

He had never heard of that before, and it made him wonder who knew about it.

His list of wrongs to right was getting longer.

"Well, well, well. Who do we have here?"

Iver slowly lifted his gaze, and then straightened up. He still had the SAL in his hand but given that two other SALs were being leveled at him, and he knew his was out of darts, he dropped it to the ground.

"Wise choice." Bret looked at him intently, and then swore.

"What, boss?" The man beside the camp leader was tall, thin and twitchy, as if he was out of his element.

"Iver Sugotti." Bret swore again, and then kicked out at a stone near his foot.

"Turns out, I'm difficult to kill." Iver lifted his hands and shoulders. "Before we go on about me and how much of a bastard I am, one of your guards has been stabbed and may still live if you get him help. The other was hit in the head with a stick and is probably concussed. Wait--!" He stepped into the path to block it as the thin man began to rush past. "Be careful. The fumes from the TellTale after-burn seem to trigger unnecessary violence. That's why that scene around the corner looks like it does."

Bret narrowed his eyes. "Trying to cover for yourself, Sugotti?"

Iver shook his head. "I was watching from the trees. When I went to help and felt the same rage rising up in me, I came out here for some fresh air."

Bret put a hand on his subordinate. "He was breathing heavily when we found him. Put on a mask just in case, Baxter."

Iver watched as the scientist--he was sure the man wasn't part of Bret's security team--found a mask in his pack and jogged around the corner.

"What are you doing here, Sugotti?"

Iver considered an answer that would keep Hana safe, and then Baxter gave a panicked shout.

"What will I find around that corner?" Bret took a step closer, his SAL aimed at Iver's chest.

"Your wounded security guards, and two others with SAL darts in them."

Bret reared back. "There's no one conscious?"

"Your people shot a smuggler, the smugglers hit one of yours with a stick, stabbed another, and I shot the two who were left, then felt the effects of the fumes and came out here to get some clear air."

The scientist ran back around the corner, the mask flapping around his neck.

"He's right about the fumes." He stopped, gulping in air. "I felt like hitting Luki while I was patching him up."

"With the mask on?" Bret asked.

Baxter shook his head. "I decided to see if he was telling the truth, so I took it off for a bit."

Bret looked up at the sky for a moment, then breathed deeply as he focused back on Baxter.

"Run and get three others, whoever's available, and come back with two stretchers."

Baxter looked like he wanted to argue, but with a look from Bret he gave a nod and ran off.

"One of your scientists, looking for what's powering the shield?" Iver asked.

Bret shot him a sour look. "Seems like you know more than you should."

"Lancaster was chatty before someone blew him up." He might as well blame it on Lancaster, rather than reveal he'd been snooping around the night before.

Bret went still. "Now why would Lancaster tell you anything?"

"He was about to kill me at the time. He didn't see any reason to hold back."

"You killed him instead?" Bret kept the question casual.

"No. I shot him with a SAL, left him in his Dynastra, and was barely clear of it when someone blew it to bits."

"Shit." Bret shook his head. "Did you see who?"

"I was a bit busy dodging burning debris."

Bret lowered the SAL to his side. "And the woman? Our prisoner until last night. What's she to you?"

Iver crossed his arms over his chest. "What woman?"

"Please. She was traveling with a man who managed to escape. Then someone frees her last night. And now here you are." Bret nodded his head slowly. "It also explains what she was doing in the back of the lander. Somehow you suspected or knew it was coming here. You got in it with her to see if it would deliver you to the camp."

Iver sighed. "Your friend Banyon sort of gave that away with his ranting outside the Touka City headquarters."

Bret kicked at the stone again, this time sending it into the stand of trees, where it smacked against a trunk. "How compromised are we?"

Iver quirked his lips, lifted his shoulders. "What do you think, given I'm right here?"

"Yeah, but there's no army with you. The VSC special forces are nowhere in sight. For some reason, you chose to do this alone."

Before Iver could answer, a loud moan came from the clearing, and Bret lifted the SAL again, used it to indicate to Iver to go first down the path.

Iver stopped before the path widened out, where the air was hopefully a little clearer, and put out an arm to stop Bret before he stepped into the open space himself.

"Fumes, remember."

Bret took a hasty step back.

Roj had started to move, and he was holding both hands to his head, as if he could barely move it.

"Looks like he's got a headache." Bret didn't sound too sympathetic.

"So will your people. And it's not as bad now as it was before. The breeze has cleared some of the stink out." Iver edged back a little more and coughed.

Bret grabbed the back of his jacket collar and pulled him back even further, as he started to cough as well.

Roj turned suddenly and vomited.

"I'm sure I've got a mask in my pack. Let me at least bring them out of the clearing." Iver didn't like the gray hue of Roj's skin.

Bret took Iver's pack off his back and retreated a few steps. "Don't move." He set the pack on the ground and opened it up, keeping his arm raised, the SAL pointed at Iver, his gaze jumping from Iver to the inside of the pack and back.

"All right. Here it is." He tossed a mask to Iver. "You carry them out here, and if you try anything, I swear I'll shoot you and leave you lying in the after-burn."

Iver nodded, secured the mask.

Roj fought him, batting at him like he'd forgotten how to throw a punch, and eventually Iver got him on his feet and wrangled him away from the clearing.

Luki was still unconscious, and Iver didn't dare move him alone, not with his wound still sluggishly seeping blood from around the patch Baxter had put in place.

Instead, he lifted the women up, one by one, carrying them to where he'd put Roj.

"Set Jeera down here," Bret said when he brought the woman who'd been on patrol with Grimms. "I don't want her close to the other two."

Iver did as Bret asked, then went back for the last man, whose name he didn't know.

"Russ can be laid down next to Jeera."

When Iver stepped back, something brushed his ankle, and he looked down, found Roj trying to grip the bottom of his pants.

"Sick." Roj turned, vomited again, and Iver held out a hand to Bret.

"My pack. He needs some water."

Bret didn't hand the pack over, but he crouched beside it again, and tossed Iver a water bottle.

Iver carefully held it to Roj's lips, let him sip at it.

"What now?" he asked Bret.

Bret angled his body, so he could keep an eye on everyone as well as the path from the river.

"Now we wait for my people, and then we find out who these people sent that TellTale too."

"How you going to do that?" Iver had a bad feeling he knew.

"Any way we have to." Bret's gaze rested on Roj and Lia, and Iver was glad Hana was no longer in his clutches.

CHAPTER 22

SOMETHING HAD HAPPENED.

Something violent.

Hana could think of no other reason for the four people from the camp running along the path Iver had taken, carrying two stretchers between them.

If Iver was one of the people hurt . . .

She took a deep breath. If he was, she couldn't do anything to help him right now.

She needed to watch and see what was going on before she ran down and got herself recaptured.

It didn't take long for the group to come back around the curve of the hill again.

One of the people holding the end of a stretcher was Vras, the medic who'd tended to her the day before. He and the other two men and one woman helping him all seemed ill at ease.

They negotiated the river carefully, all four of them carrying first one and then the other injured person on the stretchers over the rocks.

Iver wasn't on either.

Hana focused back on the path again.

Two people came limping into view.

One of the woman who worked at the camp was supporting a fellow guard.

He was unsteady on his feet, his hand to his temple.

The woman looked in better shape, but her stride was uncertain.

Behind them came the woman who'd followed Grimms and her friend along the river and discovered the camp. Now that she was facing Hana and walking slowly, Hana recognized her as Lia, Brynja's friend from the valley ambush. Her hands were clasped behind her head.

Iver came behind her, doing the same.

Hana swallowed back bile as a heavy weight settled in the pit of her stomach at seeing him captured.

He seemed all right, though. Uninjured at least.

She would have to get him out and it would be a lot harder for her than it had been for him to rescue her.

They would be on alert now.

Especially because the smugglers had sent a TellTale. Bret knew the camp's location was no longer a secret. They'd be on their guard now.

Finally, last in line, came Bret. He was holding a SAL, pointed at Iver's back.

He obviously thought Iver was the more dangerous of his two prisoners, he kept his focus on him, and Hana could see Bret hadn't noticed that Lia was moving a little faster along the path, putting more distance between them. She was a little unsteady on her feet but there was a determined look on her face as she suddenly dodged right, breaking into a run as she aimed for the trees.

She was mid leap when she collapsed, a SAL dart in her back.

Iver started toward Lia and then stopped, turned to face Bret. Hana couldn't hear their exchange from the hillside, but it looked heated. Eventually, Bret waved the SAL at Iver and he approached Lia slowly, then crouched beside her.

He said something to Bret, and they argued a little longer before Iver picked her up.

Hana saw blood on Lia's forehead as her head hung limply over Iver's arm.

Iver carried her to the river, then put her over his shoulder as he jumped the rocks to get across.

Bret was right behind him, standing over Iver as he set Lia down on the other side.

"Can you hear me?" Bret shouted.

Hana frowned. Who was he calling to? Iver could definitely hear him, he was only a couple of arm-lengths away.

"If you don't come in to camp by dusk tonight, Sugotti here is going to get hurt."

He was shouting at her, Hana realized. Calling to *her*.

Iver very carefully didn't look up the hill at her. He shook his head and moved his arms around, arguing with Bret, although he spoke too quietly for her to catch what they were saying to each other.

Bret made a gesture that even from up the hill Hana could see meant conversation over, and in response, Iver ran straight at him.

He had taken Bret by surprise.

The camp leader jumped back, but Iver took him to the ground. They wrestled for the SAL and Bret threw it down the path.

Iver shoved him to the side, leaped to his feet and started to run.

Not toward her.

He was being careful to keep her safe from discovery.

He headed along the river bank, following the curve of the valley.

But Bret was already back on his feet, lunging for the SAL. He must have been a crack shot during the war, because Iver collapsed moments after he took aim and shot, the dart sticking out of the middle of Iver's back.

Bret ran toward Iver and stood over him, then looked down the valley and then up the hill, turning slowly, just as Grimms had, as if trying to spot her.

Then he kicked Iver in the ribs, a hard, vicious lashing out.

"He says you're too sick to move. That you won't be able to get to the camp by nightfall. Just know I'll do a lot worse than this to him if you don't come in, but I'll give you until tomorrow morning." Bret put hands on either side of his mouth to shout his threat. "Don't keep me waiting."

Some of his people were coming down the path from the camp, carrying stretchers. They loaded Lia up on one, while the others made their way to Bret. While she couldn't catch his every word from where she lay, she could hear temper in the snap of Bret's voice as he gave them instructions. They loaded Iver up and walked back to camp.

Bret did a last turn, saying nothing this time, and then walked after them.

Message delivered.

Hana slid back from the edge of the rock, deeper into the undergrowth, and turned onto her back, looking up at the impossibly blue, clear sky, before she sat up and took off her boot.

Her foot was healing now she was out of the null zone of the camp, but the magfield was high out here, and her upgrade was sluggish.

She had until tomorrow for it to do its work, but she didn't dare push Bret on the timing. She'd have to be there shortly after dawn.

Iver wouldn't want her to hand herself in to the enemy. He'd tried to break free of Bret even though his chances were almost zero rather than put her in that position, but she wouldn't--couldn't--let him get hurt if she could prevent it.

She knew what Bret wanted.

And if she had to, she would use that knowledge to get what she wanted in return.

Iver.

Hana was careful to limp heavily as she approached the camp. She couldn't see the wall, and she ran into it, rapping her knee. She swore softly, then braced her hands on the top of it, sat, and then swung her legs over.

Her upgrade seemed to die within her from one moment to the next, and she fell to the ground on the other side, dry heaving.

"You're not looking so hot." The voice seemed to come from a long way away, and Hana ignored it as she breathed in and out, trying to get herself under control.

Her arms shook and she couldn't hold herself up. She collapsed, face down, and breathed in the spicy green scent of the ground covering.

Hands grabbed her around the waist and lifted her, and she bent over and retched again before slowly straightening up.

"She really as sick as she seems?" Bret spoke and she glanced to the side, saw him watching her with narrowed eyes.

"She feels clammy with fever." The voice that responded was deep.

Bret moved around to stand in front of her, and seemed to be pleased with what he saw. "You do look pretty bad. I'm guessing you won't be running off in any hurry."

"I'm here, as demanded. Now what do you want?" Hana tried to see any sign of Iver, but it was just the guard who'd been shot yesterday near the river by one of the smugglers and Bret standing in the early morning light.

"Just wanted you where I could see you. Not that you'd have been any threat to us given the state of you. But I like knowing where everyone is." Bret waved a hand at the guard. "Put her with Sugotti. Might as well keep them together seeing as they're so cozy." He tried to reach for Hana's pack and she stumbled away from him, clutching it to her chest.

"It's got my clothes in it, and some stuff to keep my foot from getting infected."

Bret studied her a moment with dislike, then flicked a glance at the guard. "Check it for weapons, she can keep everything else."

The guard grabbed her arm in a firm grip and pulled her toward one of the huts ranged in a curve beside the ruins.

As they got closer to the ancient building, the rhythmic thump she'd sensed the day before overwhelmed her. It felt as if it were rattling her bones with every beat.

She turned to the side and heaved again.

The guard cursed, loosening his grip, and she stood, bent at the waist, feeling light-headed.

"Come on." The guard grabbed her again, but he let her set the pace.

A door opened as they got close to one of the huts, and Iver stepped into the doorway, face tight, his movements stiff.

"You're hurt." Well, she knew that already, had seen Bret kicking him while he lay unconscious on the ground, but the lines of strain around his mouth had her heart beating double-time in panic.

"I'm okay." His voice was a croak, and he cleared his throat. "I wish you hadn't come."

She stopped in front of him and gently ran a finger down the bruise on his cheek. "You would have." She didn't need to say any more than that.

He went still, then gave a nod and stepped back inside.

Hana followed him in, leaving the door open behind her.

The big guard stood in the doorway, blocking the light, although there were sky lights in the roof overhead, illuminating the space in lieu of windows. He held out his hand.

"Oh, the pack." She handed it over reluctantly and he set it on the ground and crouched down to go through it, pulling out each item and placing it on the floor.

"Stay in the hut," he said when he was done. He left everything on the ground and walked away empty-handed.

"What's his name?" Hana asked, leaning against the doorjamb to watch him go.

"Kyle." Iver joined her, moving carefully, and she turned to him, worry pressing hard on her chest.

"They aren't going to lock us in?"

Iver shook his head. "The huts are the usual VSC military temp accommodation with standard electronic locks. They don't work here. None of the doors lock, and they don't seem to have any restraints of any kind, so they're counting on our injuries to keep us tethered to camp."

She nodded, distracted by the way he favored his side, and reached for the hem of his shirt to have a look.

"I'm all right." He caught her hand in his instead, gave it a squeeze. "Just my ribs."

She'd had broken ribs before, from a particularly bad crash in the war, so she knew how much they hurt. She bent down, looking for the medication from her pack to ease his pain and help with healing.

"What about you?" Iver put a hand on her shoulder. "You're so pale. You look worse than you did yesterday. Save the medication for your foot."

She shook her head as she rose up with what she needed for his side. "My foot's fine." She inclined her head toward the ruin, visible through the open doorway. "That's what's making me feel bad."

He frowned at her. "The ruin?"

She leaned closer to him, put her lips near his ear. "What's under it. The engine."

He pulled back, eyes wide, although he kept his arm in a hard band around her waist, anchoring her to him. "You can hear it?"

"I can't hear it, but I can feel it." She swallowed audibly and touched her fingers to his chest, drummed out the timing. "It reaches right in and makes me sick."

"How?" He caught her fingers in his.

"The same way I could feel where that tracker was in your back. The same way I can hear runners coming from miles away. The same way I can fly like I'm one with the machine." She turned her face away from his, unable to look at him. "Because I *am* one with the machine."

"Whatever you're thinking, whatever you believe about yourself, don't make the mistake of thinking for a moment it's going to change how I feel about you, Hana." Iver grabbed her chin between his fingers and tipped her face up to his. "I already knew some of what you've just told me and it didn't stop me for a second."

She gave a nod and then tried to eke out a smile. "We should probably have talked about this yesterday morning, uh, before things got a little heated between us.

"We're talking about it now."

She heard the implacability in his voice, and shot him a genuine grin. "Understood. No straying from the topic." She gave a Themis military salute and then lifted his shirt, juggling the medical supplies in one hand.

He kept his gaze on her and she sighed.

"It's hard to talk about because I don't fully understand it myself. That's why I was planning to spend a couple of days in the Spikes. I was going to look for answers, seeing as this is where I changed." She admired his chest as he finally shrugged out of his shirt, and then got down to applying the cooling gel to his ribs.

He closed his eyes in relief. "How? When?"

"During the war, I crash-landed in the Spikes. I went down deeper than where we are now. I was piloting a Dynastra, flying out to fetch a team of soldiers retreating from their position, and I was the only one onboard. There was a sudden storm, one of those ones that just blow up out of nowhere in the Spikes, and I had to veer off course. I hit a dead zone. I'd had to fly lower than usual because of the storm, and I flew straight into it. I fought to get the engines started again, but I got caught in a downdraft and went down like a stone." She applied the wrap band to Iver's chest as she spoke, and as soon as the two ends were joined together it expanded and then settled across his ribs.

He took what she guessed was his first deep breath since yesterday.

"I don't think I've ever heard of anyone encountering a dead zone at that altitude." He tilted his head toward the ruin. "It wasn't . . .?"

She leaned back against the doorjamb and crossed one ankle over the other, closed her eyes and tipped back her head, enjoying the sun warming her eyelids and cheeks. "Maybe. It's crossed my mind a few times since I arrived here."

"It would explain how your engines cut out, even above the mountain tops." Iver pulled his shirt back on. "What happened next?"

"At the time, I thought I was dead. I remember the crash, remember seeing the Dynastra was on fire, and I crawled out of it." She finally lifted her gaze to his. "And then, I don't remember. I sometimes think there was a necklace of silver beads. That it was wrapped around my wrist, across my palm, like I'd grabbed it up off the ground as I was crawling away. The next thing I remember, I was awake, the Dynastra was still burning, but I was feeling better, and I got up and started walking. A rescue team found me a couple of hours later."

"The military never went back to find your runner?"

She shook her head. "I told them it was burned out. I was the only one onboard and I was safe. They had better things to do than risk another runner looking for a useless Dynastra in a dead zone."

He gave a nod. "And after that?"

"After that, I knew I was different. There was something inside me. I thought I was going mad some of the time. But I was also faster, healed quicker, heard better." She paused. "But the magfields on Faldine affect my performance. Flying--that's where I shine. High up, I'm at my best. Until I got a job working for you, and moved to Bero. Then I was at my best at home *and* at work."

He tilted his head. "Is that why you applied for the job?"

"No." She sighed. "I was bored with my old job. I needed more excitement, and I thought working for the head-of-planet would give me that. I didn't realize Bero was as free of magnetic interference as your headquarters. It was a wonderful bonus."

"You could have left Faldine. Got away from the magnetic fields altogether. And there are places where the VSC military would have given you a lot of interesting things to do."

She gave a nod. "Special Forces offered me a job a couple of times. But I couldn't leave Faldine until I worked out what had happened to me. This is where I got my upgrade, and I didn't want to go until I'd figured it out."

"Your upgrade?" His eyebrows rose up.

She ducked her head and laughed. Shrugged. "That's how I think of it. In the beginning, it was separate to me. I had to force it to do what I wanted, not what it thought I should do. But now, after nearly two years, it's mostly part of me. Integrated."

"You're thinking some kind of nanotech?"

She gave a slow nod. "I keep remembering the string of beads. If each bead was made up of microscopic nanotech, and all of them somehow found their way inside me . . ." She shrugged again. "I'm surprised I don't rattle when I walk."

"You never told anyone?"

She huffed out a laugh. "No."

"And if you do manage to find out where you went down. Find some clue to what happened to you? Would you ask for help in working it out?"

She studied him. He was holding tightly to his control.

"You think I should?"

It was his turn to shrug, but it was a little too casual. "I understand why you didn't."

"But?"

He sighed. "But nothing. It's your decision. I probably would have said something, and then regretted it for the poking and prodding that would have followed. But you might consider that the nanotech itself might have tried to influence you into keeping quiet."

"No." On this, she was completely sure. "Its imperative is my safety and well-being. There were times I was almost out of my mind with worry about what was happening to me, what it was doing to me. And I could sense it urging me to get checked out."

"Its priority is you?" He blinked. "You feel that?"

"It's the one thing I'm absolutely sure of."

"So if it is nanotech of some kind, it was developed to help its host. That's its sole purpose."

"Yes."

"I'm on the Scientific Council, and I can tell you that nanotech has been discussed many times. It's helpful in fulfilling a task programmed into it, repairing cells, or bone. But it has a limited life-span, and it has a limited function. What you're talking about is nanotech that has been waiting possibly hundreds or even thousands of years in the open, that had the intelligence to find you when you landed near it, and then the ability to integrate with you, a being for which it couldn't have been designed, and that it retained and still does retain, two years later, the mission to keep you alive and well at all costs."

"I have wondered if I really am a being for which it wasn't designed." She threw out her most outrageous theory.

Might as well.

Iver frowned. "What do you mean?"

"I will need to find the place where I crashed again. It's a dead zone, so if I crashed there, maybe someone else crashed there, too, long before me. Maybe someone looking to settle on Faldine, which is relatively close to the other planets of the Verdant String. Who's to say the VSC planets are the only ones settled by our common ances-tors? They had success settling the Verdant String, but what if they had some failures as well? What if Faldine was one of those failures?"

Iver stared at her. "You think your nanotech has integrated so well with you because it was designed for our ancestors who settled the Verdant String planets?"

"Yes."

"But then we'd know about it, wouldn't we? At least some of us would have that nanotech in us."

Hana shrugged. "It's just a theory, but when I think it, it feels . . . right. As if my upgrade is agreeing with me. That's why I want to find the place I crashed. See what evidence I can find."

Iver blew out a breath. "I want to be with you when you do."

She grimaced. "First we have to escape Bret's clutches." She brought an arm around her middle, breathed in and out as she hugged herself tight.

"It's getting worse?"

She shook her head. "Not worse, it just isn't very pleasant."

"And your foot?"

She wriggled it. "It's fine. I stayed out of the camp as long as I could to give it time to heal."

"You're saying the magnetic fields are strongest inside the camp?"

"Either that, or the shield somehow affects my upgrade in a very similar way to high magfield interference."

Iver looked over at the ruins thoughtfully. "Maybe I can sow a little discord here with that information."

Hana nodded. "I've also taken some steps to make things difficult."

Iver looked over at her. "What did you--?"

The sound of shouting cut off what he was about to ask, and they both stepped out of the hut to see what was happening.

Although Hana had a good idea.

She'd orchestrated it, after all.

A group of people approached the camp from the river.

Craven, Brynja, Barre and Tillis. The fifth person was a man who, unlike the rest of the smugglers, looked like a serious soldier. His uniform was pristine, and clearly not cobbled together.

So, maybe not a member of the group.

Maybe whoever was circling Faldine in a nearspace capable ship, waiting for the TellTale, had decided to imbed someone in with the smugglers.

They were shouting, and Tillis was hitting a flat metal sheet with a metal spoon as they approached.

"What the fuck?" Bret had come out of a hut a few doors down from them. "You led them here. You must have." He turned slightly and pointed a finger at Hana.

"All I did was come to camp as you insisted. If they were watching the camp and followed me, that's not on me, that's on you." She leaned against the hut wall and stared Bret down, unable to help the shiver that went through her.

His eyes were dead.

Bret turned away, but Hana noticed the flush on his cheeks.

He had made a mistake, and there was no way for him to shift blame. He had been the only one throwing orders around yesterday and issuing ultimatums.

"She's right. You didn't think it through, did you?" Grimms limped out of a hut, and put a hand on her hip, watching the approaching group. She was holding a SAL. She flicked a look at Bret and then started limping toward the wall.

Two guards jogged down the side of the wall, one from the direction of the camp's entrance, one from behind the ruin.

Kyle had stepped out of the hut right next to Iver's soon after Grimms and he gave them a hard look before he walked over to join her.

"That looks like all they've got in terms of defense," Iver's voice was quiet.

It wasn't a lot.

There had been others yesterday, but Hana recalled how many had been carried back to camp on a stretcher, and guessed this was the best Bret could do.

The camp leader pulled a SAL from the back of his pants and walked toward the other four. "Shoot them."

Grimms glanced back at him. "Why are they making a noise." She kept her voice low. "This could be a diversion. Others could be coming over the wall on the other side."

Bret conceded her point with a nod. "We still shoot them. Tie them up. Then go shoot their friends."

She shared a glance with Kyle, then nodded.

Bret stepped between them, right up to the wall, lifted his SAL and shot Brynja in the chest.

She went down after a few steps, and as the others opened fire, those on either side of Brynja crumpled to the ground.

"Now what?" Kyle asked.

"Now we drag them over here and tie them up."

Hana glanced at Iver. Tilted her head to indicate the back of the hut.

"You're up to something," Iver whispered as they edged their way around the back.

She nodded. "Do you think you can walk out of camp?"

"I can."

She would be stronger as soon as they were over the wall, but she was very aware someone might just decide it was worth their while to track the two of them down--whether Bret or Craven won this round she'd set up.

She would love to have been able to steal the lander, but that wasn't going to happen now.

Craven and his people had taken the information she'd left them and run with it.

"What did you do?" Iver's breath was short, as if every lungful hurt.

"Left a message for the smugglers on the road out of the valley. Told them to watch the river this morning and follow the person entering the camp, and I warned them everyone has SALs."

"A distraction for our escape." He narrowed his eyes. "How could you be sure they would notice the message in time?"

Hana shrugged. "I used one of the emergency flares in the pack and left the message beside it. It was the best I could do with what I had."

She stopped at the low wall at the back of the huts and scanned the area for any smugglers that might be coming in the back way.

Iver came to a stop beside her and did a sweep of his own. "Looks clear."

"Yes."

Sudden shouting erupted behind them, and spurred on by it, she jumped over the wall, then turned to help Iver.

Iver was easing himself over when he stopped, his gaze snapping to a spot beyond her shoulder.

Hana closed her eyes, blew out a breath. "Who?"

"One of Bret's," Iver murmured. "Baxter."

Hana turned, found a SAL pointed at her face. The man holding it was the scientist from yesterday who'd returned from the TellTale launch site with Iver and the others.

"What's going on in the camp?" Baxter asked.

"Bret and the others are fighting the smugglers," Hana answered.

"What did you have to do with that?"

"Nothing. It's possible the smugglers followed me or saw me coming in to camp, but I couldn't do anything about that. Iver and I saw the fight and thought it might be a good time to go our own way."

"Sorry to disappoint you." Baxter indicated with the SAL, and with a sigh Hana swung back over the wall.

As soon as she was on the other side, she fell to her knees and had to breathe carefully to prevent herself throwing up.

"What's wrong with her?" Baxter toed her ribs with a boot.

"She's got an infection in her foot from a trap the smugglers set in the valley. She's feverish."

Baxter grunted and Hana tried to get to her feet. She didn't like the vulnerable feeling she had of being on the ground, and she didn't want Iver to have to bend down and help her up.

It would be agony for him.

She was too late. He knelt beside her, put an arm around her shoulders.

"That's got to hurt," she said, turning her face to his. She rested her cheek against his neck, suddenly aware that sweat had combined with dirt from her walk through the valley last night to leave her face streaked with the fine black dust of the Spikes, and that she'd needed a shower for the last two days.

He gave a choked laugh, turned his head and kissed the side of her temple. "I'll live."

They stood together, each supporting the other, so they were leaning against each other when they finally straightened up.

"It wouldn't exactly have been difficult to run the two of you down," Baxter said.

Hana ignored him and rested her head for a moment on Iver's shoulder.

She really had never felt this bad.

"What have we here?" The man who stepped around the hut was the stranger amongst the group of smugglers, the man Hana suspected was working for whoever was trying to steal the engine from Bret.

"Who the hell are you?" Baxter demanded, moving his SAL from Hana and Iver to the new threat.

The stranger aimed and they both shot each other at the same time, although only Baxter went down.

The man looked down at Bret's crumpled form, and plucked the SAL dart out of his shirt.

"Body armor." Iver sounded approving.

The man looked at him, a slow perusal. "You're Iver Sugotti."

Iver shrugged.

The man narrowed his eyes. "I think you need to come with me."

CHAPTER 23

HANA WAS NOT WELL.

Iver was worried about the gray cast to her skin, and the perspiration that beaded on her forehead and at her hairline.

That he knew the reason for it didn't seem to help.

He probably didn't look that well himself, he acknowledged. His ribs were better since Hana had seen to them, but he could still feel the throb of the bruises on his face and side.

Hana affected an exaggerated limp as they were herded toward the others, and he decided it wouldn't hurt for him to make himself look more injured than he was, as well.

Bret and his people stood together in a tight knot, surrounded by the smugglers. Craven's people had taken their SALs, and he noticed they looked a little surprised at their own success.

"Did you know they had Iver Sugotti prisoner here?" The man who'd shot Baxter was looking at Craven as he herded them toward the group.

"What?" Craven turned to stare at Iver. "So it is." He looked over at Bret's group. "How?"

No one answered, and Craven grabbed the nearest person, who turned out to be Jeera, and shoved his SAL against her throat.

"He came with her, we think," Jeera said, after a moment's hesitation. She flicked a hand at Hana.

"With--?" Brynja took a step to the side to look him over. "*He* was the second person we were chasing? The one you were supposed to track down?" She directed the last sentence to Barre.

"As he was busy stealing supplies from the back of my lander instead, that would have been hard for him to do." Fraen, the lander's driver, didn't hide his scorn.

Barre snarled at him, raised his SAL, and Craven clamped a hand on his forearm. "What's this?"

Barre turned his head to look at Craven, and tried a nonchalant shrug. "Lies."

"Truth," Bret said. "Not that we were complaining. Our getting hold of Sugotti ourselves because you were too busy stealing was worth the equipment you took."

"Much good it's done you now." Barre bared his teeth at the camp leader.

Bret's lips twisted in a wry smile. "Obviously, things could be going better for us."

"Quiet." Craven's hand slashed through the air. He looked long and hard at Barre before finally turning back to Iver.

Iver took the opportunity to give the smuggler as thorough a perusal as Craven was giving him.

He looked to be about 50 standard Arkhoran years, and like the rest of his group, was more than a little wild. His clothing was dirty and ripped in places, and he obviously hadn't bathed in a while.

Iver glanced down at himself and acknowledged he probably didn't look much better.

"What are you doing here, Sugotti?"

"Well, they tried to kill me," Iver tipped his head toward the camp crew, "and I decided to come out here and find out why."

"Tried to kill you?" Brynja's eyes widened.

"Ask your friend here," Iver said, taking an educated guess as he looked over at the hard-eyed stranger who'd forced them back to camp. "He'll know all about it. My guess is Lancaster was feeding him information about what was happening here at camp before he was killed."

The stranger took a step back, hands raised, as every eye focused on him.

"Lancaster was involved with this lot?" Bret asked, waving at the smugglers.

"I don't think so. I'm guessing he was talking to whoever this guy represents." Iver nodded to the stranger. "Shortly after Lancaster made the error of admitting to whoever he was dealing with that he hadn't killed me as originally planned, he was killed himself, and my guess is they thought I was dead along with him." Iver smiled. "That seems to happen to me a lot."

"But why did they try to kill you?" Brynja persisted.

"Because he was about to build his sky lane right through this camp," Bret said.

"Shit." Brynja turned and looked up and then down the valley. "They'd have tripped over you."

"Obviously everyone's plans have been disrupted," the stranger said. "But let's get down to it. Where is the engine?"

Bret gave a laugh. "Didn't Lancaster tell you about that?"

"Tell me what?"

"That we're still looking for it."

There was silence as the stranger stared at him, a growing silence that had even Craven twitching a little. "He said you had it." The words were so quiet, it was hard to hear them.

"He told me he was loyal and wouldn't let me down. Neither of us got the truth out of him." Bret lifted his hands.

The stranger narrowed his eyes at the whole group, looking from one to the other. "I don't believe you."

"Why do you think the shield is still up if they've found and removed the engine?" Hana asked.

Everyone's heads snapped in her direction, as if they only just remembered she was there.

"Maybe they've found it but haven't yet removed it."

"Maybe." Hana's lips quirked in a smile. "But then what are they still doing here? The lander that was intercepted yesterday was full of supplies, as your little thief there knows full well. Why were they stocking up if they were done?"

"What's it to you one way or the other?" Craven asked.

"Nothing. Except I'm stuck in the middle of this. I want to get back to Touka City, get some actual help for my foot, and Iver needs to let the VSC battalion know he's still alive, before Admiral Valerian shows up in force to look for the head-of-planet."

"They don't know you're alive?" the stranger asked, skeptical.

"I was a little busy running for my life to check in with the fleet." Iver shrugged. "I'm sure the head administrator of Touka City contacted them after my Sig was shot down."

"And what's your stake in this?" Bret turned to Craven. "You working for him?" He pointed at the stranger.

"Working *with* him," Craven corrected smoothly. "We've got a mutually beneficial deal."

"And who is he?" Iver asked.

"You're asking the questions now, are you?" The stranger moved his SAL just a little higher in implied threat.

"He a Caruson liaison?" Grimms asked, absolute disdain in every word.

"What? No!" Craven shook his head. "I'm not dumb enough to get into bed with that lot. They've got no allegiance to anyone who isn't from Caruso."

"So who, then?" Bret asked.

"Not a word." The stranger moved slightly, so the SAL was pointing in Craven's direction.

"Silence was part of the agreement. I keep my word." Craven looked unhappily at the SAL.

"See that you do." The stranger did a slow sweep of the camp.

"Put half the group in one hut, the other half in another, and lock them in."

No one commented on that, something that Iver found interesting. Either they didn't realize the locks didn't work, or they didn't care to let their employer know it couldn't be done.

"Except you. I want to talk to you." The stranger turned to Iver, his gaze passing over Hana as if debating whether she was worth questioning as well.

There were risks to her both ways, and Iver couldn't work out which would be worse. He kept his body relaxed, his face neutral.

"You, too," he said at last, pointing his SAL at Hana. "I don't like mysteries."

The couch drew her.

Hana limped toward it, aware of Craven's consternation as she angled away from him and flopped down, stretching out and closing her eyes.

She concentrated on breathing away the nausea, happy to be lying down in comfort.

Craven hovered over her, and she fought back a smile.

She had really needed to lie down, but putting their captors off balance was a nice bonus.

"Now you have us in private, would you care to introduce yourself?" Iver's voice was smooth and implacable.

"You can call me Jake." She heard the amusement in the stranger's voice, as if he thought the idea of an introduction was quaint.

She doubted it was his real name.

She heard Jake set down the black case he'd carried over to the admin building with him and then the sound of chairs scraping against the floor as Iver and Jake took a seat.

"What's wrong with her?" Jake asked.

"She's got an infection in her foot from a metal trap Craven set in the valley." Iver kept his tone neutral.

"A metal--?"

"A device my people put out to catch some game." Craven's clothing rustled as he stepped behind the couch, toward the table. "You know, because your lot reneged on sending us the supplies you promised."

Nothing was said for a long moment.

"You know why we couldn't." Jake's voice was quiet.

"Sure." Craven sounded skeptical, but he didn't say anything else.

"So, she's injured." Jake seemed to want to move on. "And so are you, by the way you're moving."

"Bret likes to kick people when they're down." Hana could almost see Iver's shrug. "I want someone to check Hana out in the medbay."

Jake laughed. "That's not going to happen. You complicate things for me, Sugotti. When Bret's people were going to kill you to stop the sky lane and make it look like an accident, that was one thing. When they screwed it up, that created a whole new set of circumstances. We don't have the luxury of time now, we have to get hold of the shield engine and get out, because the VSC will be scrutinizing every runner leaving the planet."

"I'd say that's a certainty." She heard Iver shift in his chair. "When you blew up Lancaster's runner, Admiral Valerian would have sat up and taken notice. A Special Forces team was on the way two days ago, and if it isn't already on-planet, it will be soon."

"You blew something up?" Craven's words rose, thin and high.

Jake said nothing, and Hana finally couldn't resist opening her eyes. Craven's agitation was clear in the movement of his body.

"You said this would be quiet. Stealthy." Craven's back was to her, and he threw out a hand, fist clenched. "Most of us were taken prisoner in the war. None of us want to go back to that."

"You knew this wasn't legal." Jake's voice was dismissive. "If you were concerned about repercussions, you shouldn't have gotten involved."

Craven turned away, his face set. He caught Hana's gaze, and his mouth contorted with fury. "And who the fuck are you, anyway? I still haven't gotten an answer on that."

"Lashing out at someone else isn't going to change reality." Iver poured contempt into his voice. "Especially someone you harmed."

Craven swung back to Iver, just as he must have intended. "Fuck you, Sugotti. You were the one who imprisoned me and my crew during the war. I'm onboard with killing you here and now."

"Good thing it's not up to you, then." Jake's chair scraped as he stood. "We can use him as a hostage if things get sticky. If you were thinking clearly, you'd realize that."

"And her?" Craven waved a hand back to her. "She's nobody, as far as I can tell."

"She's somebody to him." Jake stared at her from his place by the table, his expression thoughtful. "They were helping each other over the wall when I caught them, and I got the impression they're close. Could be that Sugotti will be more cooperative if he wants his friend to stay safe."

"Fine." Craven turned again, glared at her. "I'm going to see if my people need anything."

He stalked out.

"Volatile," Iver commented.

"Needs must." Jake shrugged. "Not much choice when it comes to boots on the ground out here."

The lights flickered overhead, went out, and then flickered back on.

Jake was still standing, and from her position on the couch, Hana saw him glance up at the ceiling, a frown on his face.

"They must be chewing power on something," Iver commented. "Or there's something wrong with their array."

"What are you talking about?" Jake's gaze snapped to Iver.

"Seems they have to cable power in over the wall. They can't generate it inside the camp." Iver waved in the direction of the array. "Can't receive any comms either."

"The shield blocks comms signals?" Jake frowned.

Iver shrugged. "I only stumbled in here yesterday. But it seems so."

Jake lifted up the black case and swung it onto his shoulder, then stalked out. He shouted for someone to come guard the door, and then disappeared.

For the first time since he'd captured them, they were alone. Private.

"You all right?" Iver was suddenly sitting on the edge of the couch, a hand on her shoulder.

She struggled to sit up. "Yes--" Before she could say anything else, Brynja appeared in the doorway.

She stared at them for a moment, then moved inside a little way, and leaned against the doorjamb, a SAL in her hand. "Your foot causing problems?" She tilted her head.

"What do you think?" Iver asked, eyes narrowed.

"All you civilized lot from Touka seem to be really outraged by that trap." Brynja shook her head. "We grew up in the Havens, mostly old runners that our parents landed on Faldine and then couldn't launch again. Traps like that kept us fed until the VSC finally caught up with us."

"And then what kept you fed?" Hana asked.

Brynja shot Hana a look. "I'm supposed to be grateful to be made a beggar?"

"No. You never were a beggar." Hana hooked an arm under her head and turned to watch Brynja's foot jiggle in agitation. "You're a citizen of the VSC, and entitled to a citizen dividend. And you weren't responsible for what your parents did to the Halatians."

"You say that, but a lot of others thought different."

Hana curled onto her side, making more room for Iver on the couch. "What are you trying to achieve now?"

"A new place, that the VSC won't try to take."

"A new place?" Iver asked. "Another planet's DND order

broken? Like here? Like on Veltos? How are you even going to get off of Faldine? In what?"

"Jake's people have a runner, they'll take us. They need people like us."

"People like you?" Iver asked.

"Survivors." Brynja's lips formed a tight line and she turned her head to look out the door.

"And who are Jake's people?" Iver asked.

Brynja shook her head, a sharp, angry movement. "I'm not telling you."

"Fine." Iver leaned back, at ease. "But Jake's gone off over the wall to contact his friends with his comms unit, hasn't he?"

The power flickered again, and Brynja glanced up at the ceiling, then at Iver.

"So what if he has?"

"No reason." Iver leaned back further on the couch and rested a hand on Hana's shoulder.

She shared a look with him.

Jake had been rattled to learn the shield blocked comms. She'd thought he glanced down at the case more than was normal while he'd been seated at the table.

"He was waiting for a message," she whispered to Iver. "He didn't look happy to discover he can't receive anything in the camp."

Iver gave a slight smile. "Not happy, at all."

CHAPTER 24

WHO WAS JAKE COMMUNICATING WITH?

Iver shifted a little at the outside table where they had been taken to eat some lunch, trying to see where he'd gone.

He wasn't in the camp, unless he was behind the buildings, near the entrance, but given that Craven kept glancing out toward the river, Iver guessed he'd gone that way.

It was obviously bothering the smuggler that his collaborator was keeping himself out of sight and out of earshot.

Hana sat beside him, and worry spiked in his chest just looking at her.

There were dark circles under her eyes and she was listless.

She folded her arms in front of her and rested her head on them, after having barely touched her food.

"We're going to have to do something about her."

Iver looked up, found Lia watching him. She had a big bruise on her right cheek where she'd fallen the day before after Bret had shot her in the back, and her posture was as stiff as his own.

When he said nothing, she moved closer, blocking the sun so he could look straight up at her. "She needs the medbay."

Iver nodded. He thought so, too, but Hana kept insisting that she was fine. "Jake says she'll have to tough it out."

Lia huffed out a breath. "I know you carried me yesterday after that bastard shot me. Thank you."

"You're welcome."

She was the youngest of the group, and she thought she owed him. She would maybe help them, if the right opportunity arose, but Brynja had swung her attention in their direction as soon as they'd started talking, and Tillis started moving, circling the table and chairs set out on the grass like a predator circling its prey.

Bret swiveled on his bench as Tillis moved, slowly biting off pieces of the thick bread in his hand. He and Brynja had given each other a nod of recognition at the start, but hadn't said anything more to each other. If they had known each other during the war, as Hana told him Bret had said, then they hadn't been close.

The tension between the two groups had been evident since the start, but it seemed to be ratcheting up.

That wasn't completely bad, Iver thought, as long as he and Hana could run while the two teams fought it out. But Hana didn't look like she could walk right now, let alone run.

He leaned back in his chair and pushed his empty plate away, pulled Hana's barely touched food in front of him and looked around for a knife. The meal was just bread, cheese and fruit, but it was a welcome change from the military fare they'd had up until now.

"I need to cut this up a little more," he said.

Lia looked over at him, hesitating, and then walked to the table where her team mates were sitting, got a knife, and brought it back to him.

"Make sure he doesn't keep it." Tillis had sat back down to eat and he leaned forward, elbows on the table. He went back to shoving food into his mouth like he hadn't seen any for a long time.

The trap they'd set for game made a little more sense, now. They had been desperate.

"What animals were you trying to catch with your trap in the valley?" He took the knife from Lia with a nod of thanks. He hadn't seen any big wildlife since he and Hana had slipped out of the lander in the valley, only small mammals and insects, and not many of them, either.

He also hadn't seen any birds.

He should have noticed that sooner. Faldine was known for its birdlife. The colors on most of the birds of prey alone were considered worth a trip to the planet.

The thought caused him to look up, but there was nothing in the sky above.

That was really strange.

"We usually catch drenma, and there's plenty of them where our base is, but it's been slim pickings here. No water birds either, which is what we usually use as a stopgap between getting a medium sized drenma." She leaned against the table, watching him cut up the fruit, bread and cheese into smaller, bite-sized pieces.

It was the shield around the camp, Iver realized. The animals and birds must be able to sense it, somehow, and it kept them away. If Jake did manage to find the engine and escape with it, that was at least one indicator the VSC could use to find any shielded bases he might set up.

A shout from the ruins had everyone turning in that direction, and Barre stepped out of the arched stone and waved.

Craven appeared from a building and walked over to him.

Iver watched them confer, heads together, and then Craven ran to the wall, hopped over it, and disappeared. Off to tell Jake the news.

"That's bullshit. They haven't found it." Baxter lifted a cup to his lips with shaking hands, and then turned away from the ruins altogether.

"How do you know?" Tillis challenged.

"Because I've been looking for six months, and I haven't found it yet. You telling me you lot are just going to walk in and discover it in a few hours?"

"Maybe we have something you don't have." Brynja jutted out a hip.

"Yeah? What?"

She smirked, then turned her attention back to the ruin.

Iver sat up a little straighter as he smoothed his hand over Hana's tangle of wild hair.

He was suddenly sure they did have a way to find it. Brynja looked too smug.

This wasn't just a fishing expedition. Jake hadn't come in on the hope Bret and his people had found something. He had come to take it, whether they'd found it or not.

Hana twisted her head to look at him, and he pushed her plate toward her.

"What do you have that they don't?" he asked Lia, as Hana propped up her head on her hand and took a small piece of fruit delicately between two fingers.

He gave a grunt of approval when she swallowed it and reached for another.

When he looked back at Lia, she was shaking her head. She turned away from him, so as not to meet his gaze.

Hana straightened a little, her gaze on his face.

"All right?" he mouth at her.

She nodded, closed her eyes for a moment, and then pushed slowly to her feet. "Can I have a shower?"

Lia spun back. "What?"

"I think a shower will help me, and some clean water on my foot wouldn't be a bad thing. Can I have one?"

"He can't go with her," Brynja said, pointing at Iver.

"Who will help her, then?" Iver asked.

"I will." Lia nodded toward one of the huts, and Hana slid out from the bench, her balance a little off. She glanced over at him, gave him a nod of reassurance, and then hobbled away.

Iver watched her until she disappeared into the hut.

"You left her before. When she got trapped. But seeing you now, the way you look at her, I don't understand why you did." Brynja was staring at him, arms folded across her chest. "Didn't you realize what had happened to her?"

"Does it matter?" Iver answered.

"I suppose not." Brynja stared at him a few moments more. "She's too injured to run, and I don't think you'll leave her again."

As she turned away, Iver's gaze went back to the hut.

It should have dismayed him that Brynja had read him so well, but lucky for him, Hana was not too injured to run. Brynja was right about one thing, though. He wouldn't be leaving her behind again.

***

Jake had come back from wherever he'd been when Hana emerged from the hut. He and Craven were standing in front of the ruin, talking quietly.

Hana limped her way back to the table where Iver sat waiting, feeling fresh and clean for the first time in days.

She still felt the throb of the shield engine, but somehow, fresh clothes and a shower made all the difference.

She could think clearly again.

"You don't look much better." Bret commented, a sneer on his face.

His gaze kept going to Craven and Jake, and she saw his hands were trembling as he straightened them, then fisted them, over and over.

Craven's people didn't look much happier, even though theoretically they should have been overjoyed. They had taken the camp and they seemed to have found the engine.

But Bret and his crew had them on edge.

It was very obvious that even with the extra SALs they'd taken from Bret's team, the situation hung on a knife's edge.

All it would take was for one person to attack, and things would go sideways, fast.

Luki hadn't appeared once, so Hana guessed he was still in the medbay, but Kyle looked like he could probably do a lot of damage before he was taken down, if he had a mind to.

And it looked like all of them had a mind to.

The idea that Craven had taken the engine from under their noses was clearly unbearable.

She sat back down beside Iver and he turned toward her, swinging one leg over the bench, and she gave a sigh of relief as she leaned back against his chest. His arm came around her, anchoring her to him.

"I never heard you were in a relationship, Sugotti," Grimms said, tapping a finger to her lips as she looked over at them. "Then again, we can't get comms here."

Hana looked up at her, surprised.

"It isn't because you don't get comms," Lia said, latching on to a neutral topic with what sounded like relief. "We do get comms at our camp and I didn't hear about it either."

"Who cares?" Tillis asked.

"He's head-of-planet, and he's got himself a partner. There's been speculation for months as to why he was alone at all those planetary functions and now we know." Grimms lifted her eyebrows at Tillis, making her contempt for him clear.

"You were seeing her that whole time in secret?" Lia asked into the silence that followed.

Hana could feel Iver tense behind her.

"No." His answer was curt.

"What he means is he was trying to get my interest that whole time. Hard to do if you're taking other women to planetary functions." Her voice came out a little husky, a little raw.

She had the feeling she was balancing the peace with gossip.

Jeera leaned forward on her elbows from her place between Bret and Vras. "And did it work?"

"As you can see." Hana fluttered a hand and Iver's grip on her waist tightened.

"You look familiar." Brynja watched her, face thoughtful. "I've seen you somewhere before. I didn't notice it earlier, but now you're cleaned up and look a little less ragged . . . I know I recognize you."

"She's ex-military. Got to be." Roj, who'd been quietly eating at the same table as Tillis, looked up from his empty plate. "Why else would she be so unwilling to say who she is? Besides, even sick you can tell she's always alert. It's clear."

"Is that so?" Brynja asked. "You fought for the VSC in the war?"

Hana kept her face blank.

"Yes." Bryjna took a step closer. "You did." She spoke slowly. "I remember now. I saw you."

Hana cocked her head to the side. Looked at Brynja again. She didn't recognize her at all. "I don't think so."

"I did see you. I was captured in the second year of the war. Rounded up, and then they flew us to containment. You . . ." Brynja stared at her, then shook her head. "I can't remember what you were doing, but I never forget a face."

The sound of a runner, screaming down the valley at top speed, cut off the speculation in Brynja's eyes, and everyone turned and looked up.

A Dynastra was coming toward them, low enough to be clear in every detail.

Hana reached out and grabbed Iver's hand, getting to her feet in the same motion.

"It's going to--" She ran out of words as it reached the camp, hit the dead zone, and the engine shut off.

For a moment--it felt longer--no one spoke or reacted in the sudden silence, and then the runner was past them, dropping fast.

A beat later it disappeared from sight, into the river.

A plume of water and soil shot up and the ground beneath their feet shuddered.

"What was that?" Jake ran out of the admin building, and Lia took a step back from him.

"A runner."

Jake stared at her, confused. "Where is it?"

"In the river." Roj rose to his feet. "It hit the shield over the camp, the engine died, and it crashed."

Jake flinched. "Shit. Watch the prisoners." As he ran toward toward the wall, a thin wisp of white smoke drifted across the blue sky and Hana heard Jake swear again as he ran.

"What happens now?" Brynja asked, looking between Roj and Lia.

Neither responded, and Craven came running out of the ruin.

"What's going on? Did the runner land?"

"It landed, all right." Lia pointed toward the river as Jake leaped over the wall and disappeared down the path.

"We're fucked." Roj hunched his shoulders.

"Everyone, back to the huts." Tillis pushed away from the table he was sitting at, a SAL pointed at Iver. "Now. Quick."

Bret's people got to their feet reluctantly, and then Kyle made a sudden move, leaping toward Tillis.

Tillis shot him and the big guard went down hard.

Everyone stared at him.

Tillis motioned with his SAL. "I've taken out your biggest threat, and I'll do it to anyone else who even looks at me wrong. You got it?"

Bret crouched beside Kyle and carefully rolled him onto his back. "We got it."

Grimms took his feet and Baxter took Kyle's other side, and they lifted him, moving back to the huts.

"You, too, Sugotti."

Tillis was including her in that, too, Hana had no doubt.

They followed Bret and his team into the hut and Brynja shut the door behind them.

Luki was lying on the floor against the far wall, his eyes closed. It shocked Hana. She'd thought he was in the medbay. Another man, one she thought she recognized as having been supported over the river by Jeera the day before, lay beside him, although he was awake.

Vras, the medic who'd treated her, walked over and crouched between both men, checking them.

No one said anything, and in the silence, they all heard Jake shouting, the words indistinct.

"Well, at least they destroyed their own runner." Grimms leaned against the wall and then slid down it to sit with her knees bent.

"That's true." Bret nodded. "They aren't going anywhere for now."

"They could take the lander." Baxter sounded defeated.

Everyone thought about that for a moment, and then slowly sat down as well.

"Maybe they'll send for another runner." Fraen rummaged in a bag and pulled out some water, took a sip.

"That was a Dynastra. There aren't that many of them, and I don't think you can easily get one. Isn't that so, Sugotti?"

Bret looked over at Iver.

"No. I can only guess Lancaster helped them get that one."

"Fucking Lancaster." Jeera turned narrowed eyes on Bret. "He was playing both sides."

"Three sides," Iver reminded them. "I thought he was a friend and a colleague."

Outside, there was the sound of running, more shouting.

"How many of them are out there?" Bret asked suddenly.

"Jake, Craven, Tillis, Barre, Roj, Lia and Brynja." Fraen counted them off on his fingers.

"There's another woman," Hana said. "She was with Craven when they ambushed your lander."

Fraen nodded slowly. "Yes. I haven't seen her here in the camp."

"I never saw Roj in the valley when they ambushed you. But he's here now. Makes you wonder how many of them there really are." Like Hana, Iver was still on his feet, leaning against the wall beside the door.

"Is he right?" Bret asked Fraen.

The driver nodded. "Yes. Impossible to say how many there are.

My guess is not too much more than what we've seen, though. They were trapping for food out there, so they didn't have the supplies to sustain a lot of people."

Bret nodded. "Right, so beware, people. There could be a cordon around the camp, or at least someone watching where we go if we manage to get out of here."

"We can hardly run." Jeera nodded toward Kyle, Luki and the third man lying on the ground.

"We can take the lander and get out," Bret said.

Before anyone could comment, there was an argument near the ruin.

Hana could hear raised voices, and knew if her upgrade was working, she'd have been able to make out the actual conversation.

The shouting stopped, and for a long while no one spoke and they heard nothing from outside.

Eventually, she slid down the wall herself, and Iver followed her, looping an arm over her shoulder.

She was half dozing against his side when it felt as if her skin caught on fire.

She convulsed, twisting away from Iver to retch to the side, her whole body shaking.

"What's wrong with her?"

She put her hands out, bowing her head between them as she struggled to get control. She felt Iver's hands on her, holding her up, and gritted her teeth against the waves of nausea.

Slowly the fire in her blood abated and she slid back onto her heels.

She rose up, Iver rising with her, keeping an arm around her for support. When she was steady on her feet, she walked to the small bathroom to one side to rinse out her mouth and splash some water on her face.

When she came out, Iver was looking at her, and she gave a tiny nod.

"What just happened?" Bret watched her suspiciously.

She glanced at Iver again, wondering if she should tell them the engine was disconnected. That Jake and Craven had managed to find it and somehow switch it off.

But she didn't have a good reason to explain how she knew.

It wasn't as though she was free of the magfield--it was still Faldine, after all--but it was not nearly as strong as it had been before. She could feel her body humming.

"I said--" Bret took a step forward, and she raised a hand, palm out.

"Shh." She moved to the door, listening.

"What the--?" Bret's voice rose.

"She said keep quiet." Iver's voice was a low rumble behind her as he cut the camp leader off.

"There's no one outside the hut." Hana turned to look at them. "They're either down by the river, helping the people in the crashed runner, or they're in the ruin, getting the engine out of its hiding place. No one is watching us."

She stepped toward the door. Opened it.

The whole camp looked deserted.

"She's right." Grimms pushed past her and stepped into the open.

Jeera followed her, and then Bret, the three of them fanning out.

Hana followed behind them, Iver on her heels.

"What's going on?" Bret swung around, staring at her. "How did you know there was no one here?"

"I have good hearing." Hana turned away from him, stepped close to Iver. "What now?" she whispered.

"Speak up." Bret was suddenly right next to them.

"What does it matter what they're doing? We're free and we can take the lander," Jeera said. "Let's go."

"She said they had the engine. How do you know that?"

"They already told us they found it, and why else would they leave us unguarded?" Hana shrugged. "Their two priorities are getting out of here and taking the engine, and they're spread too thin to do either well and also watch us. That's what the argument was about a little while ago. There was a fight about resources."

"Come on, Bret. Let's get Luki and the others and leave." Grimms tugged at his arm.

Bret shook her off. "I'm damned if I'm letting that bastard get my engine. We've been here for months looking for it. I'm not walking away."

Baxter was out of the hut now, too, and his focus was on the ruin. "I agree. I've got a SAL in my room and we've got other weapons lying around. Let's take this camp back."

Grimms looked from one to the other. Gave a slow nod.

Jeera made a sound of dismay.

"The others aren't in good shape, Jeer. They shouldn't be moved. Especially Luki. And even in the lander, the going'll be rough. Besides, this is *our* engine." Grimms put a hand on Jeera's shoulder.

Jeera looked over at the lander, then back at the ruin. Gave a reluctant nod.

They broke apart, running towards their huts, and Fraen and Vars emerged from the hut as well, running after them.

"What now? We could take the lander ourselves." Hana glanced over at the river, looking for any sign of Jake and whoever had gone to help him. A cool breeze, with a faint hint of smoke on it, lifted her hair, and she took a deep breath.

It felt like the first good breath she'd managed in a long time.

"I don't want the shield tech stolen." Iver put hands on her shoulders. "I can go into the ruin, see what's really going on in there, what we're dealing with, and you can wait near the lander for me."

Hana worried her bottom lip.

There was some sense in that. If Iver was hurt or caught by Barre and Craven, she could get him out, but she had the feeling in this situation, two were better than one.

"I'll come with you."

Iver's hands tightened their hold, and then he gave a nod, releasing her as he stepped back.

"We'll make it quick. If we can't stop them, we take the lander and go for help. With the Dynastra down, they aren't going anywhere right now."

Hana nodded and ran toward the ruin with him.

At last they would see what was really going on.

CHAPTER 25

IVER COULD SEE the change in Hana. She moved differently.

It wouldn't be obvious enough for the casual observer to notice, but she seemed to glide, in full harmony with her body.

She wasn't favoring her foot at all, and he could only assume it was healed.

There was a shout behind them as they ran for the ruin, and he turned to see that Bret had noticed where they were headed and seemed to be objecting.

He ignored the camp leader and stepped through the arched entrance, into the dappled gloom.

"They'll be right behind us," Hana warned.

He nodded in agreement, but kept going. The holes in the roof let in enough light to see by, but there were big pools of shadows, too, and he tread carefully.

He could hear talking up ahead, and slowed his pace even more, keeping close to the wall.

Hana was right beside him, head cocked in the direction of the noise. A beam of light from a break in the roof overhead lit her face, and he felt something rise up in him that was almost too big to contain.

"What are they saying?" he forced himself to ask, his voice rough.

"They're trying to work out how to carry the engine out. Sounds like it's too heavy." Hana's voice was barely a whisper.

The conversation was coming from up ahead, echoing and bouncing through the building as if the acoustics of the room they were in were unusual.

Hana reached out and touched the oddly angled protrusions on the wall in the passageway, the oblongs and rectangles sticking out in uneven, asymmetrical patterns.

They reminded Iver of something, but he couldn't quite remember what.

"The problem is the two minute limit." Craven's voice was suddenly clear, as if he'd moved closer.

"I know that." Barre sounded impatient. "We can't get the engine in place, though. Not with the equipment we have. Nothing works here. The magfields are too strong."

"The crew who were hired to take the environmental generator off Cepi were considering dismantling it when they encountered this problem. Better to have it in bits, and get someone to try put it back together, than not have it at all."

"Sugotti knows about it now, so we have to destroy it or take it with us, nothing in between." Barre audibly spat after he spoke.

"Sugotti can't live to see another day, whatever Jake thinks his value as a hostage is, so it doesn't matter what he knows."

Craven's response didn't surprise Iver at all. He expected it. What he hadn't expected was mention of Cepi. He'd told Hana the day before that the shield engine in the camp reminded him of Cepi's mysterious generator, but it sounded as if Craven had inside knowledge.

And the strange protrusions on the wall . . . he suddenly remembered where he recognized them from. The ruins of Cepi had looked very similar.

Craven and Barre must have been told what to look for in these ruins to get to the engine. And they could only have been told by whoever had funded the attempted theft of Cepi's environmental generator.

"Problem is, Sugotti *is* a way out if we're stopped by the VSC when we try to leave. He does have value as a hostage, Jake's right about that. We can't get rid of him yet." Barre's voice went softer as if he had turned. "Not that it matters now. We're not going anywhere until we solve this problem."

"We're not going anywhere anyway, with the Dynastra down." Craven sounded bitter. "What the hell were they doing, buzzing the valley like a VSC strike-team in the war?"

"Probably that asshole, Linnel." The sound of a stone skittering over the floor made Iver think Barre had kicked it.

He looked over at Hana, saw her eyes were a little wider, her mouth open in shock at the mention of Linnel's name.

"Damn," she mouthed. "Thought we'd gotten rid of him."

Iver nodded. He had, too.

The head administrator of Touka City had obviously not managed to hang on to the lieutenant after she'd arrested him. Most likely the mysterious Banyon had something to do with getting him free.

It also looked like Linnel had been playing Bret and his team, just the same as Lancaster had been. Because until right now, Iver thought he was in Bret's camp, but here he was, helping Jake and Craven. Either he was in with Lancaster from the beginning, or he knew what Lancaster was up to, and decided to throw in with the other side when things blew up for him in Touka City.

Iver motioned Hana to leave, and she gave a nod.

The engine wasn't going anywhere.

It sounded as though they didn't have a way to get the engine out, and as Craven said, even if they did, until the Dynastra was running again, they were stuck here.

Hana led the way back down the passage.

She stopped just before the arched door and pressed up against the wall. Iver followed her lead.

Bret and Baxter stepped through, Baxter with a SAL, Bret holding a long piece of pipe.

Bret jerked back and swung the pipe wildly as he caught sight of them.

Hana dropped, easily sliding into a crouch, and the pipe struck the wall above her head.

Iver stepped away from the wall, ready to hit him, when Hana rose up, arm coming out so fast he barely saw it move before she had the pipe in her grasp.

She yanked it, and Bret let it go, stumbling forward.

"You!" He narrowed his eyes. "Get out of here, Sugotti. The engine is mine."

"We're getting out." Iver kept his voice low, fury forcing him to breathe slowly, fight for control. "But what do you think you can do with it, Bret?"

"Sell the tech for big money to one of the Beyond planets, be that the Caruso or someone else, and use the money to set up another Haven, with the shielding tech to keep us safe."

"Safe from what?" Hana asked.

"From the VSC and its interference." Bret held out his hand for the pipe. "Get out of here, Sugotti, and be grateful I don't have the capacity to keep you a prisoner as well as fight Craven and Jake. I don't want to see you again."

Hana did not hand the pipe over, she stared him down, and for a moment Bret stared back, flummoxed, before leaning forward and yanking it from her grasp.

He and Baxter tried to move past them, but Iver stepped in front of them, blocking the way.

"Iver." Hana gave a tiny shake of her head.

Iver stared at Bret, then Baxter, the urge to strike holding him in its grip, but at last he forced himself to move and the two men edged around him and disappeared into the gloom of the passageway.

Hana took his arm and pulled him out into the sunlight. "The Dynastra next?" she asked.

He hesitated. They needed to know how badly the runner was damaged, but he'd prefer to get in the lander and just get out of here.

"If it's not too damaged, and Linnel doesn't get in my way, I could try to fly it out." Hana jogged toward the wall.

"That would be a good solution to a lot of problems." Iver didn't have high hopes, though. And he didn't want Hana anywhere near Linnel.

The runner lay at an angle, nose down in the water.

The back was propped up on the bank, and two of the air blades were dug into the turf.

"Well, that's not going anywhere." Iver sounded strangely pleased.

"Not necessarily." She glanced at him in surprise. "It doesn't actually look like its taken much structural damage. It's wedged into the river, but if they can push it off the bank into the water, and get it to float down to that wider section of the river, it might be able to take off."

"How likely is that?" Iver moved ahead of her, keeping parallel with the path below them. She followed, her gaze on the runner.

"There's Jake." Iver pointed and she saw him come around the side of the Dynastra with Lia on his heels.

Roj scrambled up the bank to the side of them, his face streaked with dirt, and then, much slower, Linnel clambered up behind him.

They conferred together, and then leaned back down the bank, to help what turned out to be Brynja and Tillis carrying a stretcher with another person on it.

They set the stretcher down, and then Jake made gestures toward the camp.

Brynja and Tillis jogged back toward it at a fast clip, and after a moment, Lia followed them.

Roj, Jake and Linnel stood around for a few more minutes, and then eventually Jake and Roj picked up the stretcher and walked to the camp as well, Linnel trailing behind them.

Hana moved as soon as they disappeared, running down the slope with Iver right behind her.

The engines were still ticking, cooling down, and Hana crouched beside them.

"Is that sand in there?" Iver spoke over her shoulder.

"Yes." She rose up, with hands on her hips. "This isn't flying without some very careful cleaning."

"How careful?"

She shook her head. "Very careful. I wouldn't fly it unless it was taken to a workshop, pulled apart, cleaned and put back together. The Sig has a better design. If they'd been flying one, they'd probably be okay, but this isn't a Sig . . ." She shrugged. The runners used on the VSC planets just didn't work on Faldine, and the solution engineers had come up with as a quick fix had been the Dynastra. They worked, but there were issues. The Sig was a massive step up, but there were only a few of them.

"So you wouldn't fly it; would Linnel?"

She shook her head. "He was one of the workshop engineers for most of my time in the military. I didn't realize he could fly at all. Unless the person on the stretcher was the pilot." She backed away from the runner. "I wouldn't have thought he would risk it."

"Except he's not behaving logically right now." Iver looked toward the camp.

"So, the lander becomes our only way out." Hana wished the Dynastra was good to fly. They could already be on their way.

"Looks like it."

She joined Iver, and he pulled her close, so they stood together on the path, entwined in each other's arms.

He kissed her, bending his head and cupping her face with his hands, his body blocking the crisp wind that blew down from the high peaks of the Spikes.

She shivered, pressed closer into him. If they didn't need to go for help, didn't need to get the VSC here to stop Jake and his friends, she'd suggest they grab their packs and walk into the Spikes.

"Maybe they're killing each other in the camp. Maybe when we get there, they'll all be dead."

Iver nuzzled her temple. "That would suit me. We could just jump in the lander and take off."

Hana rubbed her cheek against his chin. "Jake's definitely going to get a surprise when he gets back to camp."

Iver gave a hum of agreement, and she reluctantly stepped back from him.

"Do you think he didn't understand about the doors?" She faced the camp, listening for any sign of carnage.

"What do you mean?" Iver got into step with her as she started up the path.

"I noticed no one told Jake the doors didn't lock at the beginning. Do you think he didn't know?"

Iver stopped. "You think he ordered Brynja and Tillis to come and help down here because he thought the door was locked?"

She nodded. "And they either forgot he didn't know that, or were too afraid of him to tell him."

"That means he doesn't know a lot about Faldine."

"And yet, he knew about the camp, and was working with Lancaster and some of the former Faldine rebels."

Iver waved at the ruin as the top of it came into sight now the shield was down. "Did you pick up on what Barre and Craven were talking about in the ruin? About Cepi?"

Hana slowed as they got closer to the wall. "You think this has something to do with what happened to Cepi's enviro generator?"

"This ruin seemed similar to the one on Cepi to me from the start," Iver said. "And then there's the hidden generator, creating an encasing shield, just like there was on Cepi."

"You think the same people built both structures?"

"We never worked out what was powering the Cepi generator, and if this shield is as old as the ruin, I'm willing to bet it's been here thousands of years, humming away."

"So Craven and Barre knew where to find the shield engine because the team that tried to steal Cepi's generator told them what to look for?" Hana shook her head. "I thought they were all killed."

"The team that went onto Cepi was killed, but the people who were paying them, who silenced them when they realized the crew they'd sent in wouldn't be able to get off the moon with the generator--they were never caught."

"You think Jake is working for those people." Hana spoke slowly.

"I do," he agreed. "I was told by Admiral Valerian that the VSC thought the Core Companies of Garmen were behind the attempted theft."

"But the Cores are dismantled now." They were certainly living through exciting times, Hana reflected. The last year seemed to have been a series of crises. The VSC regaining control of Garmen, a former breakaway planet, was just one of them.

"The Cores are gone," Iver said. "But not everyone involved with the Cores is accounted for. Some of them scattered before they could be scooped up."

"Theoretically, what they were doing on Garmen was legal, wasn't it?" Hana wondered what the Cores executives had been involved in that they thought it better to run than stay and face whatever sanction the VSC decided to dish out.

"Not according to the footage Sofie Erdo smuggled off the planet. The owners of the Cores knew they'd be facing prosecution if they walked back into the VSC openly, so most have gone to ground."

"And you think some of them, the same people behind the attempted theft on Cepi, heard about this ruin and its shield, put two and two together, and sent Jake here to get it?"

"I do." Iver put a finger to his lips as the camp wall came into view.

Hana ducked down with him and they ran up the slope together, crouching behind the wall at a point where they had the best view of the lander.

The camp was strangely quiet, and Hana wondered what had happened when Jake had returned to find the power balance had shifted back toward Bret.

If he even knew it yet.

"Looks like everyone is hunkered down." Iver gripped the top of the wall. "Let's move now."

He glanced at her to see if she was ready and she nodded.

He stood and vaulted the wall in a fluid motion, one hand propelling him over.

Hana was right behind him and she ran for the lander, fast as she could, making for the driver's side out of habit.

Iver kept his focus on the camp rather than the vehicle, watching her back, and she jumped in and started the engine before he'd even reached the passenger door.

A shout went up as soon as the engine roared to life, and she glanced to the right, saw Jake running out of the medbay building.

As Iver jumped in, she swung the lander around and Bret came flying out of the ruin, face contorted.

He and Jake seemed to start at the sight of each other, and then Hana had no more time to watch them. She pointed the vehicle at the faint track out of the camp, and hit the accelerator.

CHAPTER 26

IVER SAW no sign of anyone as Hana raced toward the far end of
the camp.

The ramp was up, the way it had been a few nights ago when he
had watched the guards. "Stop. I'll get the ramp into place."

Hana nodded, stopping right next to it, and jumping out herself.

He was going to protest, but then saw it required two people to
maneuver it.

They worked quickly together, wheeling it to the wall and fixing
it in place, then lowering the other side down.

By the time they were done, even he could hear the shouts as
people ran from the camp toward them.

Hana pulled off as soon as they got back inside.

Iver leaned out the window and saw Grimms and Baxter running
after them.

He hung on as the lander tilted upward then bounced down the
other side of the ramp.

Hana accelerated as soon as they were on the other side and he
watched their followers disappear in a cloud of dust.

Hana gave a laugh--a whoop of relief--and he grinned.

"Out the way we came in?" Hana focused her gaze on the path in front of them.

"Yes. We at least know we can get back to Touka City if we retrace the route."

She nodded and the lander slid a little on the loose pebbles at the bottom of the slope before she turned a sharp left. The engine roared as it struggled up the steep incline, and then they reached the top, emerging into the shallower valley.

The river was narrower up here, more a stream, and the way was a lot rockier.

The lander bounced as Hana kept the speed up and Iver grunted as he bashed into the side of the door.

"Your ribs?" Hana asked, slowing down a little.

He nodded. "Don't slow down."

She gave a laugh. "This beats walking, I can tell you that. If only I could have borrowed this yesterday."

He had forgotten, totally forgotten, that she had spent the day before walking from the camp to leave a message for Craven, as a way to shake things up and hopefully create a chance for them to escape.

"Your plan worked." He knew she had done the only thing that she could, and had done it without much hope it would create the situation she hoped for, but she had gone ahead nonetheless.

"It seems to have." The road was too rough for her to look over at him, her concentration was on the ground ahead, but her lips twitched up in a smile. "Let's hope our luck holds."

"How long did it take you?"

She lifted a shoulder, her knuckles white as they gripped the steering wheel. "About two hours to get there. I waited until it was dark to move down to where they'd ambushed the lander, lit the flare and then got away as fast as possible. It took me longer to get back because I hurt my foot running away after I lit the flare."

He leaned across and put a hand on her thigh. Squeezed.

She lifted a hand off the wheel for a moment to pat the top of his. "You would have done the same. You put your life on the line to stop

Bret using you as a hostage to bring me in. I got away lightly compared to you."

"There is no scorekeeping, remember?"

She spared a moment to glance at him, then went back to watching the path. "Let's just say we watch each other's backs."

"I'm happy with that."

The hint of a smile played across her lips. "Me, too. I--"

The way she bit off the sentence, the sudden tension in her body, had him looking ahead.

"Shit."

There was a line of six people standing across the valley floor, rocks piled behind them as a barrier.

The way was blocked.

"Craven's people." Hana thumped the steering wheel with a fist. "There are a lot more of them than we thought."

"This must be their insurance, their way to make sure Bret couldn't escape."

Hana skidded to a halt, then began turning the lander.

The smugglers started running toward them, but she worked with absolute calm, swinging the wheel, reversing, and then spinning them around to face back the way they'd come.

"We're trapped." She blew a piece of hair away that had fallen over her eye.

He said nothing, his gaze ahead. "Bret's people are behind us, not Craven and Jake's. We're between two sets of enemies who won't work together. And we have a significant lead on Grimms and Baxter."

"That's true." She was looking out her window, to the right, as there was no place to turn left, the valley slope was too steep.

Suddenly, she swung the wheel, taking the lander off the path toward the stream, and he saw the place she was aiming for. The stream narrowed to a point where it would have been easy to jump from one side to the other, and she took the lander over it.

The whole vehicle shuddered as the wheels dipped into the water and then hit the rocks on the other side.

There was a scraping sound that put his teeth on edge, and then they were flying up the slope.

"This clear run isn't going to last." Hana jerked her head toward the row of rocks ahead of them that had once reminded Iver of sentinels. Now they were a blockade, barring the way up the mountain side.

She turned before she reached them, heading up the valley, in the direction of Touka City, but there was no gap wide enough to fit the lander through, and no way of going over them. Eventually, she braked.

"We're going to deliver ourselves right back to them."

They were almost back in line with Craven's people on the path below.

She put the lander in reverse and moved back, much more slowly this time, and the wheels popped and shuddered over the loose rocks.

Iver put a hand on her shoulder when they reached a point that was above a particularly sheer drop into the stream below.

She stopped. Looked from him to the drop.

She sighed. "It seems a waste, but yes. They won't be able to salvage the lander if it goes down there."

"Before we send it down, let's make sure there's nothing useful in the back." Iver jumped out and Hana joined him as he opened the back doors, but Bret had made sure the lander was completely unpacked. There was nothing left inside.

They still had their bags that they'd originally taken from it, though, so they weren't completely without supplies. Iver went to the front to grab them and Hana climbed into the lander and carefully swung the wheel so that its nose was pointing down.

She stopped when the back bumped against a rock and she couldn't reverse any more. She slid out the driver's side, leaned through the open door to release the brake, and jumped back.

The lander roared as it picked up speed down the incline, then went into free fall the rest of the way into the stream.

The impact sent a tremor through the ground and a few rocks and pebbles skittered underfoot and tumbled after it.

Iver moved forward and saw it had come to rest front first in the water.

He looked left, saw Craven's people reacting with shock as they took in what he and Hana had done.

"It's a pity." Hana sighed and he slid a hand along her shoulder and gently threaded his fingers in her hair.

Satisfaction flared inside him at the sight of the only way out for his enemies lying like vanquished prey below them. They would not be using the lander to get the engine out of the Spikes.

"No one's going anywhere now." He didn't hide his approval.

He heard a shout from the right and turned, saw Grimms and Baxter were on small buzzers, similar to the colorful dru-dru people used in Touka City but a more robust version, built for use out in the wilderness.

They had slid to a stop--like Craven's people, they were staring at the lander--and then their gazes went up to where Iver and Hana were standing.

"I don't think they're very happy with us."

Hana gave a strangled laugh. "No. I don't think things would go as well for us if we were caught again."

Then she went still, her head twisting to the left in a snap. "Someone's coming in a lander."

He turned to look, shading his eyes with a hand against the afternoon sun.

There was a glint of sunlight on glass from far down the valley, and then a lander lumbered into view. It came to a stop on the other side of the rocks that Craven's people had put in place and someone jumped out the driver's side.

Six others jumped out the back, all dressed in the security forces uniform Iver was wearing himself, taken from the stolen stores at the back of the lander.

"That looks like . . ." He squinted to get a better look.

"It's Simon." Hana's voice was soft. "Looks like Bret's got himself some backup."

A sudden flurry of shots were fired below, as Craven's people realized what was happening, and Simon's people attacked.

Everyone ducked down, taking cover behind rocks, while one of Craven's people lay sprawled on the ground with a SAL dart in their chest.

"Which way do we go?" Hana's teeth gnawed on her bottom lip. "Neither side is friendly."

"We go deeper into the Spikes." There was no guarantee they wouldn't be killed if they were caught again. They were stuck between the two factions and hadn't made friends on either side.

For now, he and Hana had done as much as they could to slow things down. It was time to think of themselves, and get to safety.

Grimms and Baxter revved their buzzers and started moving across the valley floor in their direction.

Their time to consider their options had just run out.

CHAPTER 27

THE HIGH-PITCHED WHINE of the two buzzers had long since faded, and now all Hana could hear was the cry of birds above and the wind through the trees lining the narrow pass.

That and her and Iver's breathing.

The air was thin up here, and even with her upgrade, she struggled to draw a full breath.

At least there was no sign anyone was following them.

Hana gave herself the luxury of a grin at the thought of Grimms and Baxter finding the way too rough for their buzzers. They wouldn't have wanted to risk leaving them and following on foot, not with Craven's people down below them.

Besides, with the arrival of Simon and his reinforcements they would be needed more urgently elsewhere.

Iver was right, this route was their best option. And both the groups they had escaped had more pressing things to do than chase down two prisoners. Even if one of them was the head-of-planet.

"Do you think they've given up on us completely?" She asked the question as she expended a little more effort and reached the top of the pass, pausing to lean back against the cliff behind her and pull out the water bottle from her pack.

"We can hope." Iver was only a few steps behind her and she watched him with appreciation as he walked toward her.

Despite the cool air, sweat dotted his shirt. He'd rolled up the sleeves and she could see the corded muscle of his arms. He looked competent and calm.

Like someone she'd want at her side in any situation.

A wave of lust mixed with admiration washed through her and she lifted her face to his as he stopped in front of her.

He bent down, touching his lips to hers, and then what she thought would be a simple kiss became hot and needy.

When he lifted his head and then moved to lean against the rock beside her, she was breathing hard.

"I'm sorry for all the time I wasted, before."

He looked sidelong at her.

"We could have had this a long time ago. We would have both been happier for it."

He shook his head. "Don't second guess yourself. You never played games with me. I'm fine with how things worked out." His lips quirked. "Very fine."

They stood side by side for a long moment, not speaking, and as the wind died down a little, Hana heard a faint sound of water falling.

She pushed away from the rock, working her way around it and then through a crack she had to go sideways to fit through. At the back, right against the mountain face, she found a small trickle of water running down sheer gray stone. Where it touched the rock, the gray sparkled with a silver glitter, and she drained the last of her bottle before she held it against the thin stream until it was full.

When she worked her way back, she found Iver trying to follow her and she shook her head. "Too narrow." She took his bottle to fill.

It was the first water they'd passed since they'd left the valley and the river that ran through it, and she had started to worry about it.

Their route had taken them straight up the pass and deep into the Spikes, so the part of the valley where the camp lay was no longer visible. As she walked back to Iver, who was standing at the edge of the path looking down, she could only see the open sweep of the valley as it widened in the direction of Permeo.

Iver's sky lane.

"Look." Iver pointed and she gasped in awe.

The shadow fold had begun.

The speed of it shocked her--the way the darkness traveled across the ground, eating it up. As the sun dipped below the mountains, the world below her turned to night.

"We may still be in the light now, but we won't be for long." Iver shielded his eyes against the oblique rays of the sun and stared at the gloomy world below them.

"We should set up camp here. There's water, at least, and if we move a little further along the path, there may be shelter against the wind."

He was about to answer her when they both heard the scream of engines.

Iver pulled her away from the edge, and they both crouched beside one of the boulders on the path.

A Dynastra shot overhead, flying low through the pass, between the mountains, and then disappeared.

"Jake's friends with a second Dynastra, coming to the rescue?" Hana had a feeling it was. The only other option was the Faldine military. She didn't know what measures they'd be taking right now to find Iver.

"Bret has taken the engine back now, so if that is Jake's people, they can't just load it up." Despite his words, Iver sounded grim.

Whatever reprieve they'd had had come to an end. They had to get to Touka City and mobilize the VSC forces, or they would lose something they never even knew they had.

They woke early, filling their bottles and setting out before dawn even broke.

Hana shook off the stiffness of a night on hard ground cheerfully. There had been compensations for sharing a small tent on a mountain path with Iver.

He was walking in front of her, and she grinned at his back.

Her upgrade had somehow gotten into the spirit of the occasion as they'd made love.

She hadn't had a relationship with anyone since her crash, and she knew she had never come that hard or that long before. Not even when they had made love outside the camp the day Iver got captured.

"Maybe I'm just that good," Iver told her with a smirk.

Maybe.

She grinned again.

The sound of a Dynastra overhead cut off her feeling of amusement, though, and stopped her in her tracks.

She dropped to the ground and rolled under the closest bush, and Iver crouched up against a rock.

The Dynastra circled, moving overhead in a tight pattern.

It passed them, working its way deeper into the mountains, and eventually they both got to their feet, watching it circle.

"It's looking for us." She was dismayed. She'd hoped they were no longer considered worth the effort.

"I can only think of two reasons why, and both might be in play." Iver looked in the direction the Dynastra had gone. "One, the VSC Special Forces has locked down any exits from the planet, so they need me back to use as a hostage, and two, Bret and his people still have control of the camp."

"Which means Jake and Craven want to stop us getting to Touka, to give themselves time to take it back from Bret." Hana brushed dust off her pants. "What do they think flying over us is going to do, though? It's not as if they can land. They'd need . . ."

She trailed off as she made out four tiny figures jumping from the runner.

"Combat flyers." Iver's voice held the weight she felt in her chest.

Runner diving had been a hobby. A pastime on some Verdant String planets.

The fun of using the wind and a cloth-covered frame to fly through the air by jumping from a runner, mountain or other high point.

On Arkhor they called it free flying. On Kalastoni, wind riding. On her own planet of Themis it was known as air sailing.

That hobby had become the way the VSC had dropped troops into rebel-held areas. It was the only way they could do so because of the magfields.

The tiny propelled frames that Special Forces usually used had the propensity to simply misfire midair on Faldine. They had lost at least six soldiers before they switched to a more innovative way.

Dropping soldiers down had become easy enough. It was getting them back out that caused the problems.

She watched as the tiny figures rode the wind, turning like birds of prey on the mountain thermals.

"They're going to land up ahead. They're boxing us in." Iver watched them, legs braced apart.

"So we can either go forward, see if we can slip by them, or go back." And going back wasn't an option, as far as she was concerned.

Iver shook his head as she said that. "No going back."

"Agreed." There was no benefit in it. At least if they forged ahead, they had a chance of getting to Touka City. Going back meant walking straight back into the arms of their captors.

"I can't get taken. I won't be used as a tool for them to get off planet with that shielding device." Iver sounded implacable.

"Then we have to make sure you don't get taken."

CHAPTER 28

THE TREES WERE thick as they came down the pass into the steep, narrow valley below.

Touka City was theoretically just one row of mountains beyond, but Iver couldn't be sure without a comm unit, and he doubted even if he had one that it would work.

Hana had lost a little of the otherworldly glide she had when her upgrade was working well, so he guessed they were moving through a high strength magfield.

"We'll be bumping into those combat flyers soon." She paused a little way back from the treeline, and Iver nodded in agreement as he stopped beside her.

"I was thinking the same." The sun was on the far side of the range, and they had about an hour before the shadow fold.

Most of the trees were tall, the trunks thick and with long, wide branches, with a few more slender varieties sprinkled through. They had plenty of cover here and the deep shade meant they had been able to walk down the pass without worrying about being spotted.

Hana was looking between the trees to the sunlit open meadow beyond. She pushed a tangle of dark hair that had fallen around her face behind her ears, and arched her back, and Iver moved behind her and started massaging her shoulders.

She turned her head, her gaze suddenly hot, and she twisted and pulled him close, kissing him hard on the mouth before pulling back.

"No time, too dangerous," she said with regret as she turned away and angled closer to the treeline.

He took a moment to collect himself, and followed. The path down had been narrow and difficult, forcing them a certain way. Hopefully, the thickness of the trees hid the fact that there was only one place they could really come out of into the valley, but he wasn't going to put his trust in hope.

He crouched beside her, holding onto a trunk for balance.

"Anything?"

She shook her head. "At some point, we're going to have to go out there. Do we wait for the shadow fold?"

He thought about it. "If we can go before, while its still light, we'll have a sense of the lay of the land beyond the trees, and we can make better decisions about where to hide tonight."

She nodded, eyes back on the open ground in front of them. "And if they're there, they'll have a clear view."

"Can you hear anything?"

She shook her head. "I'm pretty much neutralized. The magfield here is really strong."

"Then we move forward carefully." He took the lead. There were only three or four rows of trees left until the forest stopped and the pale green meadow began. He could hear water, so there was a river flowing through the valley.

He stepped out into the open, heard Hana's footsteps just behind him, and moved down the slope toward what looked like a small stream that was more tumbling white water than anything else.

They were over it, and making their way toward the gap in the mountains up ahead, when the glint of sun off metal had him reaching out a hand to grip Hana's shoulder and push her down.

"I saw." She swiveled toward it, crouching on her haunches.

They sat for long minutes, but there was no sound of running feet, no sound at all but the water and the wind and the birds overhead.

They carefully rose back up.

"We have to check it out." He didn't want to. He wanted to head for the pass. But he didn't want them to have whatever this was at their backs without finding out what it was.

"Yes." Hana let him go ahead again, both of them looking carefully all around them as they approached the top of a rise.

He stopped at the crest, waiting for Hana before he made his way down.

It was as if some giant hand had scooped out a second, shallower valley within the valley. A long, wide hollow.

A Dynastra lay buried on its side in the soft ground, with leaves and other debris piled up against its side. Years worth.

It wasn't alone, though.

There was something else--perhaps another ship--although nothing of it was visible but what looked like a window, buried in the side of a gentle hill.

"My Dynastra." Hana expelled the words on an exhale.

That had been his first thought. "You don't remember being here?"

She pointed to a an opening at the far side of the hollow, two rocks that formed a kind of gateway out. "I went that way. I don't remember much about it."

She ran down the slope and came to a stop in front of the strange window.

"They are trying to tell me something, but the magfield is too strong."

They. Her upgrade.

He moved past her, crouching beside the opening and looking in. There was a chill that seemed to rise up out of the darkness. Whatever this was, it was deeper than it looked.

He glanced at her over his shoulder. "What do you want to do?"

"Go in." She did a slow turn, carefully looking over the whole area. "I think I must."

He grabbed the top of the window frame with both hands and lowered himself inside, trying to gauge the depth. When he couldn't find the floor, he twisted, looking for a foothold against the wall, and when he found one, he moved to the side to let Hana in.

She swung in carefully, moving a little way below him as she found hand and footholds, and he pulled out the small light from their pack.

He pointed it down, and there below was a floor that seemed to be made of thin interlaced metal rods.

It wasn't that far down and he pushed off and dropped onto it, then turned and held his arms up to Hana.

She jumped after him, and he caught her around the waist and lowered her beside him.

"They aren't happy." She leaned back against him and took a deep breath.

"Do they think there's danger?" He wished she'd said this sooner.

She shook her head. "They don't like to be back here. They were here for so long before." She looked up at him. "Maybe thousands of years."

She ran a hand down her arm, almost like she was soothing herself.

"That way," she said, pointing.

He felt a chill lift the hairs on the back on his neck. "Hana?"

She looked over at him, blinked, and then shook herself.

"I'm okay." She tried to smile. "I've got all kinds of strange going on inside me, that's all."

He said nothing, let her show the way as their boots rang out on the metal floor. It vibrated under his feet, and made him worry he wouldn't be able to hear anyone creeping up on them.

The wide passageway ended in a set of stairs, twisting upward into the darkness.

"Notice that it's built for people of our general height?" Iver shone the light over the steps and the railing that ran beside it.

"Yes." She cleared her throat. "We have to go up."

"All right." He held the light steady and then followed behind her, lighting her way.

At the top was another wide corridor, and the faint smell of an animal, as if one of the largish rodents that lived in the Spikes had made this its home for a while.

There was a door up ahead. Iver half expected it to open for them, but it remained shut.

There was no handle or button, but there was a screen set beside it.

Hana reached out and touched it, and after a momentary flicker, an outline of a hand appeared in gray.

Hana gasped. Looked over at him.

"I see it."

She tentatively reached out again, put her hand inside the outline, and with a hiss and a groan, as if in need of lubricant, the door parted.

Hana stepped in, and then reversed out, bumping into him.

She pointed in silence, and in the diffuse light inside he saw two bodies slumped in chairs.

Two skeletons, he should say. There was nothing left of them.

A scrabble of sound came from overhead, and both their heads snapped up.

A crack ran along the ceiling, and Iver realized the air was warmer here and the light seeping in was coming from above.

"This isn't a two-person bridge." Hana turned her focus from the ceiling to the area around them and Iver played the handlight over the walls and floor for her.

It was massive, with place for at least twenty people.

"These two were the only ones in here when it crashed. Which means they sent everyone else away."

"We didn't find any other bodies so far. Maybe they managed to get out?"

"Or they died on the journey." Her voice caught a little. "And these two were all that were left."

Neither of them said anything for a long time, then she looked up at him.

"If they hit the same shield I did--and given the fact that we both landed in more or less the same spot, I'd say they did--then no one would have had time to evacuate." She looked out of the now-open door. "If they were alive and on the ship when it hit the shield, they're somewhere in here. Maybe on the flight deck. Scrambling for the runners."

He thought of that and shivered. "I hope you're wrong."

She shivered as well, and then ran both hands down her arms, hunching over as she did it.

"We're getting out of here." He couldn't stand to see her like this a moment more. It was as though she was being tortured by memories that weren't hers.

She took a deep, steady breath. "I want to. I really want to. But my upgrade is telling me there are runners on this ship. Runners that we could maybe use to get to Touka City faster."

"Runners in the place you think might be a mass grave?" He couldn't hold back the worry in his voice.

She took in another unsteady breath. "Yes."

He suddenly pulled her into his arms. "Are you sure about this?" His lips brushed her ear.

"No." She tightened her grip on him. "But I think it's worth taking the chance. If they are there, their place of rest is going to be disturbed, if not by us, then by the scientists of the VSC. And if there's a runner that will get us to Touka quickly . . ."

"A runner you can fly?" he asked.

"My upgrade says yes. I can fly it."

"All right." He knew her plan made sense, but everything in him screamed to get them out and away from here. "We'll look, and if there's nothing to find, we leave."

She nodded against his chest. Pulled back.

Her hand, when it lifted to her face to push back her hair, was shaking.

"Let's go."

CHAPTER 29

IT WAS hard to coordinate her steps.

Hana tried to soothe her upgrade, taking deep breaths as she followed Iver.

He was trying to protect her by going first, trying to see whatever horrific sight he thought was ahead before her, and stop her before she got there.

It made her chest tight.

"I'm glad you're here with me. I can't believe I was planning to do this alone."

The light in his hand bobbled, and he turned. Stared at her a beat.

"It's not too late to leave now." He searched her face, the worry on his own clear.

"I know, but I can't. It'll be all right, Iver. There's nothing here that can hurt us, and we might find something to help." As she said it, the truth of it settled over her, and for the first time, she felt like herself again.

Her upgrade calmed.

You are with me now, she thought forcefully, and felt a rush of gratitude.

Iver gave a slow nod, turned again, but he held his hand out behind him, and she grabbed it and felt a lightness at the contact.

A warmth in this cold, dark space.

"Some of what I've been feeling is an echo from my upgrade." She spoke haltingly, because she was still working through it herself. "They were here a long time, and their purpose is to help people survive in all conditions. And they had no one to help."

"You think whoever traveled in this ship had the upgrade as a way to improve their chances of survival, no matter where they ended up?"

"It's likely." More than likely, but the knowing she felt deep inside was just a feeling, and she was hesitant about voicing it.

"But if they were the same group of people who founded the planets of the Verdant String, why haven't we seen the upgrade in ourselves?" Iver swung the light downward as they stepped out of the passage onto a walkway over a massive, cavernous space.

They were amazingly high above the ground, and Iver stopped and focused the light on a dead tree, far below.

"An atrium of some kind. A greenhouse." Hana leaned against the railing and looked down on it. She felt tiny here. Insignificant.

And completely awed.

This had been a life-sustaining, traveling city.

The waste of it crashing in the Spikes, of all that potential destroyed, hurt.

Iver had gone very still, and she glanced at him, suddenly worried. "What is it?"

"This is the same as the ship Tally Riva was stuck on." He turned to her. "I read the report. The Raxian military has the ship, and they've allowed scientists from all the Verdant String planets access to it."

"I remember the incident, vaguely. It hasn't been in the news much since they found her alive, though."

"That's on purpose." Iver's lips twitched in a wry smile. "I think they're taking their time to be sure that when they come out with a conclusion, it's backed up by evidence."

"And what conclusion is that?"

"That the ship was in the same fleet of ships that traveled to the Verdant String and settled the eight planets." Iver slowly moved the light away from the tree and over dead plant beds and tanks laid out in a pleasing fashion, as if the way through them curved in a sinuous path. "It seems the fleet was bigger than we thought."

"And now we know one of them went to Faldine." It was unbelievable, and yet, made perfect sense. Faldine was a livable planet. Why wouldn't they have tried to settle here if there were more ships in the fleet?

Iver pushed back from the railing. "This whole incident is going to shake the VSC. The ruins, the shield engine, this ship. Faldine is going to become a hotbed of scientists and tourists."

"If we can get safely to Touka, and stop Jake and his friends taking the shield engine off-planet. Otherwise . . ." The responsibility resting on their shoulders suddenly struck her.

"Otherwise, if we're captured, we die, and these secrets die with us." Iver sounded grim as he began to move again.

Hana followed, peering over the railings as Iver slowly swept the light from left to right.

"The ship Tally Riva was stuck on, were there any bodies?" she asked.

"Not that I know of. No runners, either. They must have had a technical failure and taken their chances to reach a place they could survive on, rather than waiting to die in space."

The grim reality was that they had probably all died. She wondered if Tally Riva had encountered any metal beads while she was on the ship. And how she'd go about asking the Raxian without tipping her own hand, or coming across as strange.

They had come to the end of the walkway and stepped through

into another corridor that went straight as well as branching left and right.

"Straight," she said, and Iver looked over his shoulder at her and nodded.

It took more than ten minutes of walking, of ignoring corridors that branched off periodically. The size of the ship threatened to defeat her imagination. "Do you think this is all buried underground?" She tried to picture the strange dip and then rise of landscape where her Dynastra had come down, and suddenly gasped.

Iver stopped, swung around, eyes snapping to her face.

"The valley within the valley. The ship made it, gouging out the ground as it crashed, and the hill . . . the hill *is* the ship, with a layer of soil on top."

He blinked. "You're right."

She fluttered her hands. "We may not be able to get any runner on the flight deck out."

He shrugged, turned, and carried on, and she gave her own shrug. She was the one insisting they had to try. So they would try. And if they couldn't get a runner out, they were no worse off than they had been before.

<h1 style="text-align:center">CHAPTER 30</h1>

THE DOOR to the flight deck was slightly ajar.

Iver came to a stop in front of it and angled his light for a look inside.

"What do you see?" Hana leaned against him, trying to look at what lay beyond. She felt a sudden roiling of nerves batter her, and she hitched in a quick breath.

Iver cupped her cheek with one of his big hands, and tilted her head up to his. "Bodies."

They had guessed that. They had even expected it.

She forced herself to straighten. "Can we get in?"

Iver shone the light over the area beside the door, and put his hand against the screen.

The door gave a sudden screech, moved open a little more, and then stopped.

It was just wide enough for them to sidle through.

"I think there are bodies in the way." Iver's warning was unnecessary. She had already guessed that.

He went first, grunting a little as he squeezed through, and then he turned for her, hand out, but she slipped through easily enough.

"So many." She whispered it as his light moved over the bones lying scattered over the floor.

Runners loomed out of the gloom, sleek but dust-covered. It was dark inside, but not completely.

The bodies were completely decomposed here, just as the two on the bridge were, and she felt a trickle of moving air touch her face.

"There's some exposure to the outside from here. Light is coming from up front."

Iver nodded. "There are leaves." He pointed the light at the ground, and sure enough, dried leaves had drifted down over some of the bones.

They made a strange, eery scratching sound as she walked over them.

Both she and Iver kept to the walls as they explored, taking everything in, until they found the flight ramp.

It was shrouded in thick, green vines which undulated a little in the breeze blowing in from outside, letting in shafts of light every time they moved.

Iver thrust his arm through, pushed the vegetation back, and light poured in. Hana saw trees and the steep side of the valley up ahead.

She looked over at Iver, but he was crouched down, one arm still holding back the vines, the other reaching to pick something up from the floor.

She made a sound that caught in her throat, and with shock, she realized her upgrade had squeezed the muscles to stop her from calling out a warning.

She tried to lift a hand, but she stood, immobilized, as he lifted two small, shiny metal balls in his palm.

"What do you think--?"

They both watched the balls disappear.

Suddenly free, Hana coughed, put a hand to her throat, and held Iver's gaze.

"Welcome to the club." Her voice was hoarse.

He lifted his palm closer to his face. "You're saying . . .?"

"There were obviously two left."

He lowered his arm, and flexed the fingers of his hand. "I don't feel any different."

She pursed her lips. "You will. When we get out of the magfield." She closed her eyes, and raged at her upgrade. Taking her choice away was unacceptable. Unacceptable.

The tentative response she got was a series of images that blossomed in her brain. A loneliness and a sense of abandonment that had to be rectified. A desperate act in desperate circumstances.

She opened her eyes on a sigh, found Iver looking at her with that steady, calm look of his.

"It's not a bad thing. I'm certainly better for it." She shook her head. "I just wish I'd been able to warn you, so you'd have had the choice."

"You told me about the beads. I should have realized what they were." He flexed his hand again. "Nothing we can do about it now anyway."

He had dropped the curtain of vines during their conversation, but he put his hand on it again, lifting it wide enough for Hana to step through.

"Let's see how overgrown it is on the outside and whether we can get a runner out at all."

She stepped through, and then pulled up so suddenly, Iver ran into the back of her.

A man in black fatigues stared at her from the trees.

He gave a sudden, high-pitched whistle, as Iver lifted her up bodily and pulled her back behind the leafy curtain.

"They're here. The combat flyers." She felt a calm come over her. Her gaze went to the runners, and she strode over to the one closest to the opening.

She touched the side, her movements on automatic, as if she had done them a thousand times, and steps creaked out from a panel, sending dust into the air.

She coughed and wiped her eyes as she climbed up and then stopped short in the open door.

"What is it?"

She backed down the stairs, jumped the last few to join him on the ground. "Bodies. Bones." She shuddered.

She couldn't use this runner.

The sound of a shout filtered in from the outside.

"Let's try the ones at the back," Iver said. "They're more likely to be empty."

She nodded and let him go ahead with the light. One runner was still clipped into place on the deck, its struts held secure.

"Can you work out how to release those?" she asked Iver as she lowered the stairs.

She almost slumped against the door in relief when she saw there were no bones in this one, and she made her way to the pilot's chair. She wanted to sink into herself, let her upgrade take over, but fear spiked in her chest at the memory of standing frozen and helpless as Iver picked up the beads.

She could sense the apology, the regret, but not for the action, only for the loss of her trust, and she lifted her shoulders up and then let them fall.

It didn't matter now. She had to put her anger and fear aside, and get on with it.

She put her arms forward, touching the panel in front of her, and let her upgrade take control.

She tried to note with her conscious mind exactly what was being touched and swiped and pressed and in what order.

The engine started up.

"I can't find the release for the struts." Iver's shout came from the top of the runner's steps as he leaned in, and suddenly her arm reached left, and she flipped a switch. The runner lifted up a little, making Iver stagger.

"That did it." He stepped inside, and the steps folded up and the door closed behind him.

The runner lifted a little higher, making the dried leaves swirl around the flight deck.

But the way out was blocked by the other runners, and when she looked up, she saw there wasn't enough clearance to simply lift up and over them.

"I'm going to have to move the runners aside." She turned to Iver, and he came forward, looking out at the obstacles in their way.

He obviously came to the same conclusion she had.

"I'll stand guard while you move them."

She left the engine running, so leaves and dust swirled around her, stinging her eyes, as she exited.

She ran to the closest ship, Iver right behind her, and scrambled inside.

She held her breath as she stepped into what was a tomb now, bones piled together. In the pilot's seat, the bones lay on the seat of the chair and on either side of it, and she leaned across it carefully to start the engine.

She lifted the runner up just off the ground and moved it as far to the left as she could.

When she set it down and jumped back out, she found Iver standing guard at the bottom of the steps, his attention focused on the exit.

"They're there. I've seen them a few times when the turbulence opens the vines a little. All four of them."

She saw a SAL dart on the ground just past the vines and realized someone had tried to take a shot at him.

"Be careful." She touched his shoulder, just a quick caress, and ran across to the next runner, checking to see how much she would need to move it.

Once inside, she gritted her teeth at more bones, some that looked like those of children, and when she got the engine going, she angled the runner to the right, nudging the nose right up against the ships on that side.

This time, when she got to the ground again, she saw Iver had something in his hand that looked like a weapon.

She had seen a few of them lying on the ground. He must have figured it was better than nothing.

The men outside would soon work out they had nothing to lose by going on the attack. As soon as she and Iver were in a runner, they would be almost impossible to stop or capture.

Iver let out a shout and activated the weapon in his hand as two of the combat flyers ran through the swaying vines.

The sound it made was like a cough, and she stared at it.

Whatever Iver had done, the effect on the two men was immediate. One fell back with a blossom of blood on his left shoulder, and the other got his hands under his friend's armpits and dragged him back out.

Hana forced her gaze away from the vines, and she and Iver stared at each other for a long beat. He looked as shocked as she was.

He turned the weapon over in his hand, and realizing she was wasting time, she forced herself to move.

There was one runner left that blocked the way, the one she'd gotten into the first time. It was close to the vines, but the soldiers were gone for now.

She climbed the stairs and hesitated for a moment in the doorway, just as she had done before.

There were more bodies in this one than the others. It was obviously the first one ready to go and they must have loaded it up with their most vulnerable. There were very small bones in here. Babies. Children. She shuddered and forced herself to the pilot's seat and started the engine.

The proximity of the runner to the vines must have galvanized their attackers, because two ran through the vines as soon as she started it up.

Her reaction was automatic, her hand reaching out and pressing a button that lit both of them up in a strong light beam.

They had to lift their arms to protect their eyes, and while they were blinded, she moved the runner out of the way, careful to keep the nose pointed in their direction, lights on full.

She was sorry to shut things down when she was done, but she didn't want them to try and use this runner themselves, and when she cut the engine, the sudden disappearance of the beams plunged the whole deck into darkness as her eyes struggled to adjust.

Iver stood below, arms extended, slowly sweeping left to right.

"They're in here somewhere." He spoke very low, and she only just heard him over the sound of the runner at the back.

"What is that thing?" she asked, looking at the dark metal object in his hands.

"Projectile weapon. Not sure what it's projecting, but it made that strange noise, and it definitely wounded one of them."

He gestured with the weapon for her to move toward the runner, and then he shielded her as they went, putting his body between her and the now open flight deck.

She moved slowly, cautiously in the green-tinged gloom.

The soldiers wouldn't be able to hear their footsteps over the roar of the runner and the swirl of leaves and dust, but she and Iver wouldn't be able to hear theirs, either, although she felt her upgrade straining to do just that.

When they had almost reached the runner, a man leaped out at them, SAL raised in front of him.

Iver activated the weapon in his hands again, and the man fell back with a scream. His SAL landed on the ground and skittered away, and Hana crouched down and lunged for it.

There was still one more soldier in here at least, so she went back to back with Iver, shuffling with him to the steps, and then climbing them with the SAL at the ready.

The man on the ground wasn't moving, and she had a sick suspicion he was dead.

She bumped into Iver at the top of the steps, turned her head quickly to check what made him stop, and then froze.

A soldier stood in the open area behind the pilot and co-pilot seats, SAL pointed at Iver.

"Serra! You there?" His shout was obviously to his fallen companion.

Hana moved a little way back from Iver, to give herself room to move. She was in a high-level magfield, but she was still faster than she would be otherwise.

"Stay still," the soldier barked at her. "I don't want you falling down the stairs when I tranq you, but I will if I have to."

"Sure." She moved in one fast, fluid motion, lifting her hands to rest the SAL on Iver's shoulder, and shot.

Iver turned, grabbed her, and fell into the runner, twisting so she landed on top of him. She sensed rather than saw the dart the soldier had managed to get off flying over her head.

"You all right?" she asked as she scrambled off him. His ribs must be hurting, but he didn't even flinch.

He nodded as he got to his feet.

The soldier was out, the SAL dart in his chest.

"There's still one out there, but he can stay out there, as far as I'm concerned."

She nodded. "We want to bring this one along, right?"

Iver nodded, reached out and retracted the steps, and she sat in the pilot's chair again.

She carefully maneuvered the runner through the space, making sure she didn't touch the floor at any time and damage the bones.

The vines resisted her forward momentum for a beat and then gave, and the runner emerged with what must have looked like a fringe of green hair.

The fourth soldier stood just outside, beside his wounded teammate, and Hana saw his astonishment as she nudged the runner free of the deck and then lifted straight upward.

It struggled, battling the magfield and probably centuries of dust, although running the engines for a while may have burned a lot of it off.

"What fuel does it use?" Iver asked, settling in beside her in the pilot's chair.

"Whatever it uses, it's currently at three quarters power." She finally got high enough that the magfield drag diminished, and then she circled over the site.

The massive ship looked like a hill from this angle, too. Nothing special.

She looked over at Iver. "Should we circle the camp? See what they're doing before we go to Touka?"

He gave a reluctant nod. "We better."

She turned north west, keeping high, and came at the camp obliquely, circling it in a wide arc.

The downed Dynastra still lay tilted at a drunken angle in the river, and the second one was parked inside the camp itself. It lifted off as she turned for a second pass, and Iver leaned forward.

"That has to be a coincidence. They couldn't have noticed us yet."

She didn't know if he was right, but the result was the same, the Dynastra was lifting off, coming up to their level, and if this small runner had weapons, she couldn't see where they were.

The Dynastra rose up in a tight spiral, keeping directly over the camp and then heading into the Spikes, in the direction they had just come.

"They're going to look for their soldiers." Iver's hands were tense on the panel in front of him. "And . . . they've just spotted us."

He was right. The Dynastra had begun a path deeper into the mountains, when it suddenly wheeled again, turning completely to face them.

And the Dynastra, as she knew all too well, did have weapons.

Then she laughed.

"What?" Iver turned to her.

"We're high enough that we're out of the magfield's pull. I forgot for a moment." She felt a sudden sense of relief that her upgrade was an integrated part of herself again, so entwined that she'd taken it for granted.

The Dynastra shot at them, and she slid the tight, sleek runner out of the way, suddenly in the moment in a way that reminded her of the last months of the war.

They shot again, and she wasn't where they thought she would be a second time.

"You're doing this by eye," Iver said, as if suddenly realizing it. "Why isn't this picking up the laz fire and warning you?"

"Probably because this is thousand-year-old tech, and whoever designed this didn't have laz fire on the list."

Iver's bark of laughter at that made her smile.

She waited for the Dynastra to shoot again, but instead it gave another of its tight about-turns and raced into the Spikes.

Hana hovered in place, staring after it, when something slammed into them from behind.

Iver swore and turned in his seat to check the damage, but she didn't need him to tell her that the back section had been breached. Air howled into the runner, tearing at her hair and screaming in her ears.

"Who?" she shouted as she fought the runner downward.

"Looks like . . ." He swore again, a long, protracted, vicious stream of profanity, as he peered through the gaping hole in the back. "It's VSC Special Forces."

"What?" She screamed it as she applied herself to keeping them alive, as the runner shuddered beneath her and bucked and twisted as the rip in the back caught the air.

She headed for the river, trying to remember the deepest section, and then managed to haul the nose up as they came down, so they coasted on the surface for a couple of beats before sinking down.

As the runner ground against the rocks on the riverbed, she sat, hands on the control panel, eyes closed, and blew out a long, slow breath. "Bastards."

She could feel the magfield interfering with her upgrade now she was on the ground, but that was okay. She had had the skills she needed high above the ground, where it really counted.

She turned to look at Iver, who was shaking his head.

"Incredible." He stood, looking back at the gaping wound in the back of the ship.

The runner trembled in place suddenly, and the sound of a runner landing on the river bank beside them engulfed them.

"Excuse me." Hana stood herself.

Iver looked at her, one eyebrow raised.

"I've got something I need to sort out." She smiled, or tried to, but from the look on Iver's face, she did not succeed. Then she walked past him to the back, to where Special Forces had ripped a hole in her runner, jumped the short distance to the bank and headed straight for a second gen Sig that was settling into landing position. She admired it as she stalked toward it. She'd been secretly hoping Iver would invest in one of these babies for the last six months.

Two Special Forces soldiers appeared as the door opened.

She smiled. She had a few things to say.

CHAPTER 31

"WHAT'S the penalty for friendly fire due to incompetence?" She thought she kept her voice pretty calm as she called the question, even though she was raging inside.

They shot at Iver. They could have killed him. And they brought down her runner. Her runner!

They destroyed it.

Far in the back of her mind, some stray thought tried to question her strength of feeling over the runner itself, because she'd flown it for what amounted to all of five minutes, but something deeper told her no. She had spent hours in that runner. It was hers!

The man she was headed for dropped lightly to the ground as a modified exit ramp lowered at the back, and Special Forces soldiers streamed out.

She noticed in some part of her brain that their weapons were mostly pointed at her.

"Excuse me?" He looked at her like she was crazy.

"I hope you have skills beyond the armed forces, or you'll be living on the citizen dividend and twiddling your thumbs for the rest of your life after this fuck up." She openly sneered at him, and pointed behind her at the runner.

"Fuck up?" The man laughed.

Iver had followed her out and was walking toward her, and she gestured to him.

"You just shot down the head-of-planet. I don't know about you, but in my experience, that's at the very least grounds for a job-reevaluation."

The asshole obviously recognized Iver, because his eyes widened.

"We hailed you," he said to her, all humor leeched from his face. "You didn't respond."

"Because I was flying an antique that didn't have the tech to pick up your hail. I had no idea you were even there." She put her hands on her hips. "What happened to coming round to try face-to-face comms when your hail failed? That can't just be Themis military standard practice. Then you'd have seen the head-of-planet, and not shot him out of the fucking sky!" She realized her voice had risen and she drew in a deep breath to get herself under control.

At that moment, a woman appeared in the doorway, and dropped down beside the man.

"Oh." Hana drew in a deep breath and tilted her head to look at her. "You're in charge. Do you go around shooting unprovoked often?"

The woman looked at her, and then her gaze slid over her shoulder to Iver. "Planetary Commander," she said, voice tight.

"Captain Donaldson." Iver rested a warm hand on Hana's shoulder as he reached her. "You tried to kill my pilot and me."

She thought he was calm, and then she felt the tension in his hand where it held her, almost like a lifeline.

"In fact, if Hana wasn't the pilot she is, you *would* have killed us."

"Not only that," Hana was far from finished here, "you let the enemy go. They flew away, and you helped them by shooting us. Are you in league with them? Is this a takeover?"

Donaldson took an actual step back. "The Dynastra that flew away was Faldine military."

"Obviously not, as they were trying to shoot us down, and as you seem to know, one of us is the head-of-planet."

"They had the codes." The man she'd accosted first spoke up. "When we came into range, they gave the Faldine military codes and claimed they had exchanged fire with you and their weapons systems were down."

"So you happily did their dirty work for them, while they lit out. Well done."

"Who did the person you spoke to identify themselves as?" Iver's hand was rubbing her shoulder now, trying to soothe her.

"A Lieutenant Linnel." The woman shook her head. "We were played, and we fell for it. I am genuinely sorry we shot you down, and very relieved you're both uninjured."

Hana realized she wasn't ready to hear an apology right now. She wanted to do some physical damage to these people, and she took a step back and turned away, hands still on her hips, to try and breathe through it.

She heard Iver and Donaldson speaking behind her, Iver letting the captain know about the two factions fighting over the shield engine, the uncertainty they had over who was in charge at the camp at the moment, or how many people either side had.

And then she heard something else.

She turned slowly on her heel, looking toward the heart of the Spikes.

"They're coming back." She said it softly, almost to herself, and no one heard her. "They are coming back!"

She ran the few steps to Iver, grabbed his arm, and pulled him away from the Sig. "The Dynastra is coming back."

Iver didn't hesitate to move with her, and to their credit, the Special Forces team seemed to realize what that meant, because even though they might not have been able to hear the Dynastra yet, they reacted as well, moving away.

And when they could hear the approach of the runner's engine, they really started to move.

The unmistakable sound of an SD3 launching had one of the Special Forces soldiers swearing, and she realized she still wasn't over them shooting her down because she didn't feel sorry for him in the least.

The Sig ignited behind them, and then something scooped her up and threw her down the path, where she landed face down in the short pale green ground cover and felt the heat of the explosion ripple over her back.

She turned her head, found Iver lying a little way behind her, groaning as he lifted up on his elbows.

"Hana?" The panic in his voice was her incentive to push upright herself.

"I'm fine."

She looked up, saw the Dynastra was circling the camp, shooting laz fire at the ruin.

"Bret's still in charge there, then. At least of the ruin. They're trying to kill as many as they can so Craven's people can go in and take the few who are left." She rolled slowly to her feet.

"I don't think they'll risk blowing up the ruin, in case they damage the shield engine, but they don't seem to mind damaging it." Iver pulled himself up, too, and staggered over to her.

"Sugotti." It was Donaldson. "What do I need to know?"

"Your people all right?" Iver asked, his arm hardening around Hana's waist when she would have wriggled free.

"A few minor injuries, but your pilot's warning saved them." Donaldson's gaze rested for a moment on Iver's hand on her thigh and then seemed to shrug it off. "Who is shooting at who?"

"We think some of the escapees from Garmen--former Cores Company shareholders--are the ones directing the Dynastra. They're trying to kill the other group, who are probably all holed up in the ruin, so they can go in and grab the shield engine."

"And the ones in the ruin? They aren't friendly, either, you say?"

"No. They're former Faldine rebels, looking to use the shield for their own purposes as well."

"Quite the mess." Donaldson didn't seem to mind, though. She said it with relish.

While she'd been speaking to them, her people gathered around, waiting for instructions, and the soldier Hana had torn a strip off ended up next to her.

"So, where'd you get the antique?"

She looked over at him with dislike.

"Hey, don't be like that. I'm sorry we shot you down, but you said you were flying an antique, and I've never seen anything like that before. It looks pretty new to me."

"Well, it's not." Argh. She wanted to stay mad with them all, but her sense of outrage was seeping away. She gave him what she considered a cordial nod, and tried to catch up on what she'd missed of Iver and Donaldson's conversation.

"Spread out, take down everyone you come in contact with around the camp, without injury if possible. None of them are friendlies." Donaldson left it at that, and the thirty strong team melted off in various directions.

"Are you able to contact the VSC for another Sig?" Hana asked Donaldson, who seemed to have decided to stick with her and Iver.

"The Sig is set up to send a distress signal if it's destroyed," Donaldson said.

"Even in a high magfield, like here?"

Donaldson paused, gave a slow nod. "I think so. It would have been propelled upward to two thou above the ground and then begun transmission. We were told it should work on Faldine in all but the worst areas, or the deadzones, obviously."

Hana nodded, relaxing a little. That sounded pretty failsafe.

Up ahead, the Dynastra came back over the camp, strafing the ruin a second time.

Without warning, Hana's body seized and she fell to her hands and knees, then flat on the ground.

There was no sound, no sight, just paralysis for a moment, and then Iver was on his knees beside her, his body bent over hers.

"They turned it back on," she managed to gasp, forcing her head up to watch as Linnel's Dynastra disappeared completely from sight, swallowed up by the shield.

There was no sound, the shield swallowed even that, but shockwaves shook the ground, as if there had been a massive impact.

It set off a rumble up the mountain.

Behind her, she heard small stones and larger rocks bouncing and rolling down into the river.

Then suddenly, the terrible sensation of loss vanished, and she coughed as she lifted up on hands and knees, her head hanging down.

The shield engine had been switched off again.

"What happened?" Donaldson's shout had the tenor of someone who'd asked the same question a few times without response.

"The shield." Iver managed to get to his feet, and she belatedly remembered he would have been affected by the sudden shield activation as well. He was truly in the same club as her, now.

"The shield's a deadzone when it's activated. They probably switched it on to bring the Dynastra down."

He held out his hand and Hana took it and let him haul her up, then put her hands on knees, until the nausea passed.

Donaldson looked over at the camp. "I didn't see the Dynastra fall, but now it's lying crashed in the camp."

"It did fall, right in front of us, it was just shielded." Iver shrugged. "Now the shield is gone again."

"Damn." Donaldson drew the word out in astonishment. "That's some shield." She looked over at Hanna. "She okay?"

"Hana has a bad reaction to the shield. There's something in the frequency that repels people," Iver said. "She's sensitive to it."

Donaldson nodded, turned back almost as if she were checking to see if the Dynastra was still there.

"Let's go find out what's actually left of the site." Iver put out a hand for her and Hana took it.

She wondered if the Dynastra had hit the ruin, and if it had, whether it had destroyed the shield engine when it did. It might be why the engine had been deactivated again. Either that, or someone on Bret's team was still alive in there, and had turned it off.

Looking at the pillar of smoke and flame, she didn't hold out much hope.

CHAPTER 32

IT WAS AN INFERNO.

Iver shielded his face with an arm as he approached the ruin.

The huts closest to it had been crushed when the Dynastra had crashed, others further away were damaged by debris. All were burning, along with the Dynastra itself.

The three larger buildings were not on fire, but Iver could see where debris had damaged them and also where stray laz fire from the strafing had ripped into the flimsy material they were built from.

Linnel or Jake or whoever had been in charge of the Dynastra hadn't worried about who on their own side they might hurt in their quest to wrest the engine back from Bret.

There was no sign of anyone.

A few of Donaldson's people had returned when the runner crashed, to see if she needed them, and she signaled them silently to check on the buildings for signs of life.

"Even if the shield engine isn't destroyed, it will take a while to find it and get it out of there," Hana said.

She was right. Even after the Dynastra burned out, they would need to let it cool, and then somehow get it off the ruin to access whatever was left below.

He would have to ask Admiral Valerian for help with that, or one of the big mining operations on Faldine.

They might have the equipment.

Donaldson approached them, and something in her demeanor told him the news was bad.

"There is only one person still alive in the camp that my people can find, and she's unconscious." Donaldson tapped at her ear, cursed, and pulled out a tiny comm unit. "The magfield is interfering with comms, but so far, my people have found and secured a number of people further up the valley who were engaged in a fight with each other, and four lookouts who were posted on the valley slopes."

"We better check to see if Jake is one of the bodies." Hana sounded reluctant. "We don't know what happened at the camp after we left, but Craven and Jake bringing in a second Dynastra makes me think they'd have already taken back some of the camp. Just not the shield, obviously."

She was right. Most likely all of Bret's people had taken cover in the ruin, and were defending it.

"I'll do it." Iver turned to the buildings, but Hana shook her head.

"I'll come with you."

"We don't both need to see that." He wanted to protect her, to save her one nightmare, at least.

She looked at him, and then gave a slow nod. "Thank you."

It felt like a victory, and he used it to steel himself for what lay beyond the damaged, torn-up doors of the communal buildings.

He stepped into the closest one, and saw Lia being tended by a Special Forces medic.

She looked even younger lying unconscious on the ground. It hurt to look at the blood on her chest.

At least she was alive. That was more than Vras and Luki had going for them. Both men were dead, the strafing laz fire had cut them both down where they sat, tied up and resting against the wall.

Lia must have been guarding them.

And had been nearly killed by her own people.

"That's all the bodies in here." The soldier guarding the door said. "There are some in the canteen next door."

Iver strode across to it, looked inside, and blinked. Craven lay on the ground beside the conference table, and Tillis sat, slumped in a chair, his head hanging.

Had this strafing been a mistake? Or had Jake used it as an opportunity to clean house?

Either that, or if Linnel had been flying the Dynastra, as Donaldson claimed, then the psycho had simply not cared one way or the other who he killed.

"Is this it?" he asked as Donaldson appeared in the doorway.

She nodded.

"Then Jake, the Cores Company rep, isn't here. He might have been in the Dynastra. If so, we'll find him when it's safe to search for bodies onboard."

He walked out the room, disgusted with the lot of them.

Too many were dead, priceless artifacts were destroyed, and all for what?

Some twisted sense of aggrievement on the part of the rebels, and nothing short of naked greed on the part of the Cores and the former smugglers.

What a waste.

Hana stood in the middle of the camp, arms around herself, still looking at the Dyanstra as it burned.

As he walked toward her, he heard a faint sound in the distance at the same time she cocked her head to the side and turned in the direction he could hear it coming from.

"A runner?" he called to her.

She turned, eyes wide as she nodded.

He tapped his ear to tell her he'd heard it, too, and she gave him a sunny smile as she jogged toward him.

"Captain." He turned his head to shout for Donaldson, and when she stepped out of the building, he pointed upward.

"Someone's coming."

Hana had stopped running, and she walked the rest of the way toward him in a relaxed manner. "It's a Sig. So probably VSC."

As soon as she spoke, a Sig appeared from between two mountains, flew overhead and then doubled back.

"They want to know if its safe to land," Donaldson said, voice wry.

Iver looked around at the carnage. Two Dynastras, Donaldson's Sig, and his and Hana's runner from the ancient ship, all either burning or crashed.

"Can't say I blame them."

Their arrival in Touka City was a whirlwind.

Hana kept back, letting Iver handle Moiri Tanek, and then, half an hour after they touched down in the sweet, upgraded Sig, the admiral herself, come down from on high to help deal with the mess.

Moiri had turned over her offices for everyone's use, and now Hana was falling asleep on one of the comfortable couches in the large meeting room.

Her exhaustion wasn't surprising given her life recently, and when someone approached with an offer from Moiri of a hotel room, she glanced at Iver, saw he was deep in conversation with Admiral Valerian, and got to her feet to follow the staffer.

The admin gave her the room number and an access code, and she asked him to pass the information on to Iver when he was done.

The hotel was in the adjacent building, and she traveled the two floors down from Moiri's offices feeling slightly detached from her body and took the transparent sky walk between the buildings without her usual interest in the city below.

The room was a suite, and she wondered if it was where Iver usually stayed when she flew him to Touka.

She supposed she would find out soon enough, because she'd be staying with him.

The thought made her smile, and she managed to generate enough energy to have a glorious hot shower before she fell into bed.

When she woke, her upgrade told her it was only two hours later, and that there was someone in the room with her.

Someone not Iver.

She tensed, working through her options, but she had no weapons, and she would rather face whoever it was than have them take her by surprise, so she rolled off the bed and surged to her feet in one movement.

The man at the foot of her bed took a step back in shock.

Banyon.

She recognized him immediately.

She said nothing though, staring at him while she catalogued the room for anything that she might use as a weapon.

Banyon lifted his arm, and she saw he was holding a SAL.

"I should come over there and punch you in the nose in retaliation for you hitting me in Simon's warehouse." He watched her with cold eyes.

"You mean that time you had me tranqed and restrained against my will?"

He waved that away. "I need you to tell me what Sugotti knows."

She thought about it, weighed up telling him the truth, or not.

But in the end, she was just too tired to care that much.

She hoped that Iver was on his way right now, because all Banyon needed to do was pull the SAL's trigger and he'd have her down. And she couldn't think anything good would come of that.

She felt something in her upgrade stir at the thought.

"Hey! I asked you a question." Banyon took a step toward her.

"Calm down." She rubbed at her face. "I've had hardly any rest, and now you've interrupted the first genuine sleep I've had in days.

Which reminds me, how did you get in here? That staffer of Moiri's in your pocket or something?"

"Or something." He smirked. "What. Does. Sugotti. Know?"

"That you're on the Touka City council. That you authorized that equipment that Fraen drove out to the camp. That you are involved with Simon and Vannie and Lancaster. That you're in this up to your neck."

"Shit. They may be able to trace that stuff back to me, but Sugotti hasn't seen my face, he was still out of it when you escaped the warehouse. If I get rid of you, I'll buy myself some time."

"Sorry, wrong." Hana didn't have the energy to moderate her tone. "Iver and I saw you arguing with Fraen outside the municipal building. That's how we found the camp, we stowed away at the back of that lander right after you left."

Banyon stared at her, eyes narrowed, as if trying to work out if she was lying.

"'Eliminate me'," Hana used air quotes, "and you'll just add another charge to your list of crimes. If I were you, I'd run now, and run fast. They'll catch you eventually, but you'd have made the effort. Or give yourself up, save everyone the trouble. That might go in your favor."

"Sure." Banyon lifted his SAL, pointed it right at her. "That's going to happen."

Now would be a good time, Iver, she thought as she waited for Banyon to shoot. But given how things had been going lately, maybe that was too much to ask.

CHAPTER 33

IVER LIFTED HIS HEAD, suddenly wondering where Hana had gone.

Something was niggling at him, and he stood, stretching out as Admiral Valerian turned to talk to one of her aides.

Hana wasn't sitting on the couch anymore and he looked around the room for her.

A sudden onslaught of images formed in his head. A door with a number, an image of a man--he knew that man--holding a SAL at someone.

At Hana, his brain insisted. The man was pointing it at Hana.

"Where's Hana?" He called it out, causing everyone to go quiet. "Hana. Where has she gone?" He looked around at the group, and a young staffer who'd brought him something to drink earlier, pointed out the door tentatively.

He was suddenly in the man's face. "Where is she, exactly?"

He heard a sound of anger from Moiri behind him, but he ignored her.

"Now." He barked the words and the man cringed back.

"Hotel. Suite--"

"428." He had seen that number. In his head a moment ago. He ran for the door. "A little help, Valerian," he shouted, but he didn't bother to check whether she responded, or even if she sent someone with him.

He raced down the two floors, across the sky walk and along the passageway to what he realized was his usual suite when he came to Touka.

The code appeared in his head before he even reached the door. He tapped it in and burst through into the room, taking two running steps and then tackling Geral Hui, Touka City liaison to the Faldine military.

Iver heard the air explode out of Geral as he landed on top of him. He pulled himself up into a crouch, leaned over Geral's prone form, and snatched up the SAL before he had a chance to move.

"I knew you were ex-military," Admiral Valerian said from the door. "But I didn't realize how proficient you were."

Iver rose to his feet, SAL pointed down at Geral, and looked over at Hana, who was standing watching him with bright, humor-filled eyes from beside the bed.

"You have a good reason for tackling the military liaison?" Valerian eyed Hana with surprise, and stepped into the room.

"Besides the fact that he broke into my room and was pointing a SAL at me, threatening to 'eliminate me' to cover his tracks and give him time to escape?" Hana's voice was almost sweet.

Valerian really looked at her now. "Those are good reasons, but how did Iver know them?"

"I put a few things together while I was waiting for you to finish your discussion with your aide." Iver lifted his shoulders, but his gaze went to Hana, and he saw the surprise in her eyes.

She was working something out.

And he realized that everything he'd seen in his head had been from her perspective.

It wasn't that she had contacted him.

It had been her upgrade to his upgrade.

They were able to share information.

The potential of it made him want to look for a chair to sit down in.

Behind Valerian, two grim-faced Special Forces soldiers hovered in the doorway.

He used the SAL to gesture to Geral Hui. "Come collect a new prisoner. He can go with the others Captain Donaldson's people rounded up. He's part of the Bret group, not the Craven group."

"Craven group?" Geral finally had his breath back and he struggled up into a seated position. "What are you talking about?"

Iver looked down at Geral's red face and was suddenly done.

He stepped back, and the soldiers took it as their cue to grab their prisoner and march him off.

His shouted questions were still audible, even through the door to the stairwell, although Iver realized only he and Hana could probably hear that.

"You up for more of a debrief?" Valerian asked as Iver walked to the door and held it open.

"No. I'm going to bed now, and I'll speak to you again when I'm not running on no sleep or food."

Valerian nodded. "Which room is yours, in case I need to get you in an emergency?"

Iver waved his hand around the suite. "You're looking at it."

Valerian's eyebrows rose, and she gave Hana a final perusal.

"And Admiral." He waited until she was out the door, and it was half-closed.

"Yes?"

"Make sure there aren't any emergencies."

CHAPTER 34

"THIS IS SOME HIGH-LEVEL SURPRISE." Hana followed Iver through the military complex she had called home during the war, and nodded to a few of the guards she recognized as they were ushered through two security points.

Finally, they were led into a room that was almost a let down after the build up of the journey, and she took a careful look around.

Her former base commander, General Yarne, stood at the head of a long, oval table. Seated at the table was a woman and two men in civilian clothing, and then a few of the general's aides standing against the wall.

When the room's occupants noticed them, they all smiled in a very friendly way.

Hana glanced at Iver for an explanation, but it came from General Yarne.

"Lieutenant Farwell. Planetary Commander." He gestured to the free seats in an invitation to sit. "The VSC wishes to thank you for finding what is turning out to be the discovery of a lifetime."

"More than a lifetime," the man who was beaming at her said. "This is *the* discovery of the shared history of the Verdant String."

Hana lowered herself into a chair, but she couldn't help the spike of nerves at the formality of the setting.

If they had found out about the upgrade . . .

Iver's hand snuck across and grabbed hers, and squeezed it.

It was comforting.

They were in this together.

The man looked over at the general, received a nod, and stood. "You might have heard about the ship discovered by Tally Riva several months ago. A ship the Caruso were trying to steal.

"We think they wanted it because they realized the same thing we did on just a cursory look, that it was incredibly old. They no doubt wanted to take it apart, see what tech was used, looking for something new to them.

"It was an amazing discovery, one which we were very sure was part of the fleet that brought our ancestors to the Verdant String.

"Unfortunately there was no salvageable data from any of the systems, except for a single distress beacon."

The woman at the table shook her head. "What was left was a treasure trove, Jackson. It might not have held the data we would have liked, but it spoke of a sophistication we had no idea--"

"Yes, Professor Farra." Jackson cut the woman who had spoken up off. "But in terms of directly communicated information, there was nothing."

She seemed mollified by this, and gave a nod of agreement.

"Does this mean the ship we found did have information you could retrieve?" Hana asked.

"Professor Vande here." The second man leaned forward eagerly. "I'm happy to answer that. We think the ship that Tally Riva found had foundered somehow in space, and the crew abandoned it, wiping every trace of themselves away as a security measure. The ship you found . . ." Vande paused for a moment. "They didn't have the luxury of wiping anything. They were simply trying to survive the crash they could see coming."

"You said you already knew the ship Tally Riva found was from the ancestral fleet. How could you be sure?" Iver stretched out his legs, his thigh bumping against hers.

"Besides the fact that everything was built exactly for people of our physiology, we found a body. A mummified body of the one person who must have stayed onboard in case the others needed to return." The woman who Jackson had called Professor Farra spoke quietly. "We will soon be able to go public with what we know. We've only kept it quiet because we wanted to make sure we had all the facts before announcing something this big. Now we have your discovery, too."

"It will be view-altering," Jackson's words were hushed. "We cannot thank you enough for finding the ship. And that you flew one of the runners--" He sent a quick, narrow-eyed look at General Yarne, who threw up a hand.

"Special Forces have apologized numerous times for the destruction of that runner. Fortunately, there are seven others you can study, still in perfect working order."

"How did you?" Vande studied Hana, his attention a little disconcerting. "How did you fly it?"

Hana lifted her shoulders and worked on keeping her face earnest and honest. "We were under a lot of pressure. We had armed soldiers after us, and we knew we needed to get to Touka City to stop the shield engine from being stolen. I just did what looked right, and fortunately for me, the design was user friendly."

Vande nodded and sat back in his chair, but Hana wasn't sure he was convinced.

"What's happening with the shield engine, now that I mention it," she asked Yarne, as a distraction. She knew from Iver the military had taken over clearing the site.

"There's another group of archaeologists and scientists waiting until conditions are safe for them to access the ruin. Most of them were working on the ruins at Cepi before it was destroyed, so they're beside themselves at the opportunity they see in the Spikes," Yarne said.

"There was something you wanted to show us today?" Iver asked, and Yarne nodded.

"Professor Jackson agreed that as the people who discovered the wreck, you should be the first to see it."

Jackson cleared his throat. "It is . . . astonishing. Absolutely astonishing."

Hana leaned forward, felt a nervous tick start up beneath her eye.

"They had supersoldiers." Professor Farra couldn't hold it in any longer. "They had mastered nanotech, more than we have, and they used that tech on the men and women who volunteered to carry the tech in their bodies as a safeguard against any adverse conditions they might encounter."

"But if they were part of the fleet, why don't we see evidence of this nanotech in ourselves?" Iver asked. He squeezed Hana's hand a little harder.

"We don't know. It appears not everyone was comfortable with the concept. And don't forget, the first planets in the Verdant String were clearly suitable environments. Perhaps it was only the part of the fleet pushing into the unknown that thought they would need the nanotech. It doesn't come without cost, it seems. There were side effects."

"Side effects?" Hana asked, and her throat closed over the words. Her upgrade soothed her, a light touch of comfort.

"A sense of otherness, from the description. Of sharing space in one's body--" Jackson cut himself off. "Here's the comm we found. The language spoken . . . well, it is mind-bending in its similarity to Arkhoran. We had a linguist work on it and she's created the sub-titles you'll see."

He stood and activated a screen that she'd noticed in the corner of the room. It flickered on, and she saw a woman dressed in a jacket and trousers, the cut and fabric foreign, but the design not so unfamiliar.

"This is an update from Dr. Lucille Barton. All ten of our nano-volunteers have completed their latest check-up, and I'm happy that they are healthy, physically at least. All of them have said they think the tech has an artificial intelligence that has developed into a second consciousness inside them--a second opinion with the ability to control their bodies when it feels they are in danger. Every single one has said they are not afraid the nanotech means them any harm, that its primary objective--to make sure they survive at all costs--remains firmly in place." She moved in a way that spoke of concern. "I have to admit that I don't know if I can trust what they are saying. If the nanotech has advanced to that level on its own, it may also have the ability to affect their view of it. There could be a symbiosis at play, where the nanotech intends to make sure its host protects it, as much as it is prepared to protect its host." She sighed, and looked down at her notes. "I've passed the information on to the other ships in the fleet. Most of them haven't started the program out of an abundance of caution, and now I wonder if we shouldn't have done the same."

The comm cut off, and there was silence in the room.

Hana looked over at Iver, but his face was calm, and she realized she felt calm as well.

It will be all right.

The message came from Iver. Not in images, as she was getting used to, but the actual sentence, as if he had spoken in her head.

I know it will.

She answered him back, and she knew he had heard it, because he suddenly looked sharply at her.

"Amazing, yes?" Jackson switched the flickering screen off.

"Amazing." Iver's voice was deep. "Did you find any evidence of the nanotech on the bodies?"

Professor Farra waved her hands. "We are still looking, but for now, the remains are indistinguishable from each other, so until we are able to scan and assess each body, we won't know if there is a difference that we can pinpoint."

"Well, if that's all, I'm afraid I have a few things I need to discuss with the planetary commander and Lieutenant Farwell about the situation that led to them finding the ship in the first place." General

Yarne pushed off from the wall where he'd been standing through the presentation, and the scientists scraped back their chairs and gathered up their screens.

They filed out, thanking Iver and Hana again as they left, and finally it was just the general and two of his aides, who Hana noticed hadn't so much as moved from their places since she and Iver had walked in.

"The Cores?" Iver asked the general, and Yarne gave a nod.

"The Cores. The person you knew as Jake wasn't onboard the Dynastra, although the bodies of Sub-lieutenant Linnel and a few other men who used to work for Lancaster were. We don't know where Jake went, but if he saw Captain Donaldson's team arrive, he may have decided to cut his losses and run, and was never rounded up with the others."

"Do you think he's a danger to us?" Hana asked.

Yarne shook his head. "He'll be long gone. There was an unidentified ship hovering in nearspace. We know the Caruso had some kind of new shielding tech that they were sharing with the Cores, and this ship was obviously using it, because Admiral Valerian's people didn't pick it up until just before it pinched to the black. So it's gone, and likely, he's gone with it."

"At least they went empty-handed." Iver rose to his feet.

"Thanks to you and the lieutenant," Yarne agreed. "Glad they didn't get you the couple of times they tried, Sugotti."

Iver nodded. "That's on Hana. There's no pilot like her."

"We tried to keep her in our ranks, but it looks like she did the right thing going to work for you." Yarne nodded at her and Hana saluted him in response. "I have to admit, I'm as astonished as Professor Vande that you were able to fly that runner. I've seen the control panel, and it doesn't make sense to me."

"When you have to do something, you usually find a way to do it." Hana lifted her hands, and the general gave a grunt of acknowledgment as he waved them away.

As they stepped outside and walked across to the small runner they were using until Iver replaced the Sig, she decided to try her new-found skill again.

I want a week alone somewhere. Just you and me.

He didn't turn to look at her, but his hand came out and took hers. *You've got a deal, lover.*

She slid her arm around his waist and tilted her head up. "Should we be worried?" She didn't need to say what about.

He shook his head. "I wouldn't change a thing."

She felt her upgrade agree, strongly, as he bent and kissed the top of her head. "Neither would I." She turned, putting her other arm around him and lifting up on her toes to kiss his mouth. "Neither would I."

HISTORICAL FICTION NOVELS

Susanna Horenbout and John Parker series:

In a Treacherous Court

Keeper of the King's Secrets

In Defense of the Queen

Regency London series:

The Emperor's Conspiracy

Banquet of Lies

A Dangerous Madness

Other historical novels:

Daughter of the Sky

FANTASY NOVELS BY MICHELLE DIENER

Mistress of the Wind

The Dark Forest series:

The Golden Apple

The Silver Pear

SHORT PARANORMAL FICTION

Breaking Out: Part I (Short story)

Breaking Out: Part II (Novella)

To receive notification when Michelle Diener's next book is released, you can sign up to her new release notification list on her website: michellediener.com.

ABOUT THE AUTHOR

Michelle Diener is an award winning author of historical fiction, science fiction and fantasy.

Michelle was born in London and currently lives in Australia with her husband and children.

Connect with Michelle
www.michellediener.com